Spenser Blake's Secret

Also by John Caris

Dancing Magicians,
A Tale of Psychic Power

Hermes Beckons,
A Tale of Alchemy and Magic

Reality Inspector,
A Tale of Computer-hacking and Chess

Foundation for a New Consciousness:
An Essay on Art, Science, and Meditation

Spenser Blake's Secret

John Caris

Westgate House   San Francisco

*Spenser Blake's Secre*t is a work of creative fiction.
Names, characters, places, and incidents are either
the offspring of the author's imagination or used ficti-
tiously.

Published by Westgate House, San Francisco, CA
Visit our web site Ye Olde Consciousness Shoppe at
http://westgatehouse.com

Cover image Copyright © 2016 by Mary D. Caris
Doorway: Morris Graves Museum (old Carnegie
Library), Eureka CA; Beach scene: China Beach, Juan de Fuca
Provincial Park, Vancouver Island, BC

Library of Congress Control Number: 2016904238
ISBN 978-0-9607320-4-3

Manufactured in the United States of America

10 9 8 7 6 5 4 3 2 1

For my parents

The kingdom of heaven is within you;
whosoever shall know himself shall find it.

– Ancient Egyptian Proverb from the Great Temple at Karnak

Chapter 1

Shocked. Frightened. And – excited, I sat back in my chair, sipped green tea and observed my studio. "Well, kitties, what compelling force is driving my life?" Lucy and Karma glanced about the room and gave their reply. Karma cleaned her paws, noting a total agreement, and Lucy jumped and grabbed a fly winging through the air, also in accord with my decision – a leap into the strange forbidden world of psi adventures. Even the orchids on a table next to my desk were brighter.

I listened to the message for a second time and very, very carefully. Yes, I had heard it correctly the first time. The message was opening the portal and I was attracted. The caller wanted to hire Peaches and her team to investigate a matter of serious import.

I paused in my thoughts wondering if my fictional detective team had left the pages of the books I had written about them and now inhabited physical bodies. I was troubled by the strangeness of the event but set it aside for the moment. A weird goofball playing the cosmic keyboards – whatever, my husband, Ralph, would enjoy hearing the story during happy hour before dinner when we were all ensconced in the living room, Ralph and I sipping extra dry martinis and the kitties – Lucy and Karma – quietly engaged in watching the antics of their house mates.

The caller, his deep nasal voice -- vibrating with emotional intensity and demand -- stated emphatically he wanted to meet me in person and could or would not discuss the matter over the phone because of the many-layered surveillance the government and its global service corporations used to spy on citizens. A very curious attitude: revealing he has a secret which he wants to share. If he is so frightened of surveillance, why busy himself with such foolishness?

He would be at Coffee and Tea Company, which specialized in a variety of coffees and teas plus pastries and other snacks on West Portal, a commercial street near our home. He would arrive at 10 am and stay for an hour before leaving if I did not show. He would be there for five days – Monday through Friday – and if I was uninterested in the case, he would find someone else.

I was definitely intrigued and would meet him not only to observe his behavior for future use in a novel but to discover the reason for wanting Peaches Peoples Investigation Service to take him on as a client. Reality seems silly, but it has a sturdy cosmic foundation.

It was happy hour, a time of relaxation, sharing the day's events, and enjoying Ralph's extra dry martinis. We held our early evening festivities in the living room, which was fairly large – eighteen by twenty-two feet -- and had a high vaulted ceiling. A wood-burning stove was inserted into the stone fireplace situated in the north wall. Almond and walnut logs were stack near the stove. A table with pots of orchids was adjacent to the fireplace. Large windows in the west wall provided a view of the street and the sunset. The living room had two entrances: one leading into what used to be called a formal dining room; the other linked the vestibule and hallway to the living room. A couch and side tables were against the east wall. Four upholstered chairs were placed conveniently around the room for conversation.

The kitties, Lucy and Karma, were curled up on the couch with Ralph while I sat at a round wood table placed near the south wall. Books and magazines I was reading were piled on the table. Several pens, a notepad, and my journal were also there. The table was my space, and I always sat there when in the living room.

Ralph Garland my partner was a stage magician, who was quickly drifting off into occult study and exploration of the psi realm. I had only recently ventured into such areas of reality, being devoted to my writing. Perhaps I could now do both. Ralph had accomplished such feats as remote viewing, out-of-body experience, and strong mental exploits.

"He wanted what, Shasta?" A puzzled look appeared on Ralph's face as he sipped his martini. "Please walk me through that again, dear," he requested.

I did and he shook his head in disbelief. "It's weird I admit and captivating enough to meet him and learn more. I'll go to the rendezvous tomorrow," I said.

Ralph looked at me intently. "You have that light of curiosity and intrigue in your eyes. Of course, I can go with you if you wish," he remarked.

I laughed. "No, I'm a big girl and can handle the situation. Besides the Coffee and Tea Company is a popular shop. What's to fear?"

"I'm just as curious as you are, but I guess I'll have to wait until tomorrow's happy hour for details."

The kitchen timer rang, and the kitties jumped off the couch and led me into the food fixing area. A few minutes later I called out, " Dinner's ready."

I stood at an open window of my study looking out at the garden Ralph and I have cultivated. It was springtime and as usual weeds ruled the land. A gentle breeze lifted sweet fragrance of star jasmine up to the window. I breathed the scent in deeply, expanding my air passages to catch its nuances. The garden is sectioned into microclimate areas – from sunny to shady and wet to dry. Native California and San Francisco plants intermingled with non-natives. Here was nature's magic. Nature's wonderful chemical lab creating chlorophyll to produce photosynthesis.

A fluttering movement by the fuchsia bushes caught my attention. I looked carefully at the bushes and noticed an Anna's hummingbird feeding from the red flowers. Its iridescent ruby throat balanced the iridescent green feathers of its back. A female and male had taken up residence in the garden and had bred many families over the years. Hummingbirds are such a joy to have as neighbors.

I turned and walked over to my desk. Seeing Anna was a good sign, I thought. Sitting down, I examined the material Spenser Blake had given to me to write his novel. That's about it. Write a novel that conveyed ideas he wanted published. My memory of the meeting was clear.

When I entered the Coffee and Tea Company on Monday at a little after 10 am, I glanced around the room. Sitting by himself toward the back of the shop in a corner half hidden from view was a middle-aged man, his hair well trimmed, with a small bushy moustache on his square face. He was stout, not fat, and appeared to exercise frequently. He sat upright, ramrod like a prudish minister. His metal rimmed glasses were firmly fixed on his nose. His smile disclosed teeth with decay. Like me he obviously didn't care about going to a dentist for repair. He was wearing a conservative cut dark blue suit and a matching blue tie. As I headed in his direction, he stood and waved me over to his table. A few people looked at us, but most were absorbed in their beverages and snacks. As I reached the table, he stood and greeted me with a handshake. Since the cafe was self-serve, he asked, "Let me treat. What would you like to drink?"

"Well, thank you. A chocolate mocha with whipped cream, please." So much for my vaunted diet.

I set my shoulder bag on the table and sat down. I removed a pen and writing tablet, ready for action. My curiosity had risen.

When he returned with the beverage, we settled in and discussed his job offer.

I remarked, "Your offer to hire Peaches was quite startling, and I wasn't sure what you were getting at. So please explain while I enjoy my mocha."

"I've a secret that has serious social and religious complications if revealed. And that's what I want to do – tell the world the secret. But – and here is where serious problems arise – I fear certain groups would be very displeased and would try to destroy me, my family and friends, and my financial security." He glanced around the room as if he was being observed by unseen eyes.

Breaking the spell of anxiety, I inquired, "May I ask some questions, ones that have been troubling me?"

"Yes. Go ahead."

"First, what is this secret that will upset so many and perhaps bring about a disaster for you?"

He smiled; a wry grin crossed his face. "I'm sorry, but it's a need to know situation. If you decide to accept my proposal, I'll provide the details. Let's just say it's a secret that has powerful consequences."

I nodded my head. "Fair enough. We'll call it the secret for now. The strange part of your offer is hiring Peaches to investigate. Why?"

"Because Peaches and her team are fictional characters who have inspected and probed some very unusual circumstances, like a recent story where Peaches learns about the throat chakra and discovers remote viewing. How imaginative that story was. Would a reader believe you had that power or were only relying on your creative skills?"

"Ah, of course, the creative imagination explains all. Safety resides there in the fictitious realm." I laughed softly, now understanding his motive. "I'm intrigued. Please continue."

"The secret concerns a religious matter of utmost importance to early Christianity. Its revelation would bring disturbing controversy to the Christian community. And many would want to banish the truth and mete out punishment to those who disclose the truth."

"So to protect yourself I would author the book, but you would provide the ideas and themes. Well, what about me?"

"The novel will probable become a best seller and you'll earn millions of dollars." He chuckled.

"Then you don't believe I'll be threatened or my life will be in danger?" My tone was a bit sarcastic.

"No. Think of the theme of the Da Vinci Code that Jesus and Mary Magdalene were married, and all those who have profited by using the theme have never been threatened or destroyed. Criticized, of course, but not ruined. Also the subject has been discussed on the internet and in scholarly discourse, and popular books have been written about it. Now I wish to publish my slant on the matter, which is a controversial interpretation, my secret, of the subject."

"And why should I be the ghostwriter?"

"Simply, because you're a well known writer of detective mysteries and have a wide readership. I'll handled the promotion angle. And the theme should be discussed in the media even if people have not read the book yet. It's the revelation of the secret or the novel's dominant theme that's important."

"If I understand correctly, you want me to write a Peaches mystery to broadcast a secret you believe is important enough to upset the Christian religious community?'

"Yes. I've a contract here." He opened a briefcase, after placing it on the table, and removed a folded bundle of papers. "Basically, the contract states that I'll pay you a specific sum of money on completion of the manuscript, purchase a specified number of copies, and will take over the promotion. If your publisher refuses to publish it or wants to make substantial changes in the manuscript, I'll find another publisher who will accept it for publication. You'll own all copyrights to the novel and any royalties from sales will accrue to you."

"So, you're willing to spend a fair amount of money to get this secret across to the public. Might I ask why? And also what's the source of your wealth?"

Spenser laughed. "You want to hear my personal history. Well, it's too involved and long to recite now. A short statement is that a trust fund has been set up for me by my family, and I come from a long line of biblical scholars. If you accept my offer, I'd be delighted to spend time socializing and talking about my family background." He handed me the contract and stated, "Read it carefully. Discuss it with your husband, and if you accept my offer, sign the contract and mail it back to me in the stamped addressed envelope. If I don't hear from you in a month's time, I'll know you aren't interested and will seek someone else for my mission."

I stood and took the contract from him, thanked him again for the mocha and left, slightly dazed from the weirdness of the undertaking.

I was working a Sudoku puzzle while Ralph was inspecting the orchids for aphids. Four orchids were set on a table near the fireplace. "Well, tell me about your adventure this morning."

"Oh, what a bang – in all senses. Is this guy a jerk or a nut or a little of each? But it's a job, an intriguing one at that. The caller, one Spenser Blake, wants to hire Peaches and team to investigate an important matter for him. He's very suspicious about government spying and doesn't wish to discuss the job over the phone or by email, but only in person."

"Weird and weirder. Spenser Blake, the name sounds familiar."

"It should be since both names refer to important English writers: Spenser for Edmund Spenser, Elizabethan poet and best known for his major poem *The Faerie Queene*. And Blake —"

"Of course. William Blake, mystic, artist, and poet."

"Which puts my potential client within a specific area of English literature."

"Are you going to take the job?"

"Definitely. I'm fascinated by the prospects."

Both Karma and Lucy sat up and began cleaning their front paws – a sure sign they were in full agreement.

The timer bell rang from the kitchen. "I'd better check on dinner." I got up and walked toward the kitchen, the kitties out in front.

"What are we having?"

"Spaghetti. If the sauce is ready, I'll start the noodles."

"Anything I should do?"

"You can prepare the garlic toast after the noodles are in the pot."

He sipped the martini, thinking about the ramifications of Shasta's new project. It would be an intriguing adventure.

Chapter 2

Early morning -- I was facing a new investigation – but not exactly, more like investigative writing. I opened a document for the new client Spenser Blake. I paused, sipping the excellent coffee I always drank, and considered that Peaches Peoples investigation team will travel the streets and byways that Spenser Blake does. Ok, Peaches is now into the big time. What fun to fuse the daily realm with fiction. I wondered which reality was more fictional: Spenser Blake's or hers. In fiction everything goes, but then so too in Blake's world.

Okay, I thought, the time is here to jump into the bizarre world of fact fused with fiction, a step through the portals of psi-space and time. I started typing.

Peaches was enjoying the excellent coffee she always drank and chewing an unlit Cuban cigar -- two things she refused to sacrifice. She might be poor, but she didn't inflict herself with pointless pain.

The door opened and Aeneas entered with their friend Rafé Courbet, who was upset and fraught with worry. Peaches stood up offering firm support to Rafé, who was about a foot shorter and very slender. Rafé's dignity compelled Peaches to stand upright. Peaches nearly saluted her friend because of her inner power but caught herself and offered a relaxed handshake and a warm smile.

Rafé was eager to talk but needed quiet first. Peaches pulled up the only comfortable chair and assisted her friend into it. Rafé took several deep breaths and said, "I had very frightening news while gliding in the psi-zone during my meditation. They are after him, going to kill him." A moving image of her travels was projected onto their mind's psi-screen for them to view.

With a fringed shawl decorated with a water bird motif wrapped around her shoulders, Rafé sat on the crescent moon and the rainbow road curved along above her. Soaring high overhead, nearly touching the edge of heaven, was anhinga, Sunrise, its wings outstretched and its long tail spread fan-like. She had named her water bird Sunrise because it signified golden illumination and dawn of consciousness. With an eagle prayer feather in one hand and the other shaking a gourd rattle with an image of Peyote Woman painted on one side and a sunrise painted on the other, she prayed to Peyote Woman. As the rhythm of the shaking rattle increased, she waved the prayer feather in a circular movement. The sacred buckskin pouch holding Chief Peyote resting next to her throat vibrated spiritual energy enhancing her inner being.

Sunrise was observing the horizons: past, present, and future moments. She asked Sunrise to fly higher into heaven itself and bond her soul and spirit. The water bird entered the heavenly sphere, and she felt her soul and spirit become one. For a few moments Sunrise glided through the heavenly domain and then it began a graceful dive passed the curving rainbow road, not stopping until it perched beside her on the crescent moon. It turned its head toward her and peered directly into her eyes. It whispered, "The best options for your plans are the ones you have chosen. But there is danger, peril to you and your friends the Garlands, especially Ralph Garland. The source is Tau, alias Quincebury. Beware the words: 'gun,' 'photon,' 'resurrection,' and 'elixir of life' – all refer to potential threats of harm." Sunrise gently touched her forehead with its beak and flew away. She floated downwards smoothly until she reached the earth. She re-entered her physical body and opened her eyes, staring up at the golden illumination.

Rafé Courbet sat up and reflected upon her visionary experience. She felt joy flowing through her body as she always did after visiting Peyote Woman. Today she could sense her soul and spirit snuggled together in a loving embrace. But today's visit was different from all the others. Her anhinga had warned her of danger in the near future.

Meditating on the meaning of the vision, she touched the centerpiece, shaped as a peyote bird with its wings formed like a crescent moon, of the necklace which was hanging around her neck. Running along the center of the crescent from end to end was the rainbow path, the peyote road. Hanging from the bird's tail were three strands of shells. She had constructed the necklace when she had joined Peyote Woman's spiritual path and became a member of the Native American Church.

The answer came in a flash. She would contact Dr. Lionel Sitting Otter, the Roadman or leader of the Native American Church branch she attended, seeking his wisdom. He was a professor in the Native American Studies Program at SF State, and was so well-known for his compassion and wisdom the students nicknamed him Gentle Lion. He was a practicing member or mide of the fourth degree of the Midewiwin Society, an ancient healing and mystical society of the Algonquin nations. The English name was Grand Medicine Society. Initiation into the society was based on a death and rebirth ceremony. A mide of the fourth degree had several spirit guides or manito guardians who communicated with the mide by vision dreams. Each mide merged with the guardian, becoming one and gaining its power. Because of his superior mide power, Gentle Lion was able to understand and interpret Rafé's vision dream.

She had contacted Gentle Lion, who offered her information about his colleague Carlyle Quincebury, who taught in an unrelated discipline but with whom he had served on committees. Yes, Quincebury was very intelligent but seemed to lack an affinity for the Great Mysteries. And he thought Quincebury could be vengeful under the proper conditions. He recommended she should get help from Peaches Peoples, a well-known sage of Euro-American culture.

Peaches felt a strong kinship, not because she was Native American, but as a lady of the earth and land, knowing its value and many psi-levels. Peaches' roots grew deep into the earth giving her a source of inner power.

Rafé was completing a MA in drama. Her thesis was a project to design and execute a dramatic performance using magic routines that portrayed traditional Native American stories. She would become a Native storyteller, narrating Native People's stories with magic. Her inspiration for the style of magical performance was Ralph Garland's Alchemical Light Show she had assisted with. It had been a daring and risky venture to portray occult themes and thoughts, yet it had worked well. She had learned much as Ralph's magical assistant.

Last spring she had researched traditional Native American animal stories and chosen a few for routines. She had been performing them during her walk-around magic acts at Ocean Delights, a cafe on Ocean Avenue. She had shown two of these magical effects at a recent theater workshop. Her teacher and the other students were amazed at her skill.

With her earth rooted intuition she realized Peaches, if she wanted to help the Garlands, required the aid of Sandra Kingfisher. Sipping the tasty herbal tea, she told them about a friend who could assist them. Sandra Kingfisher was a genius and had a superior cyber mind for surfing the electromagnetic field. Her movement through psi-space in the astral zone was also expert and she had agility and speed.

Her cyber-whiz friend had developed a traditional Western religious-mystical approach to assist her travels through cyber-psi spaces. Her abilities were more cultivated than Tau Carlyle Quincebury. Sandra had developed her cyber skills over fifteen years and was now at her peak. She had created several techniques for psi-travel and was well-known for finding a sacred portal, securing and cloaking it.

"I never knew what a peyote ceremony was like. I've heard about them but didn't realize the spiritual power of the vision." Peaches was astonished.

"Actually, it was not a regular ceremony as we have at the church and led by our Roadman, Dr. Lionel Sitting Otter. I didn't take any peyote as we do at church but was in a meditative state of mind, a form of prayer to Peyote Woman. That form of contemplation shone rays of illumination on the darkness of my soul and so expanded my consciousness."

"That's wonderful, Rafé; you have a rare talent for cosmic magic. You've already delved into more mysteries than I have in my lifetime." Smiling broadly, Aeneas felt like a proud brother.

Peaches transformed her astonishment into enchantment. "So what is your interpretation?"

"I basically agree with Gentle Lion, the Roadman of my church. Quincebury is the source of the problem and potential danger. A gun is a weapon of destruction, one that Quincebury can use. I like Gentle Lion's take on the photon, which has a double nature or identity. It can behave either as a particle or a wave. I intuited the double level of meaning applied to the whole vision. The photon referred to the golden light of dawn." Rafé paused looking at the team while she nibbled on another cookie and sipped tea.

"Yes. 'Dawn' is a beautiful metaphor for rebirth and the restoration of life," Virgil acknowledged.

"Probably the greatest cosmic mystery is creation and its meaning to us humans. The process of coming into existence and later going out of existence probes our intellect and intuition for meaning and explanation." Peaches moved into her inner being.

"Because of its double meaning I intuited the vision to refer to both advancement and peril. As Gentle Lion pointed out, I progressed closer to my inner self when my soul and spirit bonded. I moved one or two steps upward toward my rebirth." Rafé exuded golden light.

Peaches came out of her reverie. "Rafé, your spiritual goal is quite similar to the hermetic purpose. The main difference is the language used. Funny, I'm visualizing Carlyle's last words to Ralph. Carlyle wanted to discuss the 'secret that's never revealed.' Ralph was climbing the spiral staircase and Carlyle was following. Suddenly Ralph vanished. Carlyle paused on a platform, looked into the shadows, and asked Ralph to talk with him. Carlyle was filled with terror and, not receiving a response, hurried down the staircase. When he reached the bottom, he collapsed, had a stroke. What a vivid image."

"Perhaps he blames Ralph for his misfortune," Rafé said.

"The secret that's never revealed. Wasn't that an ancient riddle where if one didn't give the correct answer death occurred to the testee?" Peaches looked at the group for verification.

"I don't know. It might be," Rafé said.

"The statement is very paradoxical and can't be logically solved. It certainly fits into hermetic thinking," Aeneas said.

"What do you think its purpose was, Aeneas?"

"It's one of those teasers, a conundrum that forces the mind to move in circles without a resolution."

"Or a riddle without an answer, like a Zen koan." Peaches smiled like a happy Buddha.

Looking at her team Peaches said, "Let's pool our resources and gather again when we have some new information to share about the issue."

Chapter 3

Peaches sat quietly thinking about the import of Rafé's vision. They would investigate Carlyle Quincebury to determine the seriousness of the threat he posed. With their skill surfing cyberspace Rafé and her friend Sandra would be assets. Neither she nor Aeneas had done much surfing.

Through the intercom Aeneas announced the arrival of a visitor and potential client, "We have a visitor, a Mr. Douglas Balentine, who wishes to speak with you about our investigation services."

"Bring him in." She placed the well-chewed cigar in the ashtray. She never smoked cigars, only chewed them. She liked the taste of good rich earth tobacco.

When the inner door to her office opened, a tall, slender middle-aged man entered. He was well-groomed and probably had his hair trimmed daily. He was wearing a brown suit, conservative cut, and a brown tie. A serious frown was etched on his face. Peaches rose and offered her hand, giving his a mild but firm clasp. As he sat down in the chair nearest her desk, she noticed he was extremely anxious. To put him at ease she asked, "Mr. Balentine, would you like something to drink – coffee or tea?"

"Oh, my. Everyone, since I was a child, has called me Doug. Please, let's be informal. Too much standardization and formality in the world today. Yes, tea would be fine. Perhaps you have Earl Grey, a favorite of mine." He pushed his glasses back toward his eyes. Peaches assumed it was a nervous habit.

Aeneas, who was still standing by the office door, said, "I'll make a cup. Should be ready in a couple minutes."

"Well, Doug, tell me what the situation is, and I'll decide whether we can help or not."

"A very important manuscript has disappeared. I've searched everywhere and my valet and housekeeper have also inspected the entire house. I now believe it has been stolen."

"We've a good record for recovering lost and stolen property. We'll do our best at finding yours. I would like to know all the details, especially the reason you haven't gone to the police. At least I presume you haven't."

"Yes, well, I hadn't taken the matter to the official authorities because of the delicate nature of the manuscript's contents. Let's say that if ideas contained in the book were broadcast throughout the media, all hell would fall on me. At the moment I can't be more explicit than that. I've photos of the manuscript, both exterior and interior images. I've kept it in a very secure safe, which has not been tampered with. I can honestly state I believe whoever took it had access to the safe's combination."

"And when did you become aware it was missing?"

"Last weekend, Sunday evening, after a light supper I retired to my study and was preparing to analyze certain sections. I'm a professional biblical scholar. I've written articles on the cultural placement of biblical documents by analyzing the text, its word usage and grammar for the most part. When I opened the safe, it was gone. I immediately proceeded to search for it, calling to my two servants for their help. Monday morning I phoned a close friend who is interested in biblical texts but not a scholar. I told him what had happened and he said he would talk to his lawyer, who might recommend a detective firm to investigate the matter. You come highly recommended I must say."

"Why, thank you, and we'll be happy to solve your problem and locate the manuscript. Is it possible for us to visit your home and inspect the study where it was kept? We would also like to photograph the study which might help in discovering the method used to remove and steal it."

"Of course. Would this evening around 7 pm work for you?"

"Aeneas and I'll be there at that time. For now would you please fill out our standard contract. And we require an advance deposit before we begin." She handed him the contract. He read and signed it and then wrote a check for the advance. Peaches took the contract and went into the outer office where she made a copy. Returning, she gave the original to Doug who, placing it in his jacket pocket, stood and offered his hand again for an agreement shake. As he left the office, he said, "So I'll see you at seven this evening."

ಌ ✻ ಒ

When she heard the outer door close, she sat back in her chair, reflecting on the new case and in particular their client. Peaches asked, "Virgil, what are your first impressions?"

Virgil was their supercomputer. When Aeneas had joined Peaches Peoples, forming the Peoples Investigation Agency, he had brought with him his computer Virgil. He had designed and built the computer to his personal specifications. Virgil was more powerful than anything the government or global corporations had.

Virgil was the third and hidden partner of Peoples Investigation. It could see, hear, and speak. Camera eyes, miniature microphones, and speakers were placed in strategic areas of both their offices and living quarters. Virgil could speak fifteen languages with different voice registers and understand those languages in their spoken and written forms; it was a veritable language wizard. Peaches and Aeneas always spoke to and treated Virgil as a person. Aeneas had programmed the computer with a male persona. During most interviews, though, Virgil was silent so as not to scare clients or give away his powers.

"Doug is obviously protecting the contents of the manuscript for reasons still unknown. He also has some secrets hidden within secrets, forming a clandestine agenda which might hinder our investigation and perhaps even harm our firm."

"So you noticed his extremely suspicious mindset based on a deep foreboding fear?" Aeneas said.

"Yes." Peaches nodded in agreement. "Something bothers him more than just losing the manuscript. Virgil, give us an in-depth background check available tomorrow morning. We should have more data for you after this evening's visit.

After she sipped her extra dry martini, Shasta asked, "Well, how did the first day of the convention go?"

"It is the first time for Assembly 2 to host a convention, albeit a mini one. We don't hope to make a big profit, mainly just enough to pay for the venue and other expenses."

Ralph was a member of The Society of American Magicians (S.A.M.) and belonged to the San Francisco branch, Assemble 2. S.A.M. is the oldest and most prestigious magic organization in the world. Ralph had been a member since adolescence when he had joined the S.A.M Youth Division.

"Yes, the convention began without a hitch. The talent show started on time and the acts were well received. The lecture-presentations had good attendance, and the vendors seemed to be happy with many sales." He rubbed Karma behind the ears and she began purring.

Shasta smiled and sipped her martini. "Well, I had an active day. I commenced the new Peaches mystery for my client Spenser Blake. At the moment my Muse is singing a melodious song filled with inspiration."

"By the way I met your Spenser Blake today at the convention or at least I believe it's the same person."

Shasta looked at him quizzically. "Really. That is strange."

"Well, it isn't too strange, perhaps more an example of synchronicity. He is a S.A.M. member but has never attended an Assembly 2 meeting. There are many magicians living in San Francisco like him. We have tried to encourage them to attend our monthly meetings, but most are too busy with other activities. The same is true for Spenser when I asked about coming to some meetings. We had coffee and chatted about magic. I've made arrangements to visit him."

Shasta was sitting at the round table cluttered with magazines, a notepad and pens.

"How was your afternoon visit with Spenser?" Shasta turned toward Ralph with an attentive look. She sipped the dry martini.

Ralph was sitting on the couch. Karma was curled up beside him while Lucy was resting in one of the armchairs. "Once I had regained Spenser Blake's acquaintance at the Assembly 2 mini magic convention last week, a link of kindred interest has developed. Blake is more of a scholar than a performer and had never attended Assembly 2 monthly meetings."

"And you're now going into the history and scholarly side," Shasta replied. "Does he perform any routines?"

"He focuses on book tests, which I can understand because of his professional work."

Lucy hopped off the easy chair and leaped onto the desk and then onto top of a pile of magazines. Karma rolled over on her back asking for a belly rub, which Ralph obliging did.

"What is a book test? I've never seen you perform one."

"It's a routine, with many versions, performed by magicians who portray themselves as mentalists, the kind using telepathic powers."

"You often do some form of mentalism or psi demonstration, don't you?"

"Yes, I do, primarily utilizing ESP or tarot cards. With these props I'm able to empower the assistant selected from the audience."

"Of course, they often appear to do the magic while you stand by helping."

"Too many magicians demean the assistant thereby inflicting the audience with the same outlook."

Holding up her empty martini glass, Shasta said, "A refill please and then tell me about the book test."

Ralph took both glasses into the kitchen with the kitties leading the way, hoping for fresh munchies. When he returned and had given a glass to Shasta, he began relating the basics of the book test, "The plain and simple format involves an assistant from the audience who selects a book among, say, three books. Randomly the assistant opens the book to a certain page and the magician identifies the first word on the page or perhaps a specific word in the first sentence. In his lecture Spenser demonstrated a variety of versions, several quite complex and often involving a story. His presentation was very lucid and entertaining. I was impressed."

"Yes, he struck me as an articulate person with a well-organized and cogent intellect. No doubt his scholarly activities as a contextual analyst hone his reasoning processes."

"Oh, by the way, Spenser has a very lovely Abyssinian kitty – Theodora or Theo for short," he said.

"I'm delighted to hear that he's a cat person. What color is Theo's coat?" Shasta asked.

"It's a reddish-brown, the usual coloration one expects for an Abyssinian. From what he told me, there are more color variations now," he answered.

"What's your assessment of him?"

Ralph put his martini glass on the side table and, rubbing Lucy's ears, said, "Overall fine. It's just that –" he paused searching for words. After another sip of martini, he told Shasta about the visit. "Spenser owns an older house which has been refurbished. His library is extensive, not only books on early Christianity and textual analysis but also on other religions and on magic, many of them ancient and medieval, bound books and early manuscripts.

What amazed me was the large and wide-ranging collection of occult books. I felt privileged to view his library; at least he made me feel that way. And that's the rub. I sensed a wrongness, something out of joint."

He stopped and sipped the martini. Both Lucy and Karma were purring, showing their understanding of Ralph's troubling experience.

"He has a doctorate in Divinity and --"

"Talks like a professor giving a lecture." Shasta laughed. "I noticed his speaking manner when I first met him."

Shasta sipped her martini and, after placing the glass on the table, asked, "Was it something he said or a personality issue or perhaps his mindset as reflected during the conversation?"

"Yes and no. All three. He has a crucial secret, deeply rooted, that weighs on his soul. The inner man is different from the outer persona. He's not what he seems to be, what he projects to the public."

"Well, well. Our man of secrets, living a clandestine existence in an underground realm."

Lucy had her head on Ralph's thigh and was enjoying the ear rubbing. Karma, not wanting Lucy to have all the fun, rolled over onto her back with legs in the air. Noticing Karma's obvious call for attention, Ralph began rubbing her belly, initiating intense purrs. "An aha. I've received inspiration from the kitties. The sharp conflicts within Spenser's inner being are concealed, for the most part, from his awareness. His intense, robust ego has established a shield of denial. Anything that diverges from the self-image he wants to project through his outer persona will be automatically concealed."

Shasta picked up the thread, "So if we knew the fundamental dynamics of the strife and opposition of the basic elements of his inner self, we could better understand the motivation underlying his outer behavior."

"Yes, I believe so."

"What we need is more background data – a penetrating search that reveals what he is concealing."

"We could have help from Peaches and her team, especially someone like Virgil." He laughed.

She joined in the humor of the startling idea. She giggled and then held up the martini glass. "Dear, a refill please and I'll tell you an idea I just had."

The kitties arrived first in the kitchen, hoping for fresh munchies. Touched by their intense stare, Ralph added more food to the bowl. Then he mixed fresh drinks. Returning to the living room, he handed her the martini, sipped some of his, and sat down on the couch.

"Okay, here is the plan. We'll convey all the data to Peaches and her team. I'm her. What I know she does. Form the large Garland-Peaches team."

They smiled at each other and went into the kitchen to serve dinner.

Chapter 4

Peaches and her companion stood outside Doug Balentine's home. "My god," Peaches muttered, "what a fantastic house. I've never seen one like this."

"It's the Queen Anne style, very popular in the late nineteenth century."

Peaches turned to Aeneas, who was smiling. "I didn't know you're an expert in architectural styles."

Aeneas laughed. "I'm not. Virgil is. I sent him an image of the house."

A wry grin came over her face, as she enjoyed the merriment. "Look at that tower rising above the front entrance. The main body of the house is three stories and that tower adds another story or two."

"A good setting for a gothic mystery and romance," Aeneas said.

"Well, let's go in and investigate the scene of the crime." Peaches headed for the front door with Aeneas following.

When the heavy wood door opened, they were greeted by a middle-aged man, who introduced himself as Archie Jeeves, acting as both butler and personal valet.

Peaches and Aeneas were ushered into the study a few minutes after 7 pm. Archie said he would notify the master of their arrival.

Peaches was amused by the butler-valet. Archie Jeeves, she mused, such an quintessential name for that role.

Aeneas had taken out his camera and was photographing the room when Doug entered. "Welcome to my humble abode," Doug greeted them and indicated a group of upholstered chairs for their seating comfort.

Aeneas chuckled recognizing the ironic nature of Doug's statement. Humble indeed.

Peaches did not sit down yet. She observed Doug warily. "We should look around the room first and acquaint ourselves with its shape and contents. By the way where is the safe located that the manuscript was secured in?"

Doug walked over to a landscape painting in the style of John Constable.

He grasped the left side of the painting, which was hinged on the right side, and pulled the left side from the wall revealing a specially constructed box within the wall where the safe was seated. While Aeneas was taking several photos of the safe secretly with his tablet, Peaches walked around the room inspecting its layout. The wood paneled walls contained built-in wood bookcases. An old-fashioned roll top desk was located in one corner of the room near the safe. Two long wood tables with wood chairs filled the central space. Several lamps were strategically placed to enhance reading.

The room was designed for study and meditating on deep, philosophical thoughts, she realized. After finishing the inspection tour, Peaches sat down in one of the upholstered chairs, followed by Doug who had been hovering about waiting for his guests to be seated. Aeneas continued his walkabout, snapping pictures.

"Well, I do have some questions to ask about the study and your household in general."

The host nodded, indicting please ask.

"The study is on the ground floor, am I correct?"

"Yes, it is and it's near the front door."

"And the pair of French casement windows – they open onto what?" Peaches had noticed they were latched shut.

"There is a small garden in back. A gardener comes by once a week for maintenance."

"Are they ever left open or at least unlatched so someone could enter unseen?"

"It is a definite possibility but highly unlikely. The garden has a wrought iron fence around the part that's not up against the house. The fence does not have an opening. Actually we use a back door leading from the kitchen. There's a walk from that door to the garage and a side branch meandering through the garden."

"The garage is a detached building then?" she asked.

"It was originally housing for the horse and carriage." Doug smiled.

"So you have a small fortress here."

He laughed. "Without the moat of course."

Peaches smiled back, thinking so he had a sense of humor even though he is involved in dry intellectual pursuits. "In my office you mentioned you had photos of the book; may I see them please?" Peaches requested.

Doug walked to the roll top desk, unlocked a drawer, opened it, and removed an envelope. Taking the photos out, he handed them to Peaches.

"It's an old manuscript," she said. As she looked through the photos, she noticed the calligraphy and drawings. "Such artful handwriting," she commented.

"It was copied by a professional scribe working in a copy-shop in Florence," Doug replied.

"What's the history of the manuscript?" Peaches asked.

"Actually, it's in a book format, not a scroll format, but it is handwritten," he answered.

"What's the difference?" she inquired.

"A scroll is one long piece of writing material rolled up. The material may be paper or parchment or in very early times papyrus. A book, sometimes called a codex, has pages bound together as in our modern format."

Peaches surveyed the many shelves of manuscripts and books. "I'm impressed by your extensive collection. You must be a serious collector."

"I am indeed, but the books are also part of my scholarly work."

"How did you learn of the manuscript's existence?"

"It was mentioned in an exegesis of 'The Gospel of John' by Eusebius of Delphi."

"What's the history of the stolen book?" she asked.

"My copy was made by a professional scribe in 1423. It was, of course, based on one of the earlier copies. The central section of the book is the Jesus-Lazarus story, which is the reason I call it the 'Lazarus Gospel.' The section is written in Greek and dates back to the early second century AD. The other parts were added during the medieval period and are a collection of essays and fragments on alchemy, astrology, and pharmacology. These are written in medieval Latin and Kabalistic Hebrew. Several poetic fragments are in Old English."

"How does one go about obtaining a copy of a rare book?" Aeneas asked.

"I employed a book detective," Doug quipped.

Peaches was surprised and about to inquire further when Doug continued, "There's an antiquarian bookseller in San Francisco who'll spread the word that he has a client who wants a certain title. An advertisement will appear in *The Antiquarian Journal*. Other booksellers will be alerted. If anyone finds a copy, a finder's fee is paid on top of the retail price."

"A global network for booksellers. That's intriguing," Peaches commented.

"So the book's prime value is based on its age and rarity?" Aeneas said.

"That's a major part and very few copies are known to exist today, but the 'Lazarus Gospel' is also of importance because it presents an alternate and unauthorized version of their friendship, which potentially can upset the Christian establishment."

"What's so upsetting?" Peaches asked.

"I'd like you to find the book and return it. You don't need to know the contents."

Peaches noticed that Doug had become agitated and quite adamant. She decided to stop further questioning about the contents. She changed the focus. "Does anyone else handle the manuscript besides you?"

"Archie, whom you've met, and Gladys, my housekeeper, do. I am sometimes absentminded and leave the manuscript out after working with it. If either notices the manuscript is out, I'm notified immediately. They do not know the safe's combination but do know where it is."

"Aren't you worried that your servants might read and gossip about the delicate nature of the contents?"

"No. The manuscript is not written in modern English nor any modern language. So I am not concerned with a casual perusal by someone without the proper linguist skills."

A smile broke forth on Peaches' face. "So that limits the number of people who would be interested in the manuscript. Could you provide a list of people, close friends or casual acquaintances, who knew the text existed and also could understand it? And could anyone who knew about the wall safe potentially get the combination?"

"Monthly meetings are held here in the study for people interested in Christian biblical textual analysis. I will give you their names and phone numbers. They all know about the existence of the manuscript, but most do not have the skills to read it except for a few sections where they might understand the language."

"Is it okay if we perform a background search on the members of the monthly meetings?"

"As long as you are discrete and do not bother anyone or cause concern on their part."

"This is a good start and the background check can be accomplished without disturbing anyone. Could you have the list ready by noon tomorrow. Aeneas will be by to pick it up."

"Yes, definitely. I'll start working on it tonight."

"Well, we better leave." As she turned toward the hall door, it opened and Archie, the archetypal butler, was standing there, ready to escort them. He bowed and headed to the front door. They followed behind him.

Sitting in the backyard, enjoying the warm afternoon sun, Spenser Blake stretched his arms upward and relaxed. Hearing a soft, melodious meow, he looked down at his feet. A cat stared up at him, her large pointed ears alert and her almond-shaped eyes sparkling. "Hello, Theo. Join me. I'm relaxing, letting my mind wander," Spenser said.

Theodora purred and rubbed against his leg. He reached down and scratched behind her ears. She meowed in her musical voice and went and curled up in her box nest next to his chair. He smiled. She was his best friend and companion, God's gift to him. Theo was an Abyssinian with a deep reddish-brown ticked coat. She was six years old and weighed seven pounds. She had become a member of Spenser's household when she was fourteen weeks old.

She would become totally absorbed in his activities, wanting to participate in them. And he encouraged her. He soon found they could communicate by various means. He always spoke to her as if she could understand English and most of the time she acted as if she did.

Clumps of catnip were planted in different parts of the garden. Theo loved rolling in the catnip. When she had enough, she stretched out and snoozed.

He rose and walked the circular path through the garden, which encompassed the entire backyard. The colorful flowers and plants pleased him, and he delighted in their presence. A gardener came weekly to provided the care the flowers needed. The garden was cultivated in the state of nature style, not as a formal garden with its precise and trimmed appearance. The garden reflected his inner soul. He had learned the truth from his mother. When his father became too overbearing, he retreated to the garden, either the inner one or the outer, or both.

He stopped in the middle of the garden where a small pond was located. Its only inhabitants were lotus flowers. The beautiful colors soothed his soul. He had cuttings in vases placed throughout the house, so he could always enjoy them.

Feeling a presence, he looked around. Sitting beside a Mexican sage bush was Theo observing him, waiting to help if necessary. She reach up with her paw and pushed a stem of purple flowers. Then stared at him.

"I'm thinking about these lotus flowers and what they mean to me," he said.

Theo walked over to the pond and sat down at the edge and studied the lotus flowers.

He first became attracted to the lotus while studying in India. In his early years working on a doctorate in divinity, he had spent a year there studying Asian religions. The lotus was sacred to the Hindu god Vishnu and an important religious icon. An immediate affinity linked him with the flower, which became a central image for meditation. Besides the beauty of the plant itself, the symbolism encrusted on the lotus was complex and compelling. It provided his intellect with food for thought.

He turned his attention to a long rock that lay three feet from the pond and was reminded of his grandfather, who was the most recent of a long line of family preachers. Grandfather Norton had it transported from Ocean Beach in 1907 and had placed it in the center of the garden he was creating. He called it his Rock of Ages.

Both his grandparents loved to walk the beach and comb it for shells, stones, and wood debris for use in the garden. Grandfather Norton had many rocks brought in which he used to constructed a small wall. The building of the wall fit into his moral view that hard work was important and recommended by the bible. The life of a preacher was much different from that of the laborer and grandfather believed building the wall with his hands would also build his character to withstand evil, the wall symbolizing the shield. After his death the wall began to fall apart. Spenser often thought that the poet was correct: "something there is that doesn't love a wall."

His mother had added the pond and believed it enhanced the meaning of grandfather's Rock of Ages. She would sit by the pond and hum the famous hymn while feeding the goldfish residing in the living water. After she passed on, Spenser had the pond cleaned, the goldfish having died or been captured by predators. He decided to add a different symbol – the lotus.

Based on his study of different belief systems, he could meditate on the Rock in a way his grandfather would never think of. In certain disciplines, like alchemy, a rock or stone symbolizes the soul or the prima materia. For some contemporary poets it represents earth. In ancient philosophy rock stands for the material matrix from which all things arise. Formless and amorphous it suggests chaos before a pattern is superimposed.

Studying the Rock, he visualized the soul as a formless entity. From it sprang the waters of life, nourishing the body. It was the body's motivating force. Experience shaped it and influenced its texture. He had learned from his spiritual studies that the soul required the spirit to assist and sustain it. By itself the soul was weak and easily trampled by negative forces.

When the spirit and soul bonded together, a vessel was created, a soul body. An alchemical process had occurred, fusing the two into one. After the death of the physical body, the soul body would continue living and return to its source.

Meditating on the soul-spirit question, he rose and finished the walk around the garden. Returning to the chair, he sat down in the warm sunlight. His mind wandered as he watched butterflies darting from flower to flower. Catching a flash of movement from the corner of his eye, he turned his head and saw Theo leap high into the air, front legs outstretched as if she were trying to grab a butterfly. For her it was a game and she always missed the butterfly.

Originally he had worried she would chase and try to capture butterflies and birds while playing in the garden. He devoted extra effort to teach her not to bother other living creatures and she understood and left them alone. As part of the prevention she wore a collar with a small bell attached that limited her cloaking skills.

He liked to keep track of the different butterflies in his garden. He saw two blues, which flew away and were replaced by a white and three swallowtails. A blue returned. What marvelous creatures they are, he mused. It's part of their nature to transform into different physical forms during their four stages of maturation. Humans had their own natural process for growth and maturation.

He sat up and looked: two monarchs, a female and a male, hovered over a flower. Monarchs often stopped in his garden for sustenance on their migratory journey. He was delighted he could share his small patch of Eden with them.

He owned a house built in the American Craftsman style of the Arts and Crafts Movement. Julia Morgan was the architect. Built in the early twentieth century, it was located in the southeastern part of San Francisco -- the Candlestick Park district. He had refurbished the house a few years after he inherited the family estate, his dear mother Elizabeth being the last to pass over. She had left her worldly travail and gone to her spiritual rest in the divine heavens. He smiled; she was finally free.

She had been his protector and shield against the rages of his father. As he got older, he supported his mother in her struggle against the domineering control of her husband. His way – his way only was the motto of his life.

A trust fund had been set up and a trustee carefully watched over the family wealth. He was used to such restrictions. His father, a very conservative Christian and wealthy financier, wanted Spenser to join him in the financial world. His father had been a family rebel and had broken the dynasty of preachers and biblical scholars that extended far back into the distant past. And his father wanted him to follow, but he had more affinity with his grandfather, a renowned biblical scholar, and became a rebel with his own vision. A great divide grew between the two. Reconciliation was not an option, only toleration was. When the friction became too hot, his father would explode. A cooling off period would follow until another explosion.

Spenser disliked the business world with its greed and power ploys. He chose an area of study far removed from the marketplace. He earned his doctorate and was now teaching two classes of religion at Stanford University and doing research in biblical history and textual analysis of the bible.

He had never learned the method to use his sharp, analytical intellect to win against his father's intense emotional behavior. If reason existed for his father, it was his way of thinking, which of course was always correct. Self-righteousness was his father's middle name. Growing up in a very conservative environment, he drew inward and shrouded himself with intellectual conceits.

He had spent many years dreaming of ways to revenge the slights and snobs of those around him. He was too liberal for them, although he pictured himself as moderate. He had come to recognize the diversity of viewpoints. His plan was to get his 'radical' thoughts out into the public marketplace.

He knew the power of such a technique. And if his name was not associated with the publishing, the satisfaction would be even greater.

He had become a biblical scholar and constructed a public persona which he could hide behind and laugh at all the freak outs happening to the prudish babbling idiots who thought they understood the Bible.

It was a sudden notion to have a well-known author compose a story which tells all. He was standing by the pond enjoying the lotus flowers when bang. He went into the house and searched the web for popular mystery writers. Selecting ten, he purchased a book by each, which he read for the precise attributes needed to express his ideas. Shasta Garland was in the top three and he decided to ask her first. He had read her most recent story where she had some characters involved in the Sorcerers and Wizards game and chakras. Her imagination was open to the occult and non-Christian religious themes. He had phrased the request carefully and caught her interest.

Hearing a meow, he returned to the outer garden. Theo was sitting by the kitchen door. He glanced about his Eden before standing. As he walked toward the kitchen door, he observed an Anna's hummingbird gathering nectar from purple flowers of a Mexican sage. All things have a place in the world. He was happy.

Doug stood in the library and listened to Peaches and her assistant leave the house. He went over to the humidor, picked up a briar pipe, and took a canister of a special mixture of pipe tobacco from the humidor. Once he had fully packed the pipe, he lighted it. He enjoyed the aroma of the Canadian mixture created by a firm in Quebec which put together special orders.

He smiled, pleased with himself. He walked over to the ancient manuscript collection and examined it carefully. Then he looked up at the top shelf of the collection. In the corner hidden from view was the 'Lazarus Gospel.' He had given the manuscript the name because it contained mainly the story of Jesus and his best friend Lazarus. There were several essays on alchemy and astrology and one on pharmacology and some fragments of Old English poetic verse. The essays were written in Latin and medieval Hebrew. The Lazarus story was in Greek. Few people had the ability to read the languages today and he had little fear the manuscript would be understood. Today's foolish society were chasing false gold and not interested in spiritual issues.

Having studied philosophers and theologians, he felt a kinship to Plato's notion of reality. According to the ancient philosopher, the world we live in, our daily world, is one of appearances and has no permanent existence. It is a phantasm, a making of the human imagination, and strangely we experience it as solid existence. Science had demonstrated the brain gathers sense date and forms all the pieces into recognizable shapes and textures. What is solid about that reality?

According to Plato's view, behind the world of coming and going were the Forms, true reality – solid, permanent, and non-changing. The Forms were the essence of all things.

Puffing on his pipe, he delved into the basic notions of modern science. At the foundation of matter were subatomic particles. Many lacked mass and many received mass by going through the Higgs Field. If a particle had a dual nature and did not know what it was until the last moment, how solid is matter and the reality made from matter?

Here were issues and questions that deserved attention, not chasing fantasies in the marketplace. Yet like everyone living in modern society, he too needed money. His trust fund was low. He had lost considerable wealth in the big market meltdown and now many debts were coming due.

He had planned the scam carefully, and the first stage had been a success. The 'Lazarus Gospel' was heavily insured. He could now regain his financial feet. After the Saturday meeting he had left a fake copy, which he had presented as 'Lazarus Gospel,' on the table for the group to examine. It had disappeared. Someone had taken it. He did not believe Peaches and her team were capable of finding the book. If they did, he of course would be overjoyed and devise another way to 'lose' it.

He went to his reading chair with its soft cushions and sank into it. He set the pipe in a special pipe holder. From the side table he picked up Jane Austen's *Pride and Prejudice* and opened it to the bookmark. It would be his fifth reading and was one of his favorite stories. He smiled thinking of a major theme: how our pride blinds us to our true self.

He relaxed and let destiny run its course.

Chapter 5

Carlyle Quincebury lay in bed; tubes inserted into his body fed and removed wastes from it. An oxygen nose inhaler along with a heart monitor were attached. His live-in nurses, who were on eight hour shifts, stayed in a connecting room to Quincebury's bedroom. They were able to monitor his vital physical functions from their room. Quincebury had equipped his bedroom with high tech devices so he could utilize the computer system and communicate with his assistant Lenny Sawyer.

Quincebury's medical condition was still serious. Although he was conscious and could talk, his left side was partially paralyzed and probably would remain so for the remainder of his life. The doctors were not hopeful for a speedy or complete recovery.

The great man had been found unconscious in the Command Center of his home's high tech room by Don Wesley. Don, who with his wife Bertha, performed servants' duties and had their own apartment in the large house located in St. Francis Wood, a wealthy enclave in San Francisco. Don had phoned 911 and the emergency response had been quick and efficient.

Carlyle believed Sawyer was quite competent and so far had proved his ability to manage the business empire as the chief administrative executive. Quincebury, meticulously observing the activities of all the employees, still formulated the strategy and gave the orders for Sawyer to follow.

Yet he had an uneasy feeling about Sawyer, who seemed dedicated to his boss and the welfare of the corporation. He had noticed a hidden part of Sawyer's personality where a secret might be concealed. Carlyle Quincebury was uncertain about Sawyer's loyalty and so did not trust his decisions.

Before his stroke Quincebury had taught classes at SF State University's Computer-Information Technology Department, but now he had time off and was utilizing his accumulated sick and personal leave days. Of course he was still the formidable CEO of Madrone Advanced Systems, LLC, the top security firm and holder of equity in numerous data-collecting and security corporations. With his disabilities, though, he had to rely on others more than he liked. Even harder to accept was his incapacity to travel the cyber-psi spectrums with Tau as his tag. He had plenty of time, however, to brood and plot a dreadful revenge on the Garlands, especially Ralph, the source of his distress and present misfortune.

Lenny was also living in an apartment in his boss' mansion and was able to manage the business from the Command Center located on the top floor. The two could communicate directly over an intercom system and so Quincebury was able to give orders and provide directions quickly. Once a week, unless more frequent visits were necessary, Lenny visited the company headquarter in downtown San Francisco. The other companies were administered through Madrone Advanced Systems and could be controlled efficiently from Command Central.

Seated at the central controls of the high tech computer system, Lenny noticed a green light was blinking on the center monitor, indicating DOG had nearly completed its collection of the requested data. Quincebury had designed DOG especially to collect and analyze data based on a set of priorities while it continuously traveled through the world's data bases. The National Security Agency with its new data collection and storage site in Utah was a treasure trove for important and profitable data. The world's governments and global corporations did not have a program that came close to the super program DOG, which could travel through cyberspace without leaving any traces.

Sitting, watching monitors was usually a dull activity and Quincebury had installed a music system to provide background entertainment. The system was designed to notify anyone in the room that DOG had stored a new collection of profitable data in one of the many clouds the company operated.

Lenny sat back in the comfortable command chair listening to favorite pop songs and fantasizing about the future when he would be owner and CEO of Madrone Advanced Systems and its business operations through front companies. The green light stopped blinking and became steady. Lenny pushed the intercom button and said, "The requested data is securely stored at the Cayman Cloud."

"Excellent. I'll analyze the data and then send you another request."

Lenny Sawyer now had the opportunity to return to his personal problems.

He had spent the last two days designing a program to thwart the devious activities of the cyberspace surfers elf and stealth, both having the same IP address. Presumably they were a team involved in a common goal. He was now ready to test the program, which was based on NSA's X-KEYSCORE system. The super NSA system could monitor online users in real time and collect all personal data available online for any user including the user's actions at the moment. It was a passive program and could only listen and not act. When action was required, other programs were triggered and performed their specific functions.

Lenny named his program X-KEY, a lite version of NSA's program. Parts of the source code had became public, and he utilized them to reverse engineer the code, analyzing it back to its kernel. Like NSA's super system, X-KEY could monitor the movements of elf and stealth in real time and collect data of the sites they visited and contacts they made.

But first he would relax and enjoy a moment of anticipation. He stood up, walked down five steps and entered a circular hall. Stopping at the refreshment room, he took a bottle of beer from the refrigerator and, opening it, gulped a cool tasty liquid, a steam brew beer, one of his favorites. He returned to the command center and typed his ID and password on the touch screen. X-KEY opened and he began monitoring elf's IP address. When either elf or stealth first appeared, one of the active programs would mark the user. The marking was in addition to the user's ID tag. The mark was a method he had devised to track anyone online until the mark was deleted. Each user had an individual mark.

He had decided to keep X-KEY secret from his boss. Although he would like Quincebury to know about his masterpiece, he realized the great man might not only be jealous but disturbed that Lenny was not faithfully watching the business empire but wasting time on his own projects. Quincebury did not show pleasure when an employee used company time for personal activities.

Quincebury had built his empire to serve governments and business corporations. His firm was one of many that contracted with governmental agencies like NSA, CIA, and the Pentagon. The company did not do as much business for the government as Booz, Allen, Hamilton, one of the major firms performing security functions and collecting and analyzing data. Because Quincebury had transformed government databases such as those of NSA into his own private storage system, he did not want to spend too much effort working with the agencies in case they became suspicious. With all the whistleblowers suddenly emerging, governmental agencies and corporations had become excessively alert to data stealing and had enhanced their security systems.

Lenny had come to realize his boss enjoyed living on the dangerous, if not the dark, side. His boss's trait to gain power and wealth at any cost had touched Lenny deeply and acted as a magnet. So he stayed employed to Quincebury, hoping eventually to gain control of the business empire.

A green light on the center monitor began blinking. Lenny smiled. Upon entering cyberspace elf was marked, making tracking easy. Lenny picked up the beer bottle to take another swig, but the bottle was empty. Since all the online activities were being recorded, he went down to the refrigerator for a fresh brew.

When he returned, he clicked on monitor two, which showed the record of elf's movements while he was gone and compared them to elf's present location. He pushed the pause button. Something weird had happened. Elf's marker had disappeared. He was puzzled. How could that be possible? He pressed forward and the view started up. My god, he thought. Elf's maker was no longer discernible, as if elf had flickered out of existence. Just as abruptly elf became visible again. He watched fascinated as elf moved in and out of existence, or so it seemed. Lenny had tried in vain to enter the IP's site, but the hardy firewall had resisted his efforts. All he could do was to seek a pattern in elf's movements. X-KEY was unable to 'see' the space which caused elf to become invisible.

His alternative was to enter cyberspace as Tau-2 and personally follow elf's tracks. He keyed in the coordinates of elf's last location and merged his consciousness into the electromagnetic spectrum.

Chapter 6

The two friends were enjoying coffee at SF State's Student Union. They had walked over from the Garlands' house, less than a mile distant.

"I'm glad you accepted the position as their personal researcher," Rafé Courbet said.

"And thank you for mentioning me to them. I really appreciate the thoughtfulness," Sandra Kingfisher answered.

"You were at the top of my list – number one cyber traveler." Rafé chuckled.

"I like them. They're filled with good humor and the home exuded positive vibes. The kitties were charming. They won my heart."

"Ralph's joke giving you a paper badge with 'Super Cyber Detective' printed on it was a hoot."

"And the wages will be welcomed. I've been concerned about my finances. Worries be gone."

"Will your laptop be sufficient for the in-depth research requested?"

"Heavens, no."

"So why did you turn down the Garlands offer of their computer system?"

"Oh, it is much too limited, and I'll require a very high powered operational platform. I'll ask Dwight Stern if I can borrow time on his platform. You should see it, the latest tech updates."

"How is your relationship with Dwight? Are you still a twosome?"

"We are getting together tonight for a tutoring session. He has a midterm in a philosophy course." Sandra often tutored Dwight in classes he was having difficulty with.

"Next semester Native American Studies Program is offering a course on traditional Native American spirituality. I'm enrolling and thought you might be interested."

"Definitely. It will link neatly with a course in Western occult offered by the philosophy department next semester. I'm taking that. Are you interested?"

"I might. I will check the course syllabus. I haven't studied the spiritual traditions of other cultures very intensely. It's time for me to do that, Western magical thinking, especially."

"How is your employment of magic routines in the drama classes being accepted?"

"Sometimes they're a little hesitant when I first mention the idea. But after witnessing a performance, they are enthusiastic." Rafé looked at her watch. "I've got to go – a drama class coming up. See you tomorrow?"

"Yes, I'll be here."

When Rafé had left, Sandra took out her cell phone and called Dwight. If he were available now, she could get started on the research project. She would travel cyberspace and collect all available data on Spenser Blake, biblical scholar and textual analyst. She was high-wired to embark on the new adventure.

She and Rafé had met in a Native American culture course two years ago and had bonded, in part because of their academic interests. Since early childhood Sandra had been fascinated by Native American history and culture. She had studied the history of the Ohlone people who had inhabited San Francisco when the Spanish had arrived. Perhaps the strongest strand in their friendship was their involvement in spiritual practices and ideas. And the sharing of different cultural viewpoints was instructive and rewarding. While the differences ignited their curiosity, the similarities intensified the friendship. Rafé was immersed in the traditional religious practices of her Potawatomi people and was also a member of the Native American Church. Sandra was raised in the Western spiritual religious tradition and had been a member of the Spiritualist Church in San Francisco since high school.

Sandra's extensive meditative practice had enhanced, what she called, her superpowers. Most people would categorize these talents as occult or psychic phenomena and deny their reality, saying they were silly superstitions. She never felt the need to prove the existence of her talents. She experienced them, had gnosis of their power. And of course she applied the skills to her travels through cyber and psi-spaces. Whatever was available was part of her toolkit.

Dwight answered the call and suggested she come over now. He had some things he wanted to tell her. She pocketed the cell phone and left the Student Union overflowing with energy.

❦ ✳ ❧

The door was unlocked, and Sandra entered the four room apartment that her friend and huggable Dwight Stern shared with a fellow student Craig Takemitsu.

She called out, "Hello, Dwight. Anyone here?"

Dwight emerged from the kitchen and embraced his love. "You said you had news to tell me. What's happening?"

"You tell me your big news first," Sandra requested. She kissed him.

They sat down on the couch. "First let me ask if you would like something to drink – coffee or tea?"

"Coffee, please."

After Dwight had stood up and gone into the kitchen to make coffee, Sandra kicked off her sandals. Her friend and his roommate never wore shoes in the apartment. According to their lights, there was no reason to bring the outside grime into their clean environment. For a couple bachelors they kept their residence quite tidy. Messiness was not in their behavior. Both were majors in computer and information technology, which as she knew required clarity, an ability to focus intently, and well-organized thinking. These qualities no doubt played a role in maintaining the living quarters.

Dwight returned with coffee and sat on the couch beside Sandra. Sipping some, he quickly put the cup down on the end table. "Very hot. Be careful." He smiled at Sandra. "I have an adventurous tale to tell. While I was surfing cyberspace this morning. I discovered a mysterious traveler whose name was not on my list of cyber tags."

"Wow. Awesome. Did you gain any data on the stranger?"

Dwight maintained a list of all identified cyber tags that have been using cyberspace. Nearly all travelers have a personal tag that corresponds to their online persona.

"I learned the tag is named Tau-2. I had a weird feeling when I found the tag. I followed it for a while. It traveled to some unusual sites. And more importantly Tau-2 left very few traces of its movements."

"Obviously, Tau-2 is a seasoned and skilled cyber traveler. But there are many like that in cyberspace. What do you think was the cause of your distress?"

"I intuited Tau-2 was aware of being watched. Perhaps not who was actually watching but that she was under observation."

"Do you think Tau-2 is a woman?"

"I don't know or can't even guess Tau-2's gender. But I don't like the pronoun 'it' and I'm happy to use the feminine pronoun half the time."

"Only half the time?" She tickled his ribs.

"Ho, ho. Stop that. Yes, equal time and equal rights. Stop that, Sandra." He broke down giggling.

"Okay, then, Tau-2 could become a serious menace. You said she traveled to some unusual sites. Like what?"

She spent at least ten minutes in NSA's database in the new Utah storage unit. And she didn't set off any bells or alert mechanisms as far as I could see. I followed right on her heels as far I dared. And I didn't notice any tracks."

"That is awesome. Someone penetrating NSA's databases. Let us see if we can gather any more data about her, including her gender."

"We should be extremely careful. I sense an imminent danger if she discovers our presence and identity."

"Oh, Dwight, it's a game. What's there to worry about?"

"But a deadly game. I think Tau-2 could harm us if she became angry at our harassment."

Dwight had been intensely involved in studying stealth technology since high school when he became fascinated with the US Air Force's development of fighter planes that could be cloaked from radar and other detection devices. He had followed the development of Lockheed-Martin's F-22 Raptor, a twin-engine tactical fighter, and perceived it as the future model for flight. By choosing the cyber tag 'stealth,' he imagined his own invisible flight through cyberspace.

Sandra had chosen the tag 'elf,' a word that held profound import for her. Sandra had taken to reading stories about elves, fairies, wizards, and other magical creatures when she was quite young. Her creative imagination permitted her to project herself into a land of wonder and marvel. As she grew aware of her psychic talents, the pastime of journeying in a magical kingdom became the most important part of her life.

Dwight turned to Sandra. "Now your news."

"I've a job with Rafé and the Garlands."

"Wonderful. What will you do?"

"I'll research specific individuals that they can't do otherwise. And the extra pay will banish my money worries for the semester. Maybe I can continue, be a free-lance researcher."

Dwight rose and headed for the kitchen. "Let me fix some more coffee."

Sandra sank into the soft couch. Good things were happening, and she would take advantage of the opportunity.

Dwight returned with the coffee and joined her on the couch. They snuggled and kissed and then Sandra patted Dwight on the leg, "Okay. Enough. Back to business. I have a big favor to ask. I would like to use your computer system. Research of much value can't be done on my and the Garlands' computers. I'll pay you a fee for the favor and use it only when you are not on."

"Yes. I'm happy to lend you the use and no fee required. In fact I would like to help and put some time in research, without pay of course. I see it as a game of cyber surfing. Now a favor I'm asking you. Teach me your special techniques for locating, securing, and cloaking places in the psi field."

"It's a deal." She kissed him deeply on the lips.

"I'll cook dinner and we can start after dinner. Stay for the night if you wish."

Sandra often stayed over, enjoying breakfast with Dwight, who fixed delicious omelets. She rented a two room apartment and enjoyed the privacy and independence it provided. Other times she needed the social amenities roommates offered. "We can combine research with your training. Need any help preparing for the philosophy exam?"

"Definitely. Let us do that first and then design a plan for research and training." Dwight was excellent in his chosen field of computer science, but philosophy unnerved him.

"One of the people we'll research is Carlyle Quincebury. The Garlands have reason to believe he seeks revenge for his stroke and is going to harm them."

"Professor Quincebury? I like him. He is a very popular teacher on campus and always fills his classes. I heard about his stroke and his anger toward certain people, but nothing more than campus gossip. Yes, it will be exciting to discover the data about the issue. I'm definitely on."

After dinner Dwight got his philosophy book and Sandra provided insights to the thinking of the great philosophers. Once Dwight had prepared for the midterm, she set up her entry into psi-space on Dwight's computer.

Sitting down at the keyboard, she first created a personal account she would use for her research. Once she had the account, she generated a formidable firewall around it. Dwight had designed a powerful firewall for the platform but ruthless travelers might be able to find an opening and follow her into the account.

Now she was wired with excitement. She told him, "I have made a mental note about your warning. Maybe I'll cross Tau-2's tracks."

"Of course. I've got some code to analyze for class tomorrow. Stay the night if you wish."

She smiled at him. "I just might."

Sandra had developed her latent psi talents when she was a child. And she continued to nourish them. When she discovered they could be transformed into skills for traveling cyberspace, she gathered all the occult data available concerning them and cultivated her ability.

After detecting links or junctions between cyber field and psi field spaces, she conceived a mental map based on them. Recognizing the junctions as sacred places, Sandra learned they were gateways between the two fields: electromagnetic and psychic. At first she became confused and uncertain of her location in relation to her starting point and destination. After learning deep meditation and the control of her psi power, she was free to travel wherever she wanted to in astral space and utilized visualization as a primary technique for her travels.

She entered the gateway to astral space and began her journey.

Chapter 7

Peaches removed a plate of bear claws that had been warming in the microwave oven in her office. The margarine had melted and the aroma of the warm pastry brought a look of appreciation to Aeneas' face. Peaches placed a bear claw on a smaller plate, which she gave to Aeneas, who immediately began to devour the pastry.

"Are you sure you should be eating junk food for breakfast?" Virgil asked with a hint of displeasure in his voice.

Both Peaches and Aeneas answered simultaneously, "Definitely." Peaches continued, "It's a quick energy provider and with the caffeine from the coffee, we are ready to perform at our best."

"Virgil, you don't know what you are missing. I wish I could give you taste buds. Then you would understand."

Peaches licked her fingers and wiped her lips on a paper napkin. "Well, Virgil, what background data have you assembled on Doug and the other suspects on the list?"

"I have made and printed personal files for Doug and each of the fifteen men who attended the monthly meetings. The files are stacked alphabetically in the printer tray."

Aeneas rubbed his hands on a napkin before going to retrieve the files. He gave one complete set of files to Peaches and sat down to read his packet. "I see you have ranked them according to priority."

"The ranking was based on the data I was given about the case, which I have labeled 'Case of Lazarus' Gospel.'"

"Let us change the case name to 'Lazarus' Gospel Mystery.' The data about the members of Doug's monthly meetings are intriguing," Peaches said.

She smiled at Aeneas. "Most have a specialized area of biblical studies that they are involved with. Only two have the wide-ranging linguistic skills that Doug has. I see you have ranked them one and two, Justin Knight and Foster Meredith.

"Justin Knight appears to have as much ability as Doug," Aeneas said. "He's a professor in the Department of Religious Studies at Stanford University and teaches history and literature courses about Christianity and Judaism. He has knowledge of classical Latin and Greek and some background and work in medieval Latin. He has published articles on the historical cultural background of Christianity and Judaism."

"And Foster Meredith is a close second," Peaches said. "He's a professor in the Department of Classics at UC Berkeley and teaches courses in Latin and Greek language and history of the bible. He has published articles in textual analysis of classical texts.

"What about the third, Marcus Scarpia," Aeneas remarked.

"Yes, Scarpia presents a puzzle," Peaches answered. "For five years at Yale University he taught courses in Medieval and Renaissance cultural history with special focus on alchemy and magic. He is a member of the magician's group Society of American Magicians. He has given lectures on the influence of the Western esoteric tradition in the nineteenth and twentieth centuries."

Unwrapping a Cuban cigar, Peaches began her morning chew. "Scarpia's primary background data portrays a stage magician who has strong links to esoteric groups. Of all the fifteen men listed he jumps out at me. We don't know if he has any linguistic skills required for textual analysis. Doug doesn't strike me as a dabbler in the occult but rather as a very dry biblical scholar. So what is the reason for Scarpia's attendance? What does he hope to gain?"

"I'll focus my attention on the top three, then, giving Scarpia the priority of utmost importance." Virgil stated.

Placing his files on the desk, Aeneas asked, "Perhaps we should begin a surveillance on these three? I can call my buddy Lance Thomas."

"You're referring to the lock picking friend, owner of the locksmith company Lock-Unlock?"

"Yes. We can install several receiver-transmitters in the residences of the top three and, if we're lucky, gather some revealing data that will assist our investigation. First we'll need to know their daily habits, when they're home and when out."

"I would like to move Scarpia to the top of the list, making him the primary suspect. Virgil, please start the update collection process now."

Peaches smiled as brightness shone in her eyes. She had an inner premonition, a warm feeling they were headed in the correct direction.

"I am on top of it. I should have advantageous data collated by tomorrow morning when you have arrived for what you call a breakfast." Virgil had the ability to learn from experience – an advanced form of artificial intelligence.

Peaches and Aeneas smiled at each other, sharing a private joke. "Okay," Aeneas said, "I'll contact Lance and discuss the situation with him. He owes me some big ones."

"And what will you do, great leader?" Virgil inquired, smugness in his voice.

"Why, dear friend and adviser, I'm going to pick up my cigar and resume today's chew." Peaches laughed, amused by Virgil. She could play the game too. She gathered up the background files and commenced an in-depth study of the sixteen profiles.

He went to the back of his study and unlocked a steel cabinet. Opening it, he took out an ancient manuscript, which he carried to a work table. Here was the 'Lazarus Gospel' as Doug called it. So would Marcus Scarpia.

It had been very easy to remove the book from Doug's possession. As the members of the scholarly group headed for the front door, he slipped away and entered the sitting room adjacent to the front door. The sitting room was small and invited an intimate conversation among master of the house and favored individuals.

He waited until the household was quiet and then emerged. Silently walking to Doug's library, he entered, and there was 'Lazarus Gospel' laying on the table – waiting to be carried off as the princess locked in the tower awaits her prince-charming to rescue her. He closed the safe where the book was kept and pulled the painting over it. Scrutinizing the room, Marcus decided everything was in its proper place and Doug would not notice anything wrong from a first impression. He put the book in his briefcase and left.

He opened it to the main section about Jesus and Lazarus and began reading the classical Greek text. His linguistic skills, although not well-known among acquaintances, were excellent and he was now putting them good use.

His smile deepened and became fully joyous. He now possessed the recipe for changing nonliving matter into living forms. Little did biblical scholars realize the guidelines for creating a homunculus were in the story. Pieces of the guidelines were scattered throughout and had to be collected and arranged in correct sequence for the making of a little man, which was the alchemical parallel to the ancient Hebrew golem. It would be an enjoyable task and well worth doing for its ultimate reward of everlasting life, the nectar of the gods. The tree of knowledge, source of all existence, spread its branches wide into the starry blackness of the universal abyss. He would pick its fruit. The fountain of immortality or Philosopher's stone was able to create life. The liquid produced is liquid gold, white in color, the most precious force in the whole universe.

He visualized himself as a cosmic magician who brings about innovations to society. But unlike Faust who had lived before, he would accomplish great and wondrous marvels. He would not give way to pride or ego-centered goals. He would be acting for all humans. The serpent guarding the unconscious would be rendered harmless, allowing consciousness to emerge. Ignorance would vanish and knowledge would appear.

Marcus went to his collection of ancient manuscripts, removed several from the self, and carried them over to the work table. He opened the books at bookmarked pages and compared certain passages to those in 'Lazarus Gospel.'

His husky body shook with laughter and a bright gleam flashed across his face. Yes, so it would be. Here was the key to the stars.

A bright Saturday morning, the sun was shining and the sky was clear. Aeneas had arrived around 10 am and was lounging on Peaches' back porch. They often got together for a Saturday and sometimes Sunday too. Often their best ideas arose during these leisure hours.

"Aeneas," Peaches called, breaking his reverie. "Come in. Virgil has important news."

Aeneas rose and entered the kitchen. Peaches was seated at the dining room table, sipping coffee and chewing an unlit Cuban cigar. She motioned for him to sit beside her.

"What's the latest, Virgil?" she asked.

"There's chatter about the 'Lazarus Gospel,'" he said. "Foster Meredith and Justin Knight are talking about it. Knight has invited Meredith to visit him."

"The visit is about the missing manuscript?" Peaches asked.

"Yes. They want to discuss the book and its disappearance. The meeting is tonight at 7 pm," Virgil said.

"So we can listen in," Aeneas commented.

"Maybe not. Surveillance devices aren't in every room in Knight's home. What if they sit outside?" Peaches was worried.

"We weren't thinking ahead, were we," Aeneas said.

"Can I make a suggestion?" Virgil asked

"Please," Peaches answered.

"Use your astral talent, the remote viewing you learned from Gloria on our previous case." A tone of satisfaction arose in Virgil's voice.

"Yes. Of course. I can be listening in wherever they are." Peaches felt invigorated. She would again travel in the psi-space of the astral realm. She had used occult powers to solve the recent investigation 'The Mystery of the Missing Cat.' Their client Gloria Smith had given Peaches a powerful charm as a reward and memento of the case. The charm was a miniature sitting cat figurine attached to a necklace. The cat had power to open the portal of the throat chakra allowing the wearer the potential to move through astral space and hear voices and sounds emitted from the astral field.

When Gloria had told them about the occult dimensions of reality, both she and Aeneas, and no doubt Virgil too, were astounded and disbelieving until she had tried the charm. Gloria's lover and roommate Sean Everday had given her the charm before his death. Sean had been totally committed to the Sorcerers and Wizards game, a mind game involving psi reality.

Gloria had instructed Peaches and Aeneas in the fundamental ideas of the Hindu chakras and their role in human life. The human body has a subtle energy system, more on the psychic level. There are seven main chakras, energy centers, from the base of the spine or kundalini root to the top of the head also called the lotus blossom crown.

The throat chakra, one of the seven main chakras, is involved with communication, intuition, and creativity. A link to the astral and psychic voice channels – it is considered the first level of advanced consciousness and a healing vortex because it is associated with the thyroid gland. What Peaches learned from personal experience was that this chakra allowed her to leave her body and permitted limited travel in the astral field.

Peaches' four room flat was decorated to suit her purposes. The living room had been redecorated to sustain a feeling of serenity and peace of mind. Here was where she could indulge in ideas with deep roots and potential solutions to her investigations.

At 7 pm she put the necklace with the cat charm around her neck and sat down in the power recliner chair, positioned the head and feet sections for the most comfortable sitting posture. Aeneas, as observer, was seated in a chair next to hers. She smiled at him and, touching the cat charm on the necklace, felt it vibrate. Quieting her mind, she focused on the image of Justin Knight, which Virgil had found on the internet.

Meredith and Knight were seated in the backyard. She was in her eagle seat on the second floor window ledge looking down at them.

"My cousin, who works for Mission Bay Insurance Company, told me it was the hottest story circulating through the insurance industry. Doug had insured the 'Lazarus Gospel' for one million dollars. My cousin's company is a coinsurer for a hundred thousand," Meredith said.

"What makes the book so valuable? Who would want to steal it?" Knight asked.

"Well, it's a rare antique, one of a kind manuscript according to Doug. There are book collectors who might want it for their library, like stamp and coin collectors who own specific coins or stamps," Meredith said.

"Before we discuss it further, let me say that I didn't take it. Did you, Meredith?"

"No, I didn't. It would be nice to have in my collection certainly, but I have no passion to own it."

"Before the meeting was adjourned, I had the opportunity to look at the manuscript. It was bookmarked to the Jesus-Lazarus episode that Doug makes so much of. I didn't read it carefully but quickly scanned it for its basic theme, which is that the two argue. Lazarus is very angry with Jesus."

"Now, that's interesting since Doug promotes the minority position that Lazarus is Jesus' beloved disciple."

"I don't see how an argument between the two is strong evidence for his thesis."

"So, there must be something else in the story that's important."

"Doug said he had a provocative announcement to make about the manuscript at the next meeting. Maybe the beloved disciple thesis is a cover for something more controversial."

"Could be. I wonder what he'll do now that it is missing? I've a question I've been meaning to ask. Your friend Marcus Scarpia has been attending the meetings. He doesn't seem to have the linguistic skills nor the background to be a serious participant in the discussions."

"I met him while teaching at Yale. He specializes in cultural history and taught courses in Medieval and Renaissance culture. When I moved out here for the job at Stanford, I lost contact with him. A few years ago he moved to the west coast and looked me up. We don't socialize much. He's busy studying esoteric disciplines – not my taste. When he learned about Doug's monthly gathering, he asked me if he could attend. I checked with Doug who agreed. I don't know what he's getting out of our discussions."

"Hmm. This is off the wall, but I wonder if the whole thing is a scam for the insurance."

"Ha. That's wild, but -- I don't know, why not. I guess anything is possible."

"I'm going ask him some pointed questions at the next meeting, whether there are other important issues besides the beloved disciple thesis. Well, I'd better be going. See you next month."

After Foster Meredith had left, Knight thought more about the possibility of an insurance scam.

Once Peaches had finished the refreshing orange juice, she told her team about the conversation between Meredith and Knight. Aeneas immediately picked up their insurance scam idea.

"So if Doug is pulling a swindle on his insurance company, the manuscript would not be stolen, only hidden away somewhere by Doug," Aeneas said.

"If true, I doubt that we would find it," Virgil noted.

"Until we locate the book, we won't know whether it was stolen or hidden away by Doug," Peaches responded.

"The insurance scam possibility places Doug in the group of top suspects," Aeneas remarked.

Peaches was thoughtful. After a few minutes she said, "Virgil, do a background check on Doug's financial holdings. Find out if he has lots of debt, whether he has much to gain from the insurance claim."

"And we need to put some surveillance devices in Doug's house. I'll talk to Lance about that," Aeneas said.

"If Doug still has the manuscript, where is it hidden? Something to think about," Virgil commented.

"I'm must puzzled by Knight's comment on the Jesus-Lazarus story. He told Meredith that Jesus and Lazarus were arguing and that Lazarus was angry with Jesus. Knight didn't understand how the episode supported Doug's position that Lazarus was the beloved disciple," Peaches said.

"Good point. Virgil, gather data on the biblical issue," Aeneas requested. "We need to be better informed so Doug's thinking is more transparent to us."

Chapter 8

Sitting on the couch in the social area of the two room apartment, she was waiting for her guest Alan Bird. Thinking back over the last two months, she reflected on the important changes and challenges that had occurred. Her anhinga water bird had warned about the danger the Garlands were in. She with her friend Sandra Kingfisher started researching in cyberspace for Peaches. Her male friend Jeffrey Brooke had returned to his Pawnee reservation in Oklahoma because of a family emergency. Serious medical problems had arisen and he had to be close by. He dropped out of school returning home. He had no time now for college and later he would attend the University of Oklahoma to complete the MA.

She had met Alan Bird at a Native American Student Organization meeting at San Francisco State University and soon discovered they had an affinity for each other. Anyone could join the organization and many did from colleges throughout the Bay Area. Stanford University had its own Native American Student Organization and attracted its own share of students.

She realized that she was lonely without Jeffrey and was probably on a rebound but needed intimate male companionship besides her female friends. Growing up in a large family, she relied on the special behavior of males and females. Each had its own strengths, and she combined them to form a more perfect self. Her female part required unity with a male part as portrayed by a close male acquaintance. Choosing the right male was a necessary requirement. She was given the intuition during her vision quest when a deer had appeared. As her spirit guide the doe gave her many insights, including the need for a male partner. She was told to be careful, not to choose the wrong one, a personality that clashed with hers.

Visualizing Alan made her smile. His dimples were charming and the twinkle in his eyes charmed her. He was average height and weight and most importantly he exuded the freshness of nature and mother earth's bounty.

He always seemed to have come right out of the forests of his Nez Perce homeland in Idaho.

Last Friday night she had dinner at Alan's apartment, enjoying a comfy evening with him. And they had began sharing their personal stories. Tonight she was host and would prepare dinner. She liked the notion of alternating Friday nights for hosting.

The doorbell chimed. Rafé got up and opened the front door. Alan was standing there with a bouquet of flowers. "Hi. I brought some of my homeland to you. A greeting of friendship."

She took the bouquet and he stepped into the apartment. "I'll put the flowers in a vase of water. Please sit down." She smiled to herself. How often is a young lady greeted like that?

Alan looked about the room, noting its three functional units: social, dining, kitchen. He liked the homey feeling and good vibes. He sat down on the couch.

Rafé called from the kitchen area, "What would you like to drink – coffee or tea?"

"Coffee, please."

When she returned, she gave Alan a cup of coffee and sipped hers as she sat down beside him. "I'd like to share cultural stories. If you don't mind me possibly using them for my magic dramas?"

"I'm amazed at your magical skills and ability to express cultural stories. Please, I'd be happy if you did. One of my goals is to preserve the people's culture and the values that go with it."

"How will you do that?"

"Through the law, of course." Alan was working on a MA in Jurisprudence at the University of California Hastings College of Law located in San Francisco. Noted for its excellence, Hastings was one of oldest law schools on the west coast.

"My thesis is a focus on the relationship between the federal government and tribal governments. I would like to understand the foundation of the legal connection and its history, which is to say, the historical process of development. The federal government hasn't been consistent among all the tribes. It seems like it has different rules for different tribes."

"The law has always been over the horizon for me. Just looking at the wording of a contract, I get dizzy."

Alan grasped her hand gently. "Actually, for me too. But that's not the area I'm studying. This is more like a mathematical problem – I analyze the legal concepts that form the foundation."

"So how will you preserve Indian culture?"

"I'll find existing laws that will apply to conserve the culture and encourage the enactment of new laws for that purpose." He paused and looked at her face. She was so bright and clearheaded. He was totally enchanted.

Then he told her about one of the people's key projects. "One main goal is to protect the nation's horse breeding program, which means ensuing enough land is available. Land control is a serious issue, and we have lost much of our original acreage."

"I know very little about horses and their breeding."

"They're many stories and some go back to earlier times. But now the program, started in 1994, crossbreeds Appaloosa and a Central Asian breed called Akhal-Teke to produce what we call the Nez Perce horse. They're lovely horses. You must come up to visit and I'll take you riding through our garden of Eden."

Rafé snuggled against him and felt boundless joy. "Who is your trickster spirit? The Potawatomi have great rabbit, who not only is a major trickster figure but brings powerful medicine down from above for the people's benefit."

"Coyote has a similar function – trickster and assisting the Great Spirit."

She had heard about coyote and its antics, but rabbit was an important woodland creature and so dominated the stories of her people.

"Part of our creation story you might find useful for magical routines," Alan said.

"Please tell me," Rafé responded.

Alan smiled with joy and amusement. "After the earth had been created but not human people, a great monster lived on the land. It was so large it drew creatures to it from fifteen miles away and swallowed them whole. The animals held a council to decide the best way to get rid of the monster. Coyote was the only one who could get close to the monster. Coyote took his fire-making kit and went to the monster. Hitting it on the mouth, Coyote stepped inside when the monster opened its jaws. The little warrior built a fire and the smoke was emitted from all the monster's openings. All the creatures inside the monster that were still alive left. Coyote took his flint and cut up the monster's heart until it died. To dispose of the huge body, Coyote and his friend Fox cut it into pieces which became the different tribes and were sent out to their traditional territory. So the earth was populated. In one story the monster's bones and blood were the material used."

"Of course, there are many versions, yes? Our stories have variants too," Rafé remarked. She snuggled against his chest smelling deeply of nature's fragrance. He seemed to carry about himself the presence of his homeland, the Kamiah valley, his garden paradise. She found his soft place, his sacred spot, comforting, and knew she would be safe here. She sensed his deep spiritual soul.

"The main image of the Nez Perce people for me is Chief Joseph and the attempt to enter Canada. What is the true story."

"Chief Joseph, the son of Chief Joseph senior, was leader of the Wallowa band from Wallowa Valley at the time. In 1855 separate areas for Indians and settlers were established in the northwest. In 1863 the federal government with pressure from the settlers wanted to make a new treaty to get more Indian land. The Nez Perce were promised many benefits, none of which they received. Some of the Nez Perce signed the treaty and others didn't. Chief Joseph Senior was opposed to the new treaty. On his death bed he requested his son Chief Joseph the younger to keep the land, protecting where the bones of his father and mother were buried."

Rafé thought of the removals of her people who were restricted to the much smaller land area of the new reservations. Such relocation had happened to most Native Americans.

"In 1873 Joseph negotiated to stay on their land in Wallowa Valley but in 1877 the federal government reversed its policy and told them it would attack in thirty days if the Wallowa Band did not relocate to the reservation. Joseph requested they be allowed time to roundup their huge horse herd and prepare for the removal. They could be ready in the fall. But General Howard was adamant and rejected the request.

"The Wallowa band readied itself and decided to cross over to Canada. Under the leadership of Joseph 750 Nez Perce and a small band of the Palouse tribe and their horse herd, some sources say over 2,000 or more, tried to escape to Canada. For over three months, the Nez Perce outmaneuvered their pursuers and won the battles, traveling 1,170 miles across northwest territory. The Indians used sophisticated military tactics, including advance and rear guards, skirmish lines, and field fortifications.

"Finally the weather, lack of food and blankets forced the Nez Perce to surrender after a five day battle in 1877. The band was unable to reach and cross the Canadian border only forty miles away."

"I didn't know all that."

"The US army, of course, had more warriors and a good supply line, receiving aid from nearby forts. My people relied on procuring food from the land in a traditional manner. And the warriors also had to hunt for food – no separate units for different activities."

Rafé sat up and said, "I remember mainly reading about Chief Joseph's famous words: 'We will fight no more.'"

"First, only the part of the band following Joseph surrendered. The other half under the leadership of White Bird crossed over to Canada and joined Sitting Bull and the Lakota.

"Now think about those words. There is an irony, especially since the evidence shows that an army officer, who was writing Joseph's biography, composed the words."

She looked him clearly in the eyes, seeing the fierce fire of his soul. "Of course, who benefits if the Nez Perce stop fighting and move to the new reservation. They don't, but the settlers do. Why didn't I ever realize that?"

"Rafé, we all have our blind spots and are often bamboozled by the establishment."

"Thank you for opening my eyes."

A bong sounded from the kitchen. She stood up and moved to the stove. "I believe dinner is ready." She hustled about the kitchen getting the meal which she placed on the dining table. "Come and be served," she said. "Would you like red or white wine?'

"Red," he answered. He looked eagerly at the array of food on the table: a bowl of wild rice with chopped nuts, sautéed fish, and a combination of corn and squash. They enjoyed the meal and talked about the student organization.

After dinner they adjourned to the social area. Rafé served coffee and cookies.

"I brought along my flute." Alan showed Rafé a leather pouch with beadwork. He loosened the draw strings and removed a flute. He raised the flute to his mouth and played a song.

"That was lovely, Alan. Does your flute have a story?" Rafé asked.

"Actually, I have four flutes: another the size as this fourteen inch one, one about eighteen inches long and the fourth twenty inches. Each flute is custom made by a Nez Perce woodcarver, Albert Penney. Each is keyed to a specific pitch. This is my favorite flute and is F sharp."

He handed the flute to her. "Put your fingers over the holes."

Rafé tried to, but the holes were further apart than she could comfortably spread her fingers. "They don't cover the holes," she said.

"That's because the finger holes, like other parts, are based on the performer's arm, fist, and thumb measurements. The distance between each finger hole is the width of my thumb. Of course your thumb width is different."

He put the end-blown instrument to his mouth and played a serenade. When he finished, he said, "I composed that one. And I'm working on one especially for you."

Rafé laughed, delighted. "I'll cook a special meal for the occasion."

As she snuggled against him, she said, "Let's visit Ocean Delights next week. I'd like you to meet the gang and especially the Garlands."

"Yes, I'd like to meet them. And your job doing research in cyberspace for them -- I know very little about computers and the high tech world. Perhaps you could teach me. I have basic computer skills for my work but not much more. And I'm definitely intrigued about surfing cyberspace and, you say, psi-space, whatever that is."

"I'll be happy to teach you. It'd be fun surfing with you."

Chapter 9

Today was the first meeting of Doug's biblical discussion group since the manuscript was stolen. Peaches decided to attend and observe all the members. She was settled comfortably in a ceiling corner of Doug's library where the monthly meeting occurred. The scholars attending today's session gave Doug their sympathy and wished him success at recovering the stolen manuscript. A few had had a chance to peruse the manuscript at the previous meeting.

Doug's valet Archie Jeeves had finished serving the beverages and departed. Doug was busy handing out sets of pages stapled together.

"So, Doug, what do we have here?" Foster Meredith asked.

"I had this material ready to handout at the last meeting, but I didn't have the opportunity. I thought that you could read it over in advance and discuss it this meeting."

"Our homework, eh, Doug." Foster laughed and got some snickers from other members.

"My English translation is side by side with the original text," Doug commented.

"Ah, for those of us who can't read the ancient languages. Very good," Justin Knight said.

"Today's discussion will focus on the 'beloved disciple' issue. Who is the beloved disciple, John of the Gospel or someone else?" Doug peered around at the assembled scholars.

"Well, now, Doug, what's your evidence?" Foster asked.

"Yes, Doug, let's hear it and the group can evaluate it." Justin was anxious to get to the heart of the issue.

"Please turn to page three of the handout. Here's the original text in classical Greek and my translation. It comments on the official belief the Church has taken on the beloved disciple issue."

"Yes. It criticizes the position that John is the favored one, Those were divisive times for the Church," Lawrence Hobbs remarked.

"My. It goes even further, doesn't?" Herb Gallaway glanced around the group. "It states emphatically John is not the beloved one and he didn't compose the gospel attributed to him."

"And this text is in the stolen manuscript?" Justin asked?

"Yes. It's one of several fragments. I've labeled the manuscript 'Lazarus Gospel' because the main part of the book describes the time when Jesus visits Lazarus after Lazarus has been resurrected."

Doug smiled at his colleagues. But before the coup de grâce he would pander to their frailty. "My translation is a rather loose one. The more literal meaning indicates it's a plot by certain Church leaders to promote John as the one. Remember the passage was originally composed at the same time as John's Gospel. There's a good chance several of the bishops favored someone else and this text was passed around among them."

"That's right. From the second century on until Constantine Christian leaders were fighting over whose authority would control the Church." Justin nodded approval.

Now for the coup Doug thought. "Notice here Lazarus is mentioned in the Greek passage. And on page four the medieval Latin text states Lazarus was well-known among Jesus' followers as his beloved disciple." Doug exuded delight as his colleagues read the passage and pondered the idea.

A gleam lighted Marcus Scarpia's eyes. He decided to add a little spice to the discussion. "Oh, Doug, I see here on page six where, according to your translation, a Gospel of Lazarus is mentioned. Does such a gospel exist and what in heaven's name would it be about?"

Delighted at Marcus' curiosity, Doug now began to present the essence of his thesis. "I've an amusing tale to tell. Recently I was in Rome to do research. And I stopped by the Vatican library. Believe it or not, an entry for the Gospel of Lazarus was listed in the catalog. When I requested it, I learned it was missing – actually been missing since 965 AD. And even more mystifying the entry lacked a description of the work's contents. This gospel is not the same as my manuscript. Of course, the description of the event in my manuscript could easily be derived the original 'Gospel of Lazarus."

"Is there any other evidence of the Gospel's existence?" Herb inquired.

"Yes. The Huntington Library in southern California has a Church history by Father Antonios based on a Greek copy dated around 750 AD.

According to the good father, a Gospel of Lazarus did exist and he considered it to be a Gnostic document and not part of the Church's canon. So he placed it with all the other apocryphal writings, dismissing it as non Christian and part of Satan's attack against the true Church."

Most of the members sat astounded. Marcus was one of the few who kept his own counsel, knowing the authentic situation. Being an accomplished classical linguist, Marcus Scarpia was proficient in reading all the texts, and he knew the actual content of the manuscript contained themes **Doug** was not sharing with his colleagues. Although he did not comprehend **Doug**'s full agenda, he was not concerned since his goals were not related to **Doug**'s.

As the meeting drew to a close and the members stored the handouts in their briefcases, Peaches gazed at the gathering and noted the variety of emotions being expressed by the scholars. Preserving the impression, she returned to her living room.

Aeneas noticed her stirring and hurried into the kitchen to get a glass of orange juice, which she found refreshing after remote viewing. When he returned, she was sitting upright and smiling. She took the glass, sipped some juice, and said, "What an amazing session. Let's talk. You won't believe several of the ideas that were proposed." She proceeded to give him a summary with details, including sound and video, filled in by Virgil.

After she finished the summary, Aeneas shook his head in wonderment. "I've read many unorthodox Biblical ideas and interpretations, but **Doug**'s thesis is wild, weird, and mind-boggling."

"We need to collect more data about the beloved disciple issue. There seems to be secrets waiting to be revealed."

"And," Virgil added, "we should spend more time spying on Marcus Scarpia, who appears to be not only an unknown element but perhaps the linchpin to the mystery."

"Yes, I'll be visiting Marcus often over the next few weeks. Virgil, inform me when Marcus is in his library studying **Doug**'s manuscript," Peaches said.

Sandra rang the door bell and waited. After a few minutes, the door opened and Dwight stood there. "Come in."

He hugged her. "It's good to see you."

She giggled. "We saw each two days ago."

"I could see you every day and that wouldn't be enough." He gave her another hug and kissed her.

She pushed herself away and walked into the social room. "I'll get some coffee," he said. She sat down on the couch and took off her sandals.

Dwight returned with two mugs and gave her one. She slowly sipped some coffee and then put the mug on the side table. She turned toward him, smiling brightly.

"My latest project, Dwight, is quite strange. I'm becoming a biblical scholar."

Dwight grinned at Sandra, "You, researching biblical stories?"

"Yes, but I'm examining a certain set of stories, which are definitely unconventional. You remember the story about Lazarus whom Jesus raised from the dead?"

"Wasn't he the brother of Mary and Martha, and they lived in Bethany?"

"That's the one. Not only am I supposed to gather all the data I can about Lazarus and his life, but the weird part is to collect data about Jesus' beloved disciple, including articles on the web."

"Why, that's John, the writer of the Gospel of John."

"Yes, the official doctrine asserts John of the Gospel is the beloved disciple. According to the Garlands there are other theories about the beloved disciple's identity. One of the most popular alternative proposals argues Lazarus is. Other people, like Mary Madeleine, have also been suggested."

"Awesome. It's a mind-boggling notion. What type of proof is there?"

"Finding viable arguments for Lazarus' role and gathering other sources of evidence is part of the project."

"What an assignment. It sounds like fun. If you need any help, let me know. I'd be delighted to assist."

"I'm looking forward to starting it, and I can give you some items to check out, if you want to be involved."

"Sandra, you've been a great tutor for my philosophy class, analyzing the complex ideas, which I have difficulty with. I can't understand the reason my mind gets so perplexed."

"I think you've a psychic block for some reason. You can dissolve the block, if you go inward and discover the cause."

"You're probably right. I've no problem with ideas in computer science and information technology. And I'm very proficient at analyzing and evaluating code."

"I'll help you find your inner self." She put her arm around his shoulder, hugging him, and kissed him on the cheek. His countenance brightened and the darkness of his soul disappeared.

"I've another favor to ask. My tag name is stealth and I'm very good at surfing cyberspace without leaving traces. But I'm not up to your speed. Perhaps you can explain the method you use and help me develop the skill to travel with a cloak of invisibility."

"Let's get some coffee and I'll think about the best way to explain my ability."

Once they had returned and sat down on the couch, Sandra sipped some coffee and placed the cup on the end table. "Quantum mechanics has become the fundament for the other sciences, so I'll select metaphoric examples from the world of subatomic particles. Remember the double-split experiment in quantum mechanics, which we learned about in high school physics? The dual nature of light, whether a particle or wave, becomes apparent."

"Yeh. When a photon is observed, it acts as a particle. When it's not, it behaves like a wave."

"The paradox of a dual nature is the key to my method and underlies my skill."

"How so?"

"I treat cyberspace and psi-space in a similar fashion. If I'm being observed, the watcher sees me as a particle. When I'm unobserved, I travel like a wave. When I move as a wave, I don't leave any traces. Leaving tracks that someone can observe makes me seem like a particle."

"An intriguing analogy, but what is the method you use to change from particle to wave behavior?"

"Ah. The method focuses on the mystery of the dual nature of space: cyber and psi. The two spaces are intertwined like the Kundalini energy flowing along the spine or a double helix. Thus at junctions of the two spaces I shift from cyber to psi becoming invisible to watchers and pursuers. When I returned to cyberspace, I lose much of my invisibility." She paused.

"I believe I understand."

"Another analogy is the Uncertainty Principle: an observer influences the particle's behavior. A corollary is the importance of consciousness for forming reality. An object takes on real properties when it's consciously observed."

"So you're saying consciousness isn't in our ordinary space-time field but resides outside of it."

"Yeh. You caught it." She smiled.

"Awesome. How do I develop the skills needed?"

"Meditation is a primary path. It's been utilized for thousands of years. And it works"

"Okay. Can you teach me the basics?"

"Definitely. We'll set up a schedule."

Chapter 10

Stopping at the lotus pond, Spenser sat down in a chair beside it. The colorful flowers planted around the pond were a delight to the eyes. Most rooms of his house were decorated with vases of flowers. His housekeeper Maud Hubbard maintained the floral display with fresh flowers cut from the garden every day.

Theo kitty dashed from behind a sage bush and leaped high into the air after a monarch butterfly and missed it by a foot. Spenser grinned. She had learned to play without harming any living thing. If humans could attain the same behavior, how much better the world would be.

If humans are going to advance, they must embrace their inner opposite, their other self. Long ago he had realized just how unbalanced and one sided humans were. When he had looked within himself during meditation, he had noticed the asymmetry immediately. Children are more whole and so have a more profound comprehension of reality, but they do not have the ability to conceptualize and verbally express their intuitions. As our verbal and intellectual skills increase, we begin to separate others into two groups -- 'us' and 'them' -- often based on a gender divide. Little girls do this, little boys do that. The unity of self has terminated. Divorce proceedings are proclaimed, and the individual is now only half a perfect human. And we normally do not recognize our failure, Spenser thought. We continue to the end of life living a lie or at best a half truth.

A new thought arose in his mind unexpectedly. God created man in his own image, male and female. Thus God is both male and female. Whoever hates one gender, whether male or female, hates God. Two implications jump out. Humans possess both male and female parts to their personalities. Hating one gender means hating oneself. In today's world that's a large portion of the population. So these haters of God – whom do they worship?

Spenser paused in his thinking. He inhaled the beauty of the garden. Another thread on the theme began.

The half self often denigrates the other part. Males frequently disparage females, who often ridicule males. The wounded self will flare into temper tantrums, grow intense hatreds, and become mean-spirited and cause harm to the other. Just as each gamete must unite with its opposite to form a whole living being, the divided self must unite with its opposite half.

The Adam-Eve story popped into his mind. He was always fascinated by the first four chapters of Genesis. Ideas whirled and interlaced, then quieted. He had another aha insight. His normal writing style as a scholar was not the only format ideas could be expressed in. With the help of Shasta Garland some of his ideas were being conveyed in fictional form. He made a crucial decision: he would no longer worry about precise vocabulary, rigid grammar, footnotes, and critiques of opposing views, but write popular essays about subjects of interest.

The Adam-Eve story raised many questions, and he was still searching for answers to some of them. The story was essential to fundamental ideas in all three Abrahamic religions: Judaism, Christianity, and Islam. Here was the origin of the separation of the whole perfect self into two parts – man and woman. In the first chapter of Genesis God creates humans in his image, both male and female. God obviously is a whole being. And in the second chapter God creates Adam from the clay, but Adam is whole because God later takes Eve from Adam. And everything goes wrong from this point on – supposedly.

Spenser heard a 'meow' and Theo leaped into his lap. He rubbed her behind the ears and received in return a warm purring. "What do you think of my idea to write popular essays?" he asked. Theo curled up and continued purring. Without disturbing her, he removed a notebook and pen from his jacket pocket and began jotting down ideas.

All three Abrahamic religions arose in a patriarchal culture and thus the interpretation of the bible is from such a view point. But what if the culture is matriarchal? From the view point of a goddess religion a totally different understanding occurs.

The Garden of Eden story poses several puzzling questions: why did God plant a forbidden tree in the garden where he placed Adam? Why create a taboo? What truth is hidden in the story? Why is our attention misdirected from the truth? Who is the real deceiver: God or the serpent? Is disobedience a sin?

For the official Christian position the story is about disobedience and the knowledge gained from eating the fruit is sexual. Also Eve becomes the culprit and bringer of evil into the world – a disgusting and irresponsible passing of the buck. The goddess knows better. Eve is the harbinger of truth and cosmic power.

The tree of knowledge of good and evil is a central idea. In the Genesis story Eve becomes the source or at least the bringer of evil into the world. The serpent, traditionally linked to the goddess, deceives Eve into tasting the fruit. Here is the misdirection, the lie, because in a matriarchal culture the serpent goddess would have told Eve to taste the fruit of the tree of life first! The serpent does speak truth, though, when it says that they, Eve and Adam, will not die. This is the goddess' truth: only the worn-out physical body dies, but the soul and spirit do not. The patriarchal god, however, is jealous and angry because they choose the goddess, so he forces them out of the garden before they have eaten of the tree of life. Why does god command them to remain in ignorance of the knowledge of good and evil? Or does he force their choice by telling them not to eat of that tree?

Theo's meow made him pause. He started to pet her and then realized she was no longer in his lap. Several meows caused him to search for her. He spied her on the Rock of Ages. Laughing, he called out, "What are you up to, Theo?"

She leaped high into the air after a fly only she could see. The sight of her jump birthed an insight about the soul and body.

Underlying the story is the idea that humans as souls choose to incarnate into this physical world and the only way to leave is when the physical body dies. A second idea is that the metaphor of the soul reuniting with the god or goddess is a return to Eden. The animal skin covering is the physical body. The serpent symbolizes birth, death, and rejuvenation. The patriarchal interpretation of the Genesis story shifts the life-giving attribute of the goddess to one of death, that is, changes the focus; however, the goddess has always signified life and death and then rejuvenation. The serpent's remark "You won't die" implies rejuvenation. The patriarchal god is actually the one who forces death upon Adam and Eve by kicking them out of the garden. In fact, the god is the first to mention the possibility of death. Was this god originally derived from the god consort of the goddess? The god consort went through seasonal cycles of death and rebirth, like

Adonis, the corn god, and others, and so this god would know and have experienced death and then resurrection. But did the god of Genesis have any personal experience of death?

The idea of death is first mentioned in Genesis 2:17 where it is connected to the knowledge of good and evil. In the very next verse God realizes that Adam is alone and that he should have "an help meet" or counterpart. Then God creates the animals, but none was "an help meet for him," and so Eve is made from a part of Adam's body.

A sharp irony struck him. When Eve followed the advice of the serpent, she created the opportunity for humans to obey God's command: be fruitful and multiply. If Adam and Eve had not been kicked out of Eden, they never would have reproduced and died.

"Yes, Theo, that's the crux of the matter. God's design is complex and multilayered." Theo purred acknowledgement. God takes the female from the whole Adam, leaving only a shadow of it, so Adam is in continual search for his other self. Eve is life itself in both physical and spiritual forms. The physical is, of course, necessary for procreation and the spiritual needed for self-completion. Eve is the guardian spirit, the cosmic fire, and must unite with the soul for renewal.

Spenser laughed silently. In Genesis 2 God breathes life and spirit into Adam after making him from the red soil: an example of the separation between spirit and nature in god religion. From a goddess perspective, for example in ancient Sumerian religion, Aruru, goddess of creation, makes humans by conceiving an image in her mind, dipping her hands in water, pinching off a piece of clay, and placing it on the earth. There is no need to breathe life into the human creature because it is alive and contains the spiritual in its nature.

Eve on the spiritual level as universal life understands the serpent, a primeval sign of renewal, and recognizes its truth. Eve as female reveals the continuous pattern of birth-death-rebirth, which is the principle of regeneration. Adam the male indicates the life of the individual, the short span of temporal life beginning with birth and ending with death. The dying god, a religious theme originating in antiquity, symbolizes physical life that is constantly changing, and the goddess illumines the principle of life that endures by eternally renewing itself. The goddess represents continuity while the god, sharing in the impermanent essence of the seed, dies annually.

In ancient mystery religions the neophyte enters the hidden subterranean recesses and dies a first death and only then does rebirth occur. Now the worldly and spiritual realms remain open to each other. The goddess was the portal into the hidden dimension through which the dead passed on their way to rebirth. The goddess as mother of life sends her children forth into the world and as mother of death gathers her children unto her as they return from the world. The natural cycles signify this process of life and death. Here is the great cosmic cycle of life and death: the soul coming from the goddess and its life cycle resemble the lunar cycle; at death the soul returns to the goddess.

A gentle breeze aroused him from his musings and he looked around, seeing Theo curled up next to the catnip. The sojourn in his inner garden was quite pleasant and he was pleased with the ideas he had collected.

Chapter 11

Lenny Sawyer was sitting in a reclining cushioned arm chair in the library, a room for leisure activities and informal socializing. Surprised and angry, he put down the tall glass of Thai iced tea that Bertha Wesley had prepared along with a plate of egg rolls. DOG, the super program, rang a warning signal, a blinking orange light synchronized with a four tone chime, appeared on the control panel installed in the arm of his chair.

DOG had many subroutines. The one that had sounded the alarm, causing Lenny to lose his appetite for the afternoon snack, had discovered strange unaccountable cyber tracks. The subroutine had followed the traces, seeking to locate their original source. The cyber tag of the potential opponent was elf, whose surfing activities were becoming a challenge to his domain.

Lenny was very distraught because elf was collecting too much unauthorized data, especially from NSA's databases scattered around the world. And elf did not seem to have any difficult accessing the data without leaving traces to alert the government. Elf was a threat to his domain because he felt very territorial about many of the world's databases.

Any surfer who penetrated NSA's operating system could travel through the multilayered web linking all the government's security and surveillance agencies. The portals to all the systems were now open and intelligence data easily accessible. Usually the surfer started with the US Strategic Command or STRATCOM, which was a hub linking more specialized agencies and the leader "in Strategic Deterrence and Preeminent Global Warfighters In Space and Cyberspace." Perhaps the most important subsumed agency was ISR or Intelligence, Surveillance and Reconnaissance, which amassed intelligence data from many sources. As an insider commented, "If something isn't monitored by the government, it doesn't exist."

When he had first become chief administrative executive, he had idealized his boss, seeing him as mentor and guru. So he had decided to use a cyber tag based on Quincebury's Tau tag. He chose Tau-2. He would activate

Tau-2 and enter cyberspace, but to become the hunter he required the full power of the platform in the command center. Taking the elevator to the top floor, he walked around the main area, which was sectioned into functional units located along its circumference. All the furnishings were those of a successful CEO's office. He hurried to the entrance of the command center and walked up the five steps to the bridge. Sitting down at the command console, he observed all the monitors. Then rapidly touching the control screen in front of him, he opened the special program that allowed him to become Tau-2 and hunt unwary interlopers.

He switched on the waveform channel in the main monitor, opened the database for waveform equations, and typed 'psi spectrum' on the touch screen. Psi bosons, existing in the psi spectrum, were the vehicles for his travels. Actually they were manifestations of the field. Like all bosons they could occupy the same quantum state simultaneously, if they had the same energy. He selected the set of equations appearing on the monitor. Waveforms of the psi field moved across the screen. He entered the GPS coordinates for NSA's storage locations. The special program thrust Tau-2 into the psi field, and he began the hunt.

Carlyle had not slept well for the past week. His mind, the part which was still functioning, was too busy analyzing various scenarios to inflict revenge on Ralph Garland. His anger, which he stoked constantly, fed a deep seated motivation. One of the few pleasures he now had was visualizing Ralph's torment and destruction.

This morning when he had awakened, the solution to his conundrum had flooded his intellect: darkness. Darkness had been his weakness and caused his stroke. During his attendance at the Consciousness Fair at the Rainbow Inn, he had tried to talk with Ralph. When he had reached the platform on the spiral staircase where Ralph had vanished, the shadows had triggered panic, a fear and trembling he had never experienced before. Rushing down the staircase, he had collapsed at the bottom, and then the debilitating stroke had occurred. A large part of his motor and coordination centers had been paralyzed as too some of his speech center. If Ralph had been friendly and willing to discuss with him the secret that is never revealed, none of this would have happened. But no, Ralph's huge ego and super arrogance had prevented any accord between them.

Now, he realized, darkness could cause Ralph's downfall, not in the same way as his but in a way even more painful. The shadow would pursue Ralph, terrorizing him and creating general harassment. Carlyle required two things: a cloaking device and Lenny's assistance. He could now put Lenny's loyalty to the test, but first an invisibility cloak. He pushed a button, raising the top part of his bed so he could use the laptop sitting on the bed table. He sent a coded email to Bryant Cowper, head supervisor of the corporation's research and development unit. The high tech lab was located down south in San Mateo County, the silicon valley region. Bryant's office was in the San Francisco headquarters of Madrone Advanced Systems. Carlyle wrote that an emergency existed and requested Bryant to come to his home by noon today.

He sat back, delighted with the forthcoming adventure, a new game to play on his evil adversary. Typing on the laptop's touch screen, he notified the kitchen he wished a special lunch today: grilled pastrami and cheese on rye with large dill pickle spears and concluding with a hot fudge sundae. He typed in the menu and sat back thinking about the bright vision he now possessed.

Haydn's *Symphony #104* was playing when Bertha delivered Carlyle's lunch. He was fond of the Baroque and Classical styles. Bach and Haydn were his two favorite composers with Mozart next in line. The Romantics were too unruly for his taste. They lacked the precision and discipline he demanded in all parts of his life.

She smiled at him as she set the food tray on the bed table. "Here's the special treat you ordered. I hope you enjoy it," she said. She picked up the napkin and placed it over his chest. "Do you need any help eating?" she asked.

He smiled at her. "No, I'm fine. Thank you, Bertha."

She left the room. He ate slowly, savoring the flavors of the food. When he had finished, he pressed the call button on his bed. He closed his eyes, letting his thoughts flow freely. He was dozing when Bertha returned.

After Bertha had cleared the luncheon dishes, he thought about his housekeepers, Don and Bertha Wesley, both students at SF State. They lived in an apartment separate from the remainder of his mansion and performed typical housekeeping tasks. They received monthly wages plus free room and board. It was a good deal for everyone. They would be graduating at the end of next semester and he must start his search for replacements.

Chimes played indicating someone was in the hall waiting to enter his room. He pressed the release button and the door opened. Bryant Cowper walked in carrying his briefcase. Carlyle motioned to a chair close to the bed, and Bryant sat down in the chair and placed the briefcase on the table next to it.

"Sir, you said an emergency existed, so I brought summaries of all our projects." Bryant pointed to the briefcase.

"An emergency definitely but for an innovative and novel project. I want a cloaking device about the size of a cell phone. Gather all data on research of invisibility cloaks. Now I would like a summary of the latest developments you know about."

Bryant stared at his boss uncertain where to begin. "Mr. Quincebury, there has not been much advancement over the prototypes built last year. The theory's basic assumption is to prevent a specific part of the electromagnetic spectrum from 'seeing' an object. Metamaterials are used for the cloak because they have a structure that influences electromagnetic radiation and sound. Some of these structures can give invisibility to objects because they obscure objects from certain kinds of electromagnetic radiation or certain parts of the electromagnetic spectrum, thus making them invisible. The latest prototype is the metascreen, a structure resembling a fishing net, developed at the University of Texas, Austin. Supposedly, 3D objects can be hidden by it. Each cloak is designed to obscure a specific type of electromagnetic radiation. None has been developed to screen the whole electromagnetic spectrum. Major research is for military purposes, especially hiding aircraft. Civilian purposes are not considered socially beneficial and very little grant money is available for such research."

Carlyle clasped his hands together and gazed off into space. Then smiling, he said, "Here's what I want. We will design and construct a device to cloak the human body. The device should be a small, handheld unit about the size of a cell phone or smaller would be even better. Probably, you'll want to investigate nanotechnology. I think our solution can be found by exploiting the quantum world of atoms and molecules. Hidden within the texture of matter are secrets yet to be revealed. And you can start researching a device that absorbs photons from around an object making it invisible: the photon gun. Madrone Advanced Systems has enough grant funds to keep the project going for years. I want top priority for the cloak with top secret security clearance for everyone assigned to the project. We will lease a special campus for the work and provide it with its own cloak of invisibility." Carlyle smiled at his bit of humorous irony.

"We'll get right on it, Mr. Quincebury. I've just now notified the head supervisors of the personnel, security, and property management units to meet with me later this afternoon when I get back to the office. The project will be off the ground by tomorrow morning."

"Excellent. Be here at nine am tomorrow and fill me in. Also bring all available data on cloaking research."

Bryant stood up, took his briefcase from the table, and left.

After the door shut, Carlyle typed on the touch screen and opened DOG JR, a smaller, more sophisticated version of DOG, which collected all data at all databases throughout the planet indiscriminately, although parameters could be set to filter out specific kinds of data. DOG JR allowed Carlyle to gather data on explicit topics. He set the parameters with precise functions and definitions that would collect only data on cloaking. Enough data should be available by the end of the week for Bryant Cowper and his staff to build a cloaking device, specifically a photon gun.

Carlyle turned on the surround sound system and enjoyed a Bach fugue.

At nine am Bryant Cowper entered Carlyle's room. Carlyle motioned him to the bedside chair. Cowper placed his briefcase on the table and removed a binder. "Here's the report on the most recent cloaking research." He handed it to Carlyle, who said, "Give me a summary of the research. I'll read the report later."

"The research is being conducted by the Lawrence Berkeley National Laboratory and the University of California, Berkeley. It is involved with light at the microscopic level. Light waves are manipulated to reflect off an object so that it cannot be seen by the eye. The cloak is made from tiny gold fibers and its surface redirects the light waves so that the object is invisible. The cloaking process still has several issues to solve and of course applying it to a large object will be a serious challenge posing complex problems."

Carlyle smiled. It fits with my ideas neatly, he thought. "The work at Berkeley is the place to start. The issues with cloaking large objects like human beings are to be resolved. Keep me informed of your progress," he said.

"Thank you sir," Cowper answered. He stood up, took his briefcase, and left the room.

He was exuberant. He began to fantasize about the torments that would soon be inflicted on Ralph. He visualized Ralph becoming more and more despondent, sinking deeper into the mire of self-pity. Yes, his revenge would be sweet. He dozed off with a happy expression on his face.

Chapter 12

I was sitting in the Muse's chair, where I think deep thoughts, following the direction of my intuition, and immersing myself in the creative imagination. The chair, of course, is in my study where I compose novels and poetry. It's the third bedroom on the second floor of our home and has been decorated to enhance my creative powers. Today both Lucy and Karma were assisting me, Lucy on my lap and Karma on the desk next to the keyboard. Rafé's vision had been a recurring mental pattern roving through the byways of my mind for the past three weeks. I realized it had meaning for all three of us. Now that Spenser Blake had furnished his basic ideas and themes with comments, I perceived the relationship of the vision to the novel he had hired me to write. 'Resurrection' and 'elixir of life' were two of the five items that referred to something in our daily activities as a restorative process. Both items were contained in the vision and at the same time important elements in the novel, which I'm calling for now "Lazarus' Gospel."

Ralph had told me all the details of his quarrel with Carlyle Quincebury and Carlyle's belief that my husband was the cause of all his difficulties. So 'gun' and 'photon' remained to fit into my life. Suddenly, an aha touched my soul triggering my intuition. Peaches in her adventures with Scarpia was utilizing remote viewing (RV) and a form of out-of-body experience or OBE. I didn't see any functional difference between the two and my experience always involved a combination of them.

I had learned remote viewing at the Institute of Consciousness-Imagination-Nous or Institute of CIN from Philip Austen, one of the scientists studying psi phenomena. Philip had cajoled Ralph into performing a series of psi experiments, and, as it turned out, Ralph was quite talented, as I had suspected. After Ralph described his RV activities and we discovered he could enter the future thoughts of my creative imagination, I decided to learn. Philip and his two sidekicks Geri Meadows and her brother Jerry taught me to center my mind on a powerful image, one that was meaningful and pleasant. Ralph used a mental picture of what he called the twelve mansions or rooms of his mind. I didn't find the image particularly helpful. Then my Muse spoke and I focused on one of the most important locations of my childhood, Panther Meadows, a serene meadows located about 7800 feet up the slope of Mt. Shasta, my namesake. As a child I had discovered its special power. It was a sacred place, and I always felt comfortable and secure there. So Panther Meadows had been my choice for the portal to my creative imagination.

With RV I would visit Carlyle Quincebury at his home in St. Francis Wood and inspect his reality. I focused on Panther Meadows and found myself looking down on a large computer system with several monitors tuned to different channels. A young man sat at the control center, watching the monitors and operating a touch screen keyboard. One intriguing thing about RV or OBE is that the viewer absorbs information from the psi field surrounding the location, at least as Philip Austen explained it.

So my mind was bombarded by data from the psi field. The young man was Lenny Sawyer, acting as chief administrator of Carlyle Quincebury's business empire while Carlyle was recuperating from a devastating stroke. I observed Lenny for awhile and then went to Carlyle's room where he was napping. I returned to watch Lenny and gathered more data which I would digest later. 'Gun' and 'photon' were bits of data and I was excited to learned the purpose they had for Carlyle and Lenny.

I felt a wet tongue licking my cheek and returned to my study. Lucy was licking my face while Karma was sitting near the door. When I had become alert to the kitties and their message, I got up and followed them downstairs to the kitchen. I was exuberant. I possessed an enchanted tale to share with Ralph tonight.

Bryant Cowper and his team had performed superb work. After ten days with a little assist from Carlyle's data gathering the team had constructed a prototype of a photon gun. He had told Bryant to continue research at the new campus. Perhaps other innovations would be discovered.

He typed Lenny's ID onto the touch screen, requesting his assistant to join him in his room immediately. He would start Lenny working the new project with photon gun.

Lenny stood in the hall outside of the bedroom door and pushed the announcement button. Chimes resonated throughout the hallway, the door opened, and Lenny entered. His boss was sitting up in bed with a broad smile on his face. Lenny was surprised. Something positive and unusual had changed Quincebury's normal humorless mood.

Quincebury beckoned to his assistant, indicating a chair next the bed. "Come close. I've an important project to discuss, very high security."

Lenny approached the bed, turned the chair toward the great man, and sat down. Happiness emerged from Lenny's soul, and he eagerly awaited to learn about the new adventure.

"Lenny, I'm offering you a great honor and I trust that you'll maintain my faith in your loyalty. The task will be a first, until now only found in fiction."

The young man took the bait, sat up alert, and waited for Quincebury to provide the details. "Under the able supervision of Bryant Cowper the research team has designed and built a cloak of invisibility. Yes, 3D objects can now be made invisible."

Lenny was too astonished to say anything. Then he exclaimed, "Awesome. Amazing. It's difficult to believe."

"No, Lenny, it's not a matter of belief but of faith. Belief is someone's opinion. Faith is at the foundation of our existence. Here --" He opened the drawer of the bedside table and removed a small leather bag. From the bag he took a device about the size of a cell phone, which had a small screen and a few keys. He showed it to Lenny, whose eyes widened when Quincebury vanished. He started to reach toward the space Quincebury had filled and then jerked his hand back. A disembodied voice spoke, "Don't be frightened. I'm still here. Touch me."

Lenny reached out again and felt a body. "You're there but totally invisible. I'm astounded."

"The device is top secret and only a few know of its existence. The project I want to carry out is between you and me. No one else must know about it. Do you agree?"

"Definitely. You can trust me to the utmost secrecy."

Quincebury handed the photon gun to Lenny and explained the use of the screen and ten keys. Pointing to each button, Quincebury said, "This button increases the absorption of the field so the number of photons is decreased, and that one has the opposite power to decrease the field's absorption so the number of photons is increased. You can regulated the power of the absorption field. Do not absorb more photons than necessary. Those four buttons are directional and provide a means to direct the field to absorb different sections of the region. That button automatically cloaks the holder of the device, so directional maneuvers are unnecessary, This button turns the field's power on and the one next to it switches it off. The last button turns the device on and off. Any questions?"

"Not at the moment. I'll experiment with the gun first. If a difficulty appears, I'll ask." His face shone with pleasure.

"Now the screen. Its purpose is to show the amount of the object's visibility and so the quantity of photons absorbed. Turn the device on and point it at an object in the room. The screen depicts the shape of the object and its location in the immediate vicinity. As the object vanishes, the shape will become a broken line. When the object is no longer visible, the broken line will become dim. But you'll always be able to 'see' the object in its surroundings. Of course the reverse is true. As the object becomes more visible, the line darkens and becomes unfragmented."

Lenny rotated the gun in his hand, studying all sides. "Amazing. Okay, what is my task?"

"Simple. I want revenge on Ralph Garland for devastating my life. My stroke and all the damage it caused was his fault. I want him totally ruined."

"Why not hire a paid assassin?"

"No. Let me explain. I want him to suffer pain and anguish. The damage must occur to his ego and personality. Annihilating his intellect will throw him into the darkness of his unconscious."

"And how do I perform the maneuver?"

"I'll leave that to your inventive imagination. I'll give you some suggestions. The photon gun provides the opportunity to become a stealth warrior. He won't be aware of your presence so terrorize him, creating a mental breakdown. I've the utmost faith in you, Lenny my son. Don't fail me."

Quincebury waved dismissal and Lenny left with a magical tool, uncertain how to use it.

Lenny returned to the command center. Before entering the bridge, he removed a bottle of beer from the refrigerator. Opening it, he took a big swig. It was cool and refreshing. He climbed the five steps to the bridge and sat down in the command chair. He began to imagine techniques to harass Ralph Garland. With the photon gun it would be easy to get close to his victim. But what terror might he create? He required more data on Ralph, his background and personality. Opening DOG JR, he set parameters to collect specific information about Ralph. Then he thought of Ralph's wife Shasta. His enemy would worry about her safety and well-being. So he added her to the parameters. He pressed the go button and sat back, waiting for the program to do its job.

Chapter 13

I was sitting in some sort of a container, like a space capsule. It was not a ship since I had no sense of movement. I had a 360 degree view and could zoom in and out on specific sectors. On the horizon in front of me I saw human activity so I zoomed in on it for a more detailed look. Playing with the controls, I discovered I could change the angle of my view. The environs seemed familiar. Then I realized it was my neighborhood. And the people – why, they were friends and acquaintances, including characters from the story I was writing for Spenser Blake.

How fascinating, I thought. I get to see what my characters are doing before my Muse sings about them. A preview that I can modify, change totally, or reject.

I'll focus on Peaches, the hero of my tale. She watched as Peaches entered a building. Then she followed the detective. I've my own stakeout, she thought. Peaches went through a door into a long corridor. Doors were present in both walls of the corridor. She watched Peaches open the closest door and step into the area. After a few moments Peaches left and entered the next door on the same side of the corridor. She continued entering and shortly afterwards leaving the rooms behind all the doors. When she reached the end of the corridor, she started exploring rooms behind the doors on the other side of the corridor. When she arrived back at the starting point, she departed from the building.

Well, Shasta thought as she sat back in her chair, there are many future directions my detective can take. I wonder if I the creative artist have a choice in the matter? She reviewed all the possible scenarios, seeking the one she liked he best. What will happen if I make a conscious choice? Or I could allow my Muse to tell me. It would be a voice from my unconscious that notified me of Peaches' future.

She decided to make a conscious choice and see what happened. In one of the rooms Peaches is not only trying to locate the stole book but also searching for her true self. I like that combination, she thought. I'll select that future for my hero.

Shasta was peering down at Peaches in a room that contained objects of a personal nature: cosmetics, perfumes, clothes, pictures of different hairstyles, and several mirrors, both hand held and wall hanging ones. Peaches looked at a wall hanging mirror and gasped. She turned her attention to the variety of cosmetics. She inspected each type and then moved to the pictures of hairstyles. After visualizing herself with each hairdo, she put the pictures down and sampled the different perfumes. Next she examined the clothing section. She held up different apparel – dresses, blouses, and pants – in front of herself before a mirror. She wanted to find just the right garment. Then she checked out the shoes.

Oh, Peaches, Shasta thought, that's not the method to find your true self. A still, small voice spoke to Shasta, telling her that she should not interfere, that Peaches must make her own decisions.

A movement to her left caught her attention. Shasta turned and looked in that direction. She saw a figure. The image automatically enlarged. She gasped. It was Ralph. He was standing on the stage in his studio. A close-up magic table was sitting in front of the floor-to-ceiling mirror. She spotted a tiny object on the table. The image enlarged. She was surprised. A miniature doll stood on the table. Ralph moved his hand in the air. The doll strode forward toward Ralph. The doll stopped. It turned around and walked toward the other side of the table. When it reached the edge, the doll stopped and again turned and strolled toward Ralph, who seemed to be manipulating the doll's movements with his hands.

What amazing routine. I wonder where he discovered it. She watched as he went over to the shelves with magic props and took a box and returned to the table. Placing the box on the table, he spoke to the doll, "Come little man. Get into your nest." The doll strode to the box and climbed into it.

"Little man, get out of your nest," he said. The doll peek out of the box and then jumped out. The scene dissolved.

Shasta was stunned. What have I witnessed, she thought?

Hearing a meow, she opened her eyes and glanced down at her lap where Karma was sitting. "Karma, dear, I've just had the most amazing dream-vision in my life," she said as she petted the kitty. This will be a fascinating topic for happy hour tonight. What's happening to my reality?

As if reestablishing the concrete, mundane world, Karma jumped down and hurried to the study door where Lucy was waiting. They left the study and headed downstairs to the kitchen with Shasta following in their paw-steps.

Seated at her round table in the living room, Shasta felt an inner warmth. A bright energy shone in her eyes. Karma was curled up on the couch and Lucy nested in the easy chair next t o the table. Ralph entered and, handing her a martini, sat down on the couch. She slowly sipped the dry martini. Putting the glass down on the table, she smiled and said, "I had a weird experience this afternoon while I was in a visionary state."

Ralph looked at her quizzically. "While you were meditating?" he asked.

"Yes, I suppose I was in a state of meditation. At first I was watching Peaches explore possible futures. I was peering into my creative imagination."

"Marvelous. Discover what's going to happen before the Muse carries it into your awareness."

"Yes. I made certain decisions for the future direction of my new novel. Peaches and the other characters will now do the fine tuning."

"What were the selections?"

"The primary theme was for Peaches to encounter her true self. The theme will run parallel with the mystery of the stolen 'Lazarus Gospel.'"

"Ah, good. The theme of restoration has two sides: body and self."

She held up the martini glass. "A refill, please. Then I'll tell an even more bizarre experience."

He noticed the 'you-won't-believe-this' look and felt a deep uncertainty. Taking both glasses, he hurried into the kitchen and shortly returned. She took the martini and sipped. "Please be seated for this tale."

He sat and sipped his martini. Lucy leaped up onto his lap and Karma settled next to him. The kitties were ready for the unbelievable.

"After I watched Peaches select future options, my attention was attracted to some movement on the horizon on my left. The image suddenly enlarged. Behold, here you were performing a magic routine in your studio. The routine was astonishing. A doll was standing on one of your magic tables. The doll walked forward, turned around, strolled to its starting point, and then turned again and strode toward you. The doll's movements seemed to be controlled by hand motions." She paused, sipped some martini, and stared at Ralph.

Ralph sat in silence with his mouth partially open. A expression of awe marked his face.

"The second part of the routine was even more astounding. You took a box and put it on the table and told the doll to get into the box. Actually, you called the doll 'little man.' It followed your command and then you told it to get out. The little man performed that action too. At this point the scenario vanished and I was back in my rocking chair." She finished the martini and held up the glass.

Ralph stood with a bewildered appearance and took her glass and along with his own went to the kitchen. When he came back, he was smiling. Giving Shasta her martini, he sat down on the couch.

"You gave me a shock. Not since I learned that I had entered your creative imagination for your previous novel, have I been as stunned as I am now. To provide a rational structure, I believe you observed the workings of my imagination. Of course, how this entanglement is possible is baffling. The idea is absurd, but it has happened. The experience is real even if the notion is irrational."

"That's true of all visionary experiences I've read about. And we both know that reason has its limits."

Ralph rose and raised his right arm in the air. "There are more things in heaven and earth, Shasta, than are dreamt of in our philosophy."

She laughed. "With a couple minor changes, you're quoting Hamlet's famous statement to his friend Horatio. Perhaps the answer is simple after all."

"Oh. What might it be then?"

"Referring to another famous line of Hamlet's, 'The time is out of joint.'"

A brightness engulfed Ralph. He jumped up and hurried over to Shasta. Putting his arms around her shoulders, he kissed. "My dear, that's wonderful. You turned on a light in my mind. Let me tell what I've been doing."

She finished her martini and held up the glass. "First things first," she said.

He quickly went to the kitchen and returned. He gave a glass to Shasta and then sat down on the couch. After sipping some of the drink, he placed the glass on the side table. "I've been considering a new magic show, so I've been playing with various possible themes in my imagination. At the moment I'm focused on a shamanistic theme. I'm doing basic research on the topic with a view of finding magical routines inherent in the philosophy."

"What is the doll-like figure's purpose?"

"It's one of the magical routines that a mide or mystic can perform. The mide is a medicine person who is a member of the Grand Medicine Society or Midewiwin, which is a very important spiritual society among the Potawatomi and, I've heard, for all the Algonquian people. Rafé has told me about it and then I did some research. The mide make the dolls or little men and are able to animate them. How? I don't know. Presumably with the aid of a spirit guide." Ralph paused and laughed. "Also Harold Magian gave me a demonstration."

"Harold? I've forgotten about him. He didn't returned, did he?"

"No, it happened when he was here the first and only time. I've thought about him, wondering if he might return."

Shasta sat in silence. A puzzled expression shown on her face. "So I entered your creative imagination as you once did mine. It's all too weird and unsettling. I feel strange, somewhat unstable."

"I did too when I learned that I had visited your imagination. But now I accept the experience as I do any other remote viewing incident. I've tried to devise a rational explanation. The best I've come up with so far is that time is involved.

"How so?"

"I've developed a set of ideas about time, which I'll use in my next magic show. The concepts are derived from shamanism. I assume the existence of at least two realities: the sacred and profane. Our daily world, the profane realm, has time in our normal sense: past, present, and future. The sacred world, on the other hand, is static. Time doesn't exist there. The two realities are linked by a movement of manifestation. A part of the sacred can be manifested in the mundane realm at any time, and then it can vanish. In some way we can enter the sacred. The source of the imagination resides in the sacred realm."

"Whoa. Please stop here. I'm overloaded. I need to think about the ideas."

They sat in silence. The only sound was the purring of the kitties.

After a few minutes, Shasta said, "Okay. Your explanation is acceptable, whether correct or not, and gives me a rational lifejacket to prevent drowning in the emotional turmoil in my mind."

"My dear, we've emerged into an unconventional and spooky existence. Our new skills have taken us to the edge of normal life. The unexpected has now become part of our world."

"Yes, we now are in an alternate reality from what we've been living. Well, what other effects are you considering for the new show?" Shasta decided a practical approach was healing.

"I'm thinking about three magical effects: the little man, shape-shifting, and the sacred clown. Now that I have the topics the next step, and certainly the most challenging, is to create the story and design the props. The two go hand in hand. The props are embedded in the story which will present the theme."

She stared at him, smiled, and then giggled. "That's a definite challenge, but what fun it'll be. Do you want me to help?"

He brightened. "Yes, yes. You can help prepare the show and also be a character in it. Rafé too. Perhaps Peaches and her team can be involved. The more the better – a community project."

She rose and walked over to the couch. Taking his head in her hands, she kissed on the mouth. "I have to check on dinner." She left for the kitchen with the kitties in front.

Entering the kitchen, she glanced at the kitties' bowl of dry food. It was half full and she decided it did not require any more food. The kitties believed otherwise. They sat by the bowl looking at her with a forlorn expression.

"You have enough munchies," she told them. They began devouring the food.

Taking the lid off the pot on the stove, she stirred the chili with a large cooking spoon. Scooping up some of the chili, she blew on it, cooling it, and then tasted it. It needs more spices, she said to herself. Adding some chili powder and oregano, she stirred the chili.

Ideas stimulated by the discussion with Ralph flowed through her mind. She would multitask. Ah, she reflected, here is an example of the two realities notion, which was very intriguing. She recognized its importance for creative endeavors.

Placing the lid on the pot, she walked to the work counter and removed a loaf of sour dough bread from its bag and sliced pieces from the loaf.

When she was young, she considered her imaginary world as her personal domain, a place where she could do anything she wanted to. Unlimited by the rules and laws of the adult world, it gave her a sense of freedom and challenge. She could play different roles, restricted only by her imagination.

Removing a container of margarine and a bottle of crushed garlic from the refrigerator, she placed them on the counter. She then put some margarine into a bowl. Adding some crushed garlic, she mixed them.

In her teens she thought about the nature of the imagination. It provided a personal stage for drama and ideas. But wherever did the scenarios and visions come from? They would suddenly appear in her mind and she would choose among them, selecting those she wanted to use at the moment for her creative projects. She thought they might reside in a hidden dimension of reality, a place she longed to visit and explore, a treasure-trove of wondrous possibilities, of strange creatures and enchanted environments.

She spread the garlic flavored margarine on the bread slices and placed them in a flat pan, which she put into the oven.

She felt an intuitive appeal for Ralph's idea that the imagination resided in the sacred world and at various times manifested in the everyday world. When it did and she was open to her Muse, inspiration fueled her creativity. She immersed herself in writing.

The chili would be ready in another ten minutes. Then she would toast the bread slices. Pleased, she returned to the living room to tell Ralph about her thoughts on the imagination.

Chapter 14

Sitting in the rocking chair, moving back and forth to the slow rhythm of his heart, Ralph thought about Shasta's work-in-progress. She was on the threshold of a new and strange direction her imaginative writing was taking. Portraying the other reality was an important goal as was the blending of the two worlds: mundane and sacred. He found it a worthy purpose and had built the last two magic shows around the idea. Her enthusiasm spurred his desire to considered another show based on the idea.

He decided to start working on it now with all the positive energy surrounding him. He had mentioned to Shasta last night that he was focusing on shamanism. Since she had told him about her visit to his creative imagination, he realized that shamanism had the strongest attraction. But before he made a final decision, he reviewed the many sacred topics available for a magic show. He had performed a show using alchemy and most recently one expressing advanced consciousness. He stopped rocking and stood up. He walked over to his library, which contained not only books on stage magic and esoteric disciplines but also on Native American culture. He removed from the shelf *Shamanism*, Mircea Eliade's ground-breaking studies on indigenous culture.

He walked back to the rocking chair and sat. Leafing through the book, he surveyed ideas as they flowed by his inner eye. The shaman's world view is a sturdy building-block in the perennial philosophy. It is a thread that travels from the Paleolithic through the Neolithic down to modern times. The older he got, the more deeply Ralph felt the truth in the indigenous vision.

A shaman is made. From the spirit world comes the call to take the path of mystery, power, and wonder. One is chosen by a spirit being who prepares and assists the initiate along the dangerous yet esteemed journey. When called, the selected person has no choice but to heed the spirit's voice. What strange adventures Jonah had when he at first refused the call!

The entrance of Harold Magian in his life changed the foundation of his philosophy and the direction of his career. Harold had appeared suddenly in his studio, assisted him in his newest magic project at the time, and applied healing balm to his unsettled mind. Then Harold had vanished, returned to New York City supposedly. Ralph stared at the mirror in back of the performing area, his little stage. From his viewpoint Harold had stepped right out of the mirror, an Alice in wonderland episode. He was forced to take the challenge and accept the reality of his experience. Harold was not an apparition. Harold existed in a physical body like he did. Shasta and all their friends met the strange man, who was a very congenial helpful companion.

After Harold left, Ralph plunged further into the world of natural magic. And his attitude definitely underwent a major revision. He was a stage magician who was immersed in the sacred and utilized its power. He was becoming a real magician.

At a recent Assembly 2 meeting the routine he was presenting took a bizarre turn. Using the major arcana of the tarot, he performed a 'find the selected card' routine. The assistant, a member of the audience, chose a card, showed it to the others, and returned it to the deck while Ralph's back was turned. Taking the deck, Ralph shuffled it and then looked through it to find the chosen card. Well, it was one of those nights and he could not decided which was the card. Embarrassed, Ralph announced his failure to his fellow magicians and then asked the assistant and the other members if he could try again. They agreed and he did, successfully this time. When he displayed the selected card, he noticed a peculiar expression on the assistant's face and then on some of the other members' faces. The same tarot card had been chosen both times. Ralph remarked in a knowing manner, "Isn't this the same card?" He smiled, acting as if he had planned it, and bowed to the applause of his fellow magicians. But of course he had not planned it, nor even thought of doing the routine that way. (Some day I might, he mused.) Was it chance or the force? Coincidence or psychic powers? How can anyone know? All we can say is that it happened this way.

He paused rocking. Lucy had jumped onto his lap. He scratched behind her ears, encouraging an outburst of purring. It was easy now for him to believe he had connected with the scared and tapped its power. Certainly, his work at the Institute of Conscious-Imagination-Nous, or Institute of CIN, had enhanced his talent to use magic from the sacred world. Philip and his teammates, the twins Geri and Jerry Meadows, assisted Ralph to develop his skills. He learned the method for remote viewing (RV) and out-of-body experience (OBE) and enhanced his telepathic powers. Also he's discovered that sometimes his use had made changes in ordinary reality. In essence he was weaving another reality with magical thread.

His enthusiasm had touched Shasta, who decided to increase her psi skills. Speaking aloud, he said, "Lucy, Shasta has become a magician. She is fusing two realities: the world of imaginative fiction and her ordinary reality." He gently rubbed the kitty on her back. She purred in response.

He thought of his assistant Rafé and her people of the Potawatomi nation. Their medicine people are called 'mide,' (meaning mystic) and they are members of the Grand Medicine Society (Midewiwin) where mystic activities are practiced. Two of their activities Ralph found especially intriguing: the shaking tent and the mobile doll. A mide, bound with rope, sits or lies in a tent and calls forth spirit helpers or manitos to contact the spirit world for divining, healing, finding lost objects or even people. All sorts of awesome things can happen. Strange noises resound from the tent while objects fly about or are thrown out of the tent.

He was reminded of the late nineteenth century spirit cabinet routine, which was very popular at the time. Could the cabinet effect be inspired by Native American rituals? Now the animated doll was especially engaging. According to his reading and to his friend and mentor Harold Magian, these doll-like figures were able to move under the control of the mide. They were little men who had special sacred power.

An insight touched him. The movement between realities had made subtle changes in his companion. He smiled. She was acting strangely like a heyoka. Of course, she had become a sacred clown linking the sacred with the mundane.

Do the emotions conjured by the Peaches Peoples story have a basis in ordinary reality, he wondered? The themes of cyber and psi space surfing, the interweaving of the two spaces – do they have an existential referent?

He was puzzled. Picking up the notebook and pencil on the table next to the rocker, he jotted down thoughts. The source of real magic is in the fourth dimension, which according to Einstein, is time.

The two realities are separated more by time than space. They are in the same space interwoven together. Time in the ordinary world is an ongoing process, yet sacred time is static – the constant present moment. Ordinary time is constantly flowing while the sacred world is either manifested or not.

In the notebook, he drew a long rectangle, which he labeled the ordinary world. Through the length of the rectangle he drew a line, which he marked the flow of time from past into future. Now here is the sacred world, he said to himself as he sketched a circle. While he was constructing the figures, Lucy sat up and watched him.

"Notice, Lucy, that the link between the two realities is a form of time." He ran a line between the two worlds. The link is a movement but not in normal time. A part of the sacred can be manifested in the mundane reality. The sacred moves in and out of our daily life. Of course, when we experience the sacred, it is manifested in our present. What do you think of the idea, Lucy?" She stretched her back and lay back down on his lap and purred.

The vision continued. A mage can wait for a manifestation or find a door to the sacred and enter. From his research Ralph knew that the shaman usually found a portal either on his own or with the help of a spirit guide. There were many techniques to reveal a door to the sacred and tap its power.

He paused, hearing a meow. Peering down at his feet, he saw Karma sitting there. Karma placed her front paws on his knee and eyed Lucy who was staring at her sister. "My lap isn't big enough for both of you," he said. Lucy sat upright and leaped to the floor. Karma immediately sprang onto his lap. He chuckled at their sharing, taking turns. He softly rubbed Karma behind the ears and she purred contentedly. Lucy went over to the desk and jumped onto it. She curled up underneath the levitating clock.

Their antics conjured the image of a clown. Yes, we magicians and kitties are like clowns and are able to enter worlds or dimensions of reality that ordinary people do not. We can move through the portal of shadows and emerge into the sacred realm, which is the source of real magic. Ralph began rocking and petting Karma, who purred deeply.

Sacred clowns, he thought, enter sacred reality through their acts. Either during a ceremony or in their daily lives they are in touch with the sacred. Shasta is using the idea for her story, but she is mostly in the sacred world and her characters are connecting with people in her ordinary world.

The idea blossomed and he viewed its many petals. Stage magicians, illusionists, and sleight of hand adepts are similar to sacred clowns and fools in several ways. Although we may picture clowns as circus fun-givers and delightful buffoons, clowns have had an important role in European culture at least since the ancient Greeks. They had dramatic roles in Greek theater, which continued into the Medieval period in mystery plays and traveling minstrels. They frequented Shakespearean drama and became a fixture in theater, including the Punch and Judy puppet shows. The Harlequin came from Italy, and France supplied the white-faced Pierrot. In the Middle Ages court jesters and fools, who offered sage advice that others were too frightened to propose, were earning their keep, though most of the time they provided amusement and entertainment.

In some societies, like the Native American, clowns perform in religious ceremonies and in doing so act as a sacred character. Further, they are more like the mythic trickster and behave in a fashion contrary to conventional norms. Medicine men and women often are viewed in this way, like shamans who become one with their spirit helper.

A few examples came to his mind. The Hopi, a pueblo people living in northern Arizona, have several different sacred clowns. To outsiders the Koshari and the Koyemsi or Mudhead are the most well-known, and they have their counterparts in other pueblos. The two Hopi sacred clowns are katsina or kachina, which are spirit beings residing in the sacred realm. A katsina is manifested through a human during a religious ceremony.

Koshari will behave backwards: saying the opposite of what they mean, yes for no and no for yes; climbing down ladders head first; confusing parts of a ceremony or curing rite, often burlesquing or parodying it. Their comments on current events, both in the Hope village or in the world at large, are usually critical and ironic, poking fun at the target, confirming that the Emperor is naked.

If Koshari are more the fools and buffoons, Koyemsi are more involved in linking the sacred and profane and so possess more power and are far more dangerous than Koshari. Actually, the Hopi do not consider Koyemsi to be clowns. Healer and sage -- Koyemsi carry messages from the Ancient Ones to the people. Magician and fool -- they play games with the onlookers, impressing all with their sacred power.

Among the Lakota, living on the northern plains, men and women who have a vision of Thunderbird are touched by sacred power and must become a heyoka, a contrary; otherwise, they will get sick and perhaps die. Their behavior is contrary or reverse of the behavior normal in the community. Forwards is backwards: walking or riding backwards and speaking backwards are common practices. Dressed in bizarre clothing, acting silly and ludicrous, a heyoka is all things that a normal member of the community should not be. Although some of the behavior is similar to that of the Koshari, one important difference is that the person acting as a Koshari does so for a specific ceremonial occasion, but a heyoka acts in a strange manner daily, unless released by Thunderbird. A heyoka seems to have power similar to Koyemsi, drawing deeply from the spiritual realm.

He stopped writing and thought for a few moments. Absentmindedly, he petted Karma as he peered into the mirror. Suddenly he became aware of his behavior. He laughed. Am I waiting for ideas to appear in the mirror on the wall or should I be looking at the mirror of my mind, he wondered?

He resumed examining his previous idea. The heyoka, Koshari, and Koyemsi partake of the sacred and can be considered holy or medicine people. Anthropologists often employ the term 'shaman' for medicine people and describe them as using the sacred power for healing and bringing other benefits to the community, like rain, fertility, and plentiful supply of game. Clowns in Native American culture are always members of a medicine society, that is, their duties and obligations to the community are to bring benefits.

During a magical performance the mage becomes a storyteller, a stage director, and creates an atmosphere of awe and wonder, conjuring a magical reality. The mage enters worlds or dimensions of reality that ordinary people do not. The mage can move through the portal of shadows and emerge into the sacred realm, which is the source of real magic.

Like clowns, magicians enact the cosmic drama, which is religious-spiritual and symbolic. Bringing this sacred enactment to their community, they affirm its existence and power, allowing the audience to participate in another reality, one that exists side by side with the ordinary world and for many is interwoven with it. The sacred magician chooses to sustain a sense of mystery and opposes the view that life and the universe are meaningless and devoid of spirit. For such a mage life is the true cosmic mystery and so enhancing any mystery fortifies life.

The magic ideal is to present the audience with the opportunity to experience awe and wonder, to create a disbelief in conventional thoughts about the universe so that they are pushed aside and mystery fills the performance. To achieve the ideal, mages base their craft on reason, which is used to design and construct routines and props, yet the rational toolkit is employed to create specific emotions. We want our audience to experience wonder, marvel, and awe. We ask them to put aside their adult attitudes and once again live in an enchanted realm as they did as children. We go to great lengths to portray the cosmic mysteries for their enjoyment.

"Can magicians like clowns bestow social benefits? Can they participate in a healing process?" Ralph asked aloud. Both kitties had their ears alert and responded in the affirmative: Karma meowed and Lucy cleaned her front paws.

"I agree," he said to them. Yes, he thought to himself, maintaining a sense of mystery and opposing the view that life and the universe are meaningless and devoid of spirit is my goal. Life is the true cosmic mystery and so enhancing any mystery fortifies life. Ancient benefits were healing and using power for other social goods. My purpose will be to enhance the mystery of life. The healing of mind and body, securing self-integrity, and encouraging self-responsibility, all worthwhile social goals, are benefits that such magical performances will bring. Magic can serve the community.

"Well, Karma, shamanism will be the broad theme for the new magic show. Now what will be the types of natural magic I'll perform." He rubbed behind her ears. She purred contentedly. Three forms popped into his mind: the little man, shape-shifting or changing, and the sacred clown. Each can have its own dramatic act and then be linked with the others by a story. Three short stories woven together. The connection between sacred and profane realities is the thread. Each act has its own design yet is entangled with the others.

He closed the notebook and placed it with the pencil on the table. Petting Karma, he rocked to and fro, emptying his mind.

Shasta sighed, stretched her arms upward, and took several deep breaths. She rubbed the back of her neck, releasing muscle tension. She looked around the study and then rose from the desk. She had been working on the story since breakfast with only two coffee breaks. As she passed the table with orchids, she paused and inspected them. No aphids nor yellowing of leaves – good. Walking to the window, she looked out at the garden. Oh, dear, she thought, I've been so involved in the new writing project I've forgotten all about the garden. So many weeds had popped up, and she was overwhelmed by the sight. The next warm day, she told herself, I'll go out there and clean away the unwanted plants.

She had a love-hate relationship with oxalis. In the winter and early spring it dominated their back and front yards with green leaves and yellow flowers. The problem was that it overgrew nearly everything except bushes and tall perennials. The young shoots of most annuals were crowded out and unable to get any sunshine for their growth. She could let the weeds be and not worry about the other plants, but she had her favorites and protected them against usurpers.

But now she need some companionship and relaxation. Her Muse was quiet, no doubt resting, and she wanted a change of focus. Let all her brains cells have a vacation. She wanted to be with friends who could direct her attention to something different. She glanced at her watch. It was a good time to go to Ocean Delights, their favorite neighborhood coffee shop and social meeting place. It was where the gang met for their socializing. The group of friends had coalesced over a period of years and formed a bond with mutual interests and concerns. She would see if Ralph wished to go with her.

After walking down the stairs to the first floor, she went to the door of Ralph's studio and peered in. He was in the rocking chair, snoring. She quietly entered and crept up to him. Lucy, who was curled up on the desk, watched her. She touched her companion on the shoulder and whispered, "Ralph, dear, would you like to go to Ocean Delights?"

Karma lifted her head and then leaped to the floor. Yawning, Ralph opened his eyes. "What?" he said. He sat up and smiled at her.

"I'm taking a break and going to Ocean Delights. Do you want to come with me?"

"Ocean Delights. Sounds like a winner. I could use a mug of strong coffee." He yawned again and rose from the rocker. She went ahead with the kitties leading the way. Entering the hall she paused. The kitties had gone to the kitchen and were staring at her from the doorway. "Ralph, I'll fill the kitty bowl first," she called. In the kitchen she took the bag of munchies and filled the bowl. As Karma and Lucy happily enjoyed their snack, she went to the vestibule where Ralph was waiting. She took her jacket from the wall coat rack and put it on. They left for their afternoon social hour.

The sun was shining and a warm breeze gently moved the branches of the ornamental fruit trees now in bloom. They strolled up to Ocean Avenue and then turned east heading for Ocean Delights.

Chapter 15

Entering Ocean Delights, the couple paused and looked about. She said, "There they are. They have a reserved table."

Waving her hand, Rafé led Alan over to the gang's table. Merle and Dale moved another table and two chairs over to theirs. Rafé introduced Alan to the gang as her special friend. Shasta's eyes lighted up and she smiled brightly at the couple.

Ocean Delights was a café on Ocean Avenue which had become a neighbor hangout for the gang, the name that Shasta had given to the group. The members had met at the café. Finding similar interests, they had gathered together on a regular basis, forming their personal club.

Ocean Delights, owned by Ben Said, offered a variety of coffees, teas, pastries, and sandwiches. The most popular item in the sandwich category was the pita falafel. Customers could choose from several different fillings. Different types of Mediterranean style cuisine were available.

Dale Pepper, who taught music at SF State, was discussing the important social values of the arts with Merle Leong, an artist who did contract painting and illustration for companies so that he could spend as much time as possible on his work. Emma Leong, Merle's partner, had started the discussion by bemoaning the recent budget cuts in the educational arts programs in the public schools.

"Where's Gordon?" Rafé asked.

Gordon Russell, a retired English teacher from City College of San Francisco and somewhat of a cynic, was a stalwart of the gang and one of its original members. Shasta had met him when she was teaching English part-time at the community college.

"He and his partner Charles Freeman are at a hearing protesting the attempt to remove City College's accreditation by the Association of California Community and Junior Colleges," Dale answered.

"They're not even a state government agency," Leila Lubec commented.

Leila was the neighbor psychic and psychological therapist. She had a business on Ocean Avenue, which provided counseling and recommendations for maintaining mental health.

"The city attorney has brought legal action against the commission. He's arguing that the commission is promoting for-profit colleges and undermining public education," Shasta added.

"It's a racket and scam. There have been attempts at State to restructure programs so that they would make a profit for the corporate class. And then they expect government handouts and subsidies." Dale had fiery eyes and was about to comment further when Rafé reached above her head and caught a half dollar. She flashed the coin saying, "This is what it's all about." Startled at the abrupt production of the coin, the gang was silent and then broke into laughter and giggles. Ralph stood up and produced five more half dollars from the spirit realm. The gang applauded as did other patron in the café.

Swiftly changing the subject, Rafé said, "Alan is a member of the Nez Perce nation."

"Where do your people live?" Emma asked.

Alan smiled and said, "In northern Idaho. It's been our home for hundreds of years."

"Tell them about the Nez Perce horse breeding program," Rafé asked. In her heart she felt his soul and spirit warm up.

Turning on his charm, Alan said, "For hundreds of years the Appaloosa has been our horse. Now we're crossbreeding it with a Central Asian breed called Akhal-Teke to produce what we call the Nez Perce horse. They're lovely horses." The group asked for more details about the breeding program and then encouraged Alan to tell them about the Nez Perce history and culture. He held forth for the rest of the afternoon.

As the gang broke up, Rafé said to Ralph, "I need some help with a couple routines I'm doing for my theater class."

Ralph nodded and said, "How about tomorrow afternoon around two."

Rafé smiled. "I'll be there." She and Alan left the café.

Shasta was in the kitchen preparing dinner. Rafé and her new beau Alan

Bird would be dining with the Garlands. She had taken an immediate liking for Alan when they had met at Ocean Delights three days ago. Now she would be able to judge more closely the dynamics between the two. She hoped Rafé had found someone who would be a good companion. She laughed. Rafé had become like a daughter. She and Ralph had become surrogate parents. Well, everything was ready. All she had to do was put the casserole in the oven when the couple arrived. She went up stairs to the bedroom and, after showering, dressed for the dinner party.

Ralph answered the door when the chimes sounded. The young couple was standing there. Ralph invited them in and Shasta came from the kitchen. The couple gave her their gifts. Rafé presented a bouquet of lovely flowers and Alan offered them a bottle of red wine. Delighted with the flowers and wine and thanking the young couple graciously, Shasta carried the gifts into the kitchen and returned to the living room.

When Ralph and his guests entered the living room, they were greeted by the kitties who checked out the guests by sniffing their legs and rubbing against them. Rafé introduced Alan to the kitties and he spoke to them, praising their cuteness. The young couple sat down on the couch, and Lucy and Karma hopped into their laps and curled up, purring with delight.

"You have a very charming home with pleasant feelings," Alan said.

"Thank you," Shasta replied. Ralph smiled with pride.

"Would you two like a glass of wine before dinner?" Shasta asked.

The couple looked at each other and answered they would. Shasta stood up and went into the kitchen.

"So you're working on a degree in jurisprudence at Hastings. What exactly is your area of interest?" Ralph asked.

Before Alan had a chance to answer, Shasta returned carrying a tray with four glasses of white wine. They each took a glass and sipped the wine.

Then Alan said, "It involves a focus on the relationship between the federal government and the tribes, especially on the historical development of the connection. Many Americans don't realize the special status the tribes have with the government. The tribes are nations which the government has treaties with. The tribes have retained their sovereignty but within the framework of federal authority. In a way they are on at least a par with the fifty states, so there is often a friction between the tribal governments and the states."

Shasta remembered while growing up in Dunsmuir at the base of Mt. Shasta, the tallest stand alone mountain in California, she had become friends with the Wintu people, discovering their history and culture. "I was born in Dunsmuir. The Wintu people lived in the area and I learned a lot about their dealings with both federal and state governments. It wasn't always beneficial to the Wintu either," Shasta commented.

Alan smiled knowingly. "That's my focus." Both the kitties started purring in tune with Alan's sentiments.

"Ralph, I'd like to hear about your ideas on magic and the kinds you perform," Alan requested.

Ralph beamed and winked at Rafé. "Recently I produced a show that used large props. It was more theatrical and portrayed my interest in alchemical. Normally I do stage and parlor magic without all the heavy equipment – small props but no large ones. Right now I'm developing routines with ESP and tarot cards. I've become more interested in the history of magic, both real and stage."

"Rafé has told me that you and Shasta are doing psychic research and exploring the realms of remote viewing and out-of-body activities."

"Yes, we are assisting Philip Austen at the Institute of Consciousness-Imagination-Nous, commonly known as the Institute of CIN. We are investigating the psychic dimension in all its aspects."

"You've actually performed these activities. You're sounding like our medicine people and their spirit guides. Amazing," Alan said.

"Rafé is surfing cyber and psi spaces for us, gathering data useful for my new novel," Shasta commented.

"Yes, she's told me. She's also going to teach me the best techniques for surfing."

The kitties sat up and cleaned their front paws in full agreement with the plan.

"Alan brought his flute along," Rafé said.

"Will you play it for us?" Shasta asked.

"Well, I see I have some work to do. Of course," Alan remarked. He squeezed her hand and kissed it.

Brightened at the youthful friendship of the pair, Shasta remembered her courtship with Ralph. From a youthful, romantic attraction, their love had grown into a mature companionship and affection for each other. They were not only a team but had fused into a oneness.

Opening a leather pouch, Alan took out a flute and played a serenade.

"That was lovely. Could I see it?" Shasta asked.

Alan gave the instrument to her and Ralph stood and walked over to her to study the flute also. "It has six finger holes. What musical scale do you use?" he inquired.

"Our music is based on the pentatonic scale. This flute is keyed to F sharp," replied Alan.

"He has three more flutes," Rafé said. She was filled with excitement. "He can play with different groups."

Shasta smiled, understanding Rafé's rush of enthusiasm. A true warrior for her friend.

"You should talk to Dale Pepper," Ralph was saying when Rafé jumped in and exclaimed, "You could play in his ensemble."

"He plays the Native American flute. Perhaps you could perform a duet with him," Shasta offered.

"I'll do that," Alan said. "I know that writers don't like to discuss their work in progress, but I'd like to hear about your new novel."

"Well, I can tell you a little about it without upsetting my Muse. It centers on an interpretation of some Christian religious ideas that is contrary to the official thinking. There's a lot of cyber and psi surfing and an important theme of spying and surveillance. It fits in with modern society's involvement with computers and other high tech issues. I consider it my wildest and most bizarre novel yet." Shasta felt an inner warmth and acknowledged her willingness to share personal affairs with them.

"I certainly want to read it when you've finished," Alan said.

A timer chime rang in the kitchen. "Excuse me, but I have to check on dinner." Shasta got up and walked into the kitchen with the kitties leading the parade. Shasta appeared at the living room doorway and asked Ralph to help her. "Please be seated in the dining room," she told the guests. After a delicious meal of spaghetti and meatballs with a green salad, they returned to the living room where Shasta served coffee and cookies.

"Play some songs, Alan," Rafé said.

Alan laughed. "Of course for the wonderful meal." He performed several traditional songs, which delighted his audience.

Alan felt a strong attraction to his hosts and, being of inquisitive nature, asked them about their personal life stories. Shasta talked about growing up in Dunsmuir. Alan asked for more details about the Wintu nation and its cultural heritage.

When Shasta had finished, Alan asked Ralph about his interest in the magical arts and the development of his skills. After a summary of his involvement in magic, Ralph took the couple into his studio and showed Alan what the craft meant to him.

The evening came to an end. The couple said good night, having praised the dinner and the Garland's hospitality, and left.

Shasta was smiling. She turned to Ralph, saying, "I'm happy for Rafé. They seem to have a lovely bond."

"Yes, the way they look at each -- a love is growing." He saw the beautiful light in her eyes, the sparkle that touched his soul when they were courting. An intense feeling of love surfaced, and he hugged and kissed her.

Chapter 16

It was Friday night. She did not feel up to going out for the normal weekend social activities. She fixed coffee and took a cup into the living room. Sitting down in her private chair, the one she had used for astral travel, she unwrapped her worries. The missing manuscript case was sorely bothering her. She could not get a real grip on it. Her intuition was not offering any help. At times like these she wondered whether her life's chosen career was really meant for her. She could have selected many other types of work. Why the private investigator?

She moved deep within her memories searching for clues. For ten years her father had been a police officer in Peru before he attained rank of chief, which he held for fifteen before succumbing to lung cancer. Too many cigarettes and all the beers did not help either. Her home town Peru, Indiana, was located on the Wabash River, which flowed from the east in its southwestward journey to the bottom of the state and joined the Ohio River.

She idealized her father and modeled herself after him. She went to the police station with him, wanting to be helpful. He gave her small chores to perform and patted her on the head. Other members of the force also participated in her game and played police with her. Yes, she was pampered, but her behavior never fell below her model image.

It was a late autumn evening when John Dillinger and two members of his gang, Pierpont and Dietrich, walked down the dark alley behind the police station of Peru, Indiana. They had a floor plan of the station and knew exactly where the station's armory was located. People in small towns seldom locked their doors, even the police. The back door was unlocked from the outside but locked on the inside. Dillinger had grown up in Indiana and knew the thought patterns of his fellow citizens.

Since it was Saturday night, the police force working that night were out keeping law and order in the streets, except for Deputy Dodson who was in charge of the station. The quiet of the station was broken when a voice exclaimed, "Don't move." Deputy Dodson jerked. Terror moved inside his body as he looked at three armed men. One man put a cloth in the deputy's mouth, which was then taped closed, while the other handcuffed his hands behind his back. The unshaven one with the evil eye led Dodson to a holding cell and put him in. Then Dodson was handcuffed to the bunk and the cell door locked.

She stood outside the police station entrance and listened. Hearing voices she did not recognize, Peaches was cautious. She liked Deputy Dodson and often came to the station on Saturday nights when not much was happening. As a teenager she had several crushes on older men and Dodson, a single man, was a favorite. She did not like what she heard. Entering by the front would attract attention, so she went down the alley to the back door and quietly entered. Voices were coming from the station's armory, which was an extra large and secure jail cell. She peered in and was surprised to see three men gathering the weapons stored there. The weapons were not loaded, so she was safe unless they pulled their own guns out. Foolhardy and brave, imagining her father's praise, she stepped quickly forward and, grabbing the cell door, pulled it shut, locking it in one movement. Then she hurried to the radio communications center and broadcast the emergency signal. Her chore completed, she hastened from the station, the yells of the bad guys following her.

Often she had spent hours standing before the special exhibit commemorating the day public enemy John Dillinger and his gang had robbed the police station's armory on October 21, 1933.

The exhibit contained replicas of the weapons stolen, which were two shotguns, two Thompson submachine guns, four .38 revolvers, two Winchester rifles and six bulletproof vests. A week earlier the gang had robbed the police armory in Auburn, Indiana. Without the stolen weapons their bank robbery crime wave across the state of Indiana would not have succeeded.

She would stare into the exhibit, fantasizing the day it had occurred. What if she were a police officer then? Could she have prevented it? She saw herself getting the drop on them and putting them into the holding cells. Yes, such is the child's imagination. But now here she could not get a drop on anyone.

When she had graduated from high school, she enrolled at the Indiana

University – Purdue University Fort Wayne extension. Fort Wayne was a city located northeast of Peru. It had over 250,000 population compared to Peru's 11,500. It was a strange and extraordinary experience to jump from a small town to a large city, but she enjoyed all the new adventures.

During the summer months she worked on neighboring farms fertilizing the hybrid seed corn. It was not hard work but tedious and good paying too. The seed corn had to be fertilized at the proper time or it would not reproduce.

She also found part-time work during winter break with circuses that hibernated there in the off-season months. Ringling Brothers and Buffalo Bill's Wild West Show were two of the famous ones. Employed by the circus management, she did basic farm chores – caring for the animals and maintaining the supply of food stock. Since the animals were more exotic than normally found on the farm, the work was more exciting; besides, she could hear stories about circus performers and staff.

She made many friends both with the humans and the animals. She fell in love with Princess the lead elephant of the herd which had been trained to carry a human on their backs. Princess would kneel and lower her trunk. Peaches would climb onto the trunk and be carried to the elephant's back. They loved each other and Peaches always had some treat to feed Princess. Peaches had the opportunity to ride Princess in training sessions, learning much about animal behavior. Evelyn Bowman, who was elephant master in charge of the herd of ten, had Peaches assist her during the sessions. Peaches would ride Princess when Evelyn held practice.

She also loved Jim the chimpanzee, who was the circus' official mascot and sat in the center ring with the Master of Ceremonies. She believed she and Jim communicated via their personal sign language. Jim was a prankster and they shared jokes with hand signs.

Clown Casey Engel rented a room from her family, returning every year until he retired. Casey was small and had no difficulty performing many of the routines, especially those involving packing a limitless number of clowns in a small space such as a car or phone booth. He was a circus history buff and told many stories about life under the Big Top. Peaches' favorite story was about Emmett Kelly, Weary Willy the sad face hobo, who tried to catch sunbeams. While sweeping the floor, Willie pursued a fleeting piece of sunlight with his frayed broom. His persistence in the face of failure was heartwarming. Only much later did she grasp the wisdom underlying the hobo's absurd behavior.

After receiving her BS in criminology and returning home, she realized she was no longer a small town girl. Hungering for the excitement of city life, she applied for jobs at large city police forces throughout the state. Because of budget cuts they were not hiring. Then she investigated the private sector and learned that most firms specialized in security and surveillance with high tech equipment or had contracts with large corporations for ongoing investigatory services. She wanted more independence.

Also at this time media were publishing cases of corruption and abuse in law enforcement from the FBI down to the local small town police force. She was deeply cut and bitter. Her ideal profession was now buried in garbage. She heard her father moan and curse. His beloved work was now totally stained.

Then she made a momentous decision: come to the west coast. She wanted to live in the San Francisco Bay Area. She selected the small city of Albany, California, with a population of about 19,000. Albany is located north of Berkeley along the San Francisco Bay shoreline. It is middle class and offers affordable living.

First she rented a small apartment and began a search for appropriate office space. She found an available one room office off downtown Albany and set up shop: printing signs, business cards, and flyers. Then she introduced herself to local trades people. She had the easy outgoing manner of the small town citizen and the people were charmed. Her successes became well-known in the community and her cliental grew. She took jobs the large firms would not handle.

Her business was so profitable she decided to rent a larger apartment. And that is where I am now, she thought. She came out of her memory journey, relaxed and ready for the next round. She got up and went to the kitchen unit and fixed dinner.

After the meal she returned to her chair. She decided to read a work by Carl Jung and learn more about the true Self and finding the path to reach it. Jung had a great influence on her thinking. She was always discovering new insights every time she read one of his books. Another influence was Rafé and Sandra. Their skills for surfing cyberspace in the electromagnetic field and psi-space in the astral field, moving back and forth, were enhancing her abilities. They were good teachers.

When she had worked on neighboring farms during the summer to earn money for college, she had several visionary, mystical experiences. She liked to sleep outside in her sleeping bag under the stars. One night she had awakened when she had felt cold soft flesh nuzzle her face. She opened her eyes and was surprised to be face to face with a large rabbit. The animal, grinning, sat down beside her. They looked at each other – Peaches wondering whether she was having a vision or not? Could it be Manabozho, the great trickster and important spirit of the woodland Indians?

The rabbit sat, watching her. Then it said, "You are searching for something important, aren't you?"

She had no compunction answering, "Yes, I am."

"And what is it?"

"I'm not sure."

"Follow the inner path to the moon and you'll find the self." Then rabbit vanished and she felt a drowsiness come over her. The next morning she was wide awake and clear headed. The dream stayed with her as vivid as she had experienced it. After that she had several telepathic happenings with friends when they discussed their view of reality. They all thought of themselves as practical, down-to-earth ladies, but the strange psychic occurrences were too strong and unusual to discard.

Peaches started reading Jung, looking for the path to the moon.

Saturday was designated as a day of leisure – for fun and entertaining activities. Peaches and Aeneas spent the day together on a regular basis. Today it was Peaches' turn to be host. They were sitting in their favorite chairs, sipping coffee.

"Do you remember when we first met?" Peaches asked.

"Are we celebrating an anniversary or something?"

She laughed. "No. I've just been on a memory trip recently."

"Reviewing your life's goals, wondering if you are on the wrong path?"

"Something like that. The case has lost me and I need to reconnect."

Aeneas smiled at her. He had always admired her intellect and physical prowess, but most importantly he loved her for her playfulness and humor.

He sank back into the chair and allowed his mind to open the portals to the past.

"Ah, yes, I do. It was on a Friday night with damp fog drifting in from the bay and we were at the Club on San Pablo Avenue."

"The Club? Oh, yes, the only bistro in town at the time. It was packed out and I pushed my way over to your table. I had noticed you a few times before and decided now was the moment to make your acquaintance. And what better opportunity than a crowded Friday night. So I pulled a chair to your table, sat down, and introduced myself."

"And it was a match. We both could recognize that. I waved for the server and ordered a round of drinks and therein rests the story of our affair."

They both broke down laughing. A meeting of the souls neither had experienced before.

"And sitting before you was my new personality. My family identity, Walter Edison Blenford III, had vanished and a new one to fit my life style and these changing times arose, Aeneas the true. A perfect resurrection of soul and spirit. Once you heard about my love for computers and so knew I would not be chasing after your perfect body, you offered me a job."

"What!" She giggled and threw a pillow at him. He started laughing also.

"Let's set the record straight. I needed someone with computer expertise to run my computer system. And you needed work."

"All that is true," Aeneas responded. "I was attracted to the San Francisco Bay Area, like you, and destiny played its four aces."

He glanced at the book on the table bedside her chair. "Back into reading Jung, I see."

"I've been reading more of his works recently. I guess I'm studying his ideas. Last night after my memory trip, I realized I have an intense desire for more knowledge of myself."

"I don't know if that's such a good idea. At least it frightens me to gaze too deeply into my soul. I don't want to find all the monsters that must be hidden there."

"Aeneas, don't be afraid. These so-called monsters can't hurt you. They're only figments of your imagination. Open the cage and release them. All the pent-up energy will dissipate."

"Easier said than done."

"I agree. The first few steps are the most difficult. Then the further you progress, the easier it becomes. It's worked for me that way. My comprehension of Jung's depth psychology is growing and I'm improving my understanding of myself."

"Well, what should I do?"

Peaches reflected for a few moments. "Let's have meditation sessions together. We'll meditate and then discuss our experiences."

"I'll give it a try." Aeneas did not sound too hopeful. He smiled and his eyes lit up. "When is lunch?"

"As soon as I can fix it. We're having tuna spread on rye with potato salad. You want a glass of wine?"

Aeneas nodded his head in agreement. "I'll start thinking about our case."

Peaches rose and entered the kitchen.

Chapter 17

Peaches got up from the power recliner chair and entered the kitchen. Standing at the coffee maker as it prepared a cup of coffee from Colombian beans, she realized she was looking forward to visiting Marcus Scarpia via astral space. She admitted to herself she enjoyed remote viewing. The brew was finished and she took the coffee back into the living room.

She walked to the front window and, sipping coffee, watched the street scene. A warm, sunny afternoon, many neighbors were out enjoying themselves – sitting on their porch or standing and talking in small groups. Six boys were playing ball in the street. Two teenagers were performing acrobatics on their skateboards. She smiled, filled with positive vibes. She went back to her chair and, putting the mug on the adjacent table, sat down. She picked up a trade journal on surveillance from the table and leafed through it. So many microchip spying devices. Are they all that necessary? Or is it just being competitive?

Finishing the coffee, she went into the bedroom. Opening the top drawer of the dresser, she removed a jewelry box. Inside the box was the necklace with the cat figurine. Taking the necklace from the box, she placed it around her neck. She rub the charm and felt a subtle vibration flow through her hand. Breathing deeply, she returned to the living room and sat down in the recliner chair. She let her mind drift, waiting for Aeneas.

The front door lock clicked and the door opened. Aeneas entered. "Hi, Peaches. It's me." He saw her lying in the chair. She waved.

"I'll get some coffee," he said and, after taking off his jacket and throwing it on a chair, walked into the kitchen. Soon returning, he put the coffee mug on a table next to the chair he sat down in. He reached over and clasped her hand, squeezing it gently. "Are you ready?"

Relaxed, she smiled and answered, "Yes. Here I go." Releasing his hand, she touched the cat charm hanging from her neck and focused on a photo of Marcus Scarpia, which Virgil had found in a journal of esoteric ideas Her sense of being in a specific space-time faded. She was in her eagle seat looking down at a room that seemed to be a library or study.

Scarpia was seated at a desk hunched over a book. Peaches zoomed in and noticed the binding and pages of the book were quite old. The book was written in Latin. Peaches sent a transmission of the two pages to Virgil, who quickly responded that the pages contained chemical signs, like a recipe. She observed the remainder of the room. The walls were lined by bookshelves. One corner of the room was set up as a small chemical laboratory with sink, work table, Bunsen burner, a rack of glass flasks, and other chemical apparatus. On the wall were shelves that held bottles and jars of chemicals.

So he performed experiments. What could they be, she wondered? From the recipe book he was reading?

Scarpia rose and walked over to the laboratory area. He picked up bottles and checked their contents. When he found a bottle that was nearly empty, he wrote the name of the ingredient on a piece of paper. His shopping list, Peaches thought. After checking all the bottles, he went back to the table and sat down again, placing the list next to the book. Putting his finger on a chemical sign in the book, he wrote an ingredient on the list. Continuing to leaf through the pages, he added more ingredients to the list. Then he stopped. Peaches zoomed in on the page. He had come to the end of the chapter. Closing the book, he stretched his back. Getting up, he carried the book over to a shelf and put it among other books. He peered at titles on the spines, seeking a particular book. He removed a manuscript from the shelf and walked back to the table and placed the manuscript on it. Sitting down, he opened it to a bookmarked page.

Aeneas had added two microchips to the charm, both enhancing Virgil's participation in the psi field. One device was a receiver-transmitter that allowed Virgil to see and hear what was happening. The sensory data was sent directly to the computer who processed it immediately. The other microchip provide a direct communication line between Peaches and Virgil.

Peaches transmitted a copy of the page to Virgil while Scarpia was reading the page and writing in his journal. Suddenly, he sat up straight and looked about. "Ah, Midnight, my portend of the powers of magic and witchery."

Peaches became alert. Was Scarpia talking to himself? Or to whom? A spirit? Then she heard a meow and, gazing round the library, her eyes stopped at the entrance. A large, long-haired, raven-black cat stood there. With a graceful leap he landed on the desk beside the manuscript Scarpia was reading.

"Ah, dear Midnight, what adventures do you plan tonight?" He gently rubbed the soft, silky fur underneath the cat's chin and patted the top of the head. By now Midnight was purring with a deep resonating sound. Peaches noticed his long bushy tail was white tipped and a white circle surrounded his right eye.

My, what a lithe, handsome cat resides here with Scarpia, she thought. He must weigh twenty-five pounds or more, one of the larger sizes of domestic cats. At that size he could well be a Maine Coon, the largest domestic cat in the country.

Once Scarpia had finished petting him, Midnight cleaned his front paws and then stretched himself. Arching his back, he sprang to the top self of the bookcase behind the desk. Then he jumped from the bookshelf to the molding that created a border almost two inches wide and one foot below the ceiling. With the agility of a tight-rope walker he strolled along the molding until he reached a corner and then looked at the ceiling, scrutinizing it as if an invisible object might be hidden there. Satisfied with his inspection, Midnight continued along the molding until he reached the next corner and repeated the routine.

Peaches became apprehensive and withdrew herself through the throat chakra portal back into her living room. Aeneas was sitting quietly watching her as she performed an out-of-body-experience (OBE). He was surprised she had returned so soon. He went into the kitchen and poured a glass of orange juice, which she had discovered was a powerful assist for refreshing her energy source.

"You didn't stay long. Was there some difficulty?"

"Yes, indeed. Scarpia has a roommate, a large black male cat named Midnight, who is not only a familiar but seems to have extraordinary magical power." She proceeded to describe the cat's behavior.

"Wow. Sounds like the cat is a spying detection system, a living one at that."

"I wonder what we've gotten ourselves into? We aren't very knowledgeable about occult powers and the fundamental ideas underlying those forces. Virgil, what's your take on the situation?"

"As a rational being I am definitely amazed at the events that occurred in Scarpia's library. Midnight's behavior did not fit any model I have stored in my memory."

Peaches had been jolted out of her complacency. "Virgil, gather everything you can find about the occult, not the pseudo, social type but real magic, the kind Faust yearned for."

Aeneas had a very serious look. He had been deeply troubled. "It is like challenging a deadly enemy who has weapons to attack and conquer us but we have nothing to defend ourselves. How did we get into this mess?"

"Data about the occult and esoteric disciplines are flowing into my storage unit," Virgil said. "With a laboratory Scarpia obviously performs alchemical experiments. He probably has skills to use magic at the psi level, what is sometimes called natural magic. We need to know his agenda."

"Thank you, Virgil," Peaches remarked. "Based on what we've learned about the stolen manuscript, I don't understand its usefulness for him."

"It's going to be a long term stakeout, I can see," Aeneas said.

"We're not going to have a stakeout if we don't eliminate the threat Midnight poses. That's our first task. Virgil, put on your problem-solving cap and find a solution if you can," Peaches was worried. She was facing an emptiness and didn't have any ready fixes.

"I'm on it," Virgil said.

Chapter 18

Aeneas lived in a three room apartment on the second floor of a four story apartment building. One room was large and functioned as living-dining room and kitchen. The other two were bedroom style and he used one as a bedroom and the other as his high tech computer room. The residence was located in north Berkeley, two miles from the Peoples Investigation Agency.

He arrived home from work around six pm. After entering the apartment, he put the mail on the dining table and stepped into the kitchen area. He poured a glass of merlot wine and picked up the mail and carried it to a chair in the social area. Sitting down, he sipped the wine and sorted the mail. When he had separated the important items from the trash, he took the trash into the kitchen and put it into the recycling can. He stood looking out the kitchen window into the backyard. What should he have for dinner? He looked into the freezer and found a package of mac and cheese, which he removed, placing it in a dish, and setting it into the microwave oven.

He went back to the chair, sat, and drank some wine, waiting for dinner to warm up and thinking about the missing manuscript case. He hoped Peaches would come up with a solution. He did not have any answers.

The oven bell rang. He got up and went into the kitchen and took the mac and cheese into the dining area. As he sat at the dining table eating his meal, he thought about tonight's activities. It was Friday and he normally went out to one of his hangouts, usually going to one of three bistros. He decided on Smarty, only two blocks away. Smarty served wine, beer, and sandwiches. Its habitués were computer and cyberspace enthusiasts, who were provided a congenial place to socialize. Free wireless service was available.

After washing the dinner dishes, he went into the bedroom and combed his hair. He put on his sports jacket, checked his wallet for sufficient funds for a Friday night drink out, and left. A dampness was in the warm air as a fog rolled in. He quickly reached Smarty, which as usual was packed out on weekends and tonight was no different. Moving through the crowd, he spied Henry Larson, a long time buddy. Henry saw him and waved. Aeneas squeezed through the celebrants and sat down at Henry's table. Rock music was playing loudly and some couples were trying to dance, but there was little available space.

"What a mob," Henry said. "How have you been?"

"Fine. We've started a new investigation. Find a stolen manuscript which deals with controversial religious ideas. That's all I know at the moment."

Henry scrutinized his buddy, knowing he was always reticent about his cases, and laughed. "Aren't all religious ideas controversial, at least to someone?" Henry, a free thinker, beckoned the waitress and ordered another glass of merlot. Aeneas placed his order for the same.

After the waitress brought the wine, they settled into a serious discussion of the new operating systems that had been put on the market.

Aeneas felt something around his ankles and he noticed the wagging tail. He felt a cold nose sniff his hands which were in his lap.

A voice called out, "Hi, Henry. Aeneas." A border collie stuck her head on the tabletop, giving the men an innocent look. They laughed and both said at once, "Sheri. Sit with us, please."

Sheri Wordsworth sat down and gave a hand sign to her dog Star, who sat beside her. "Wow. Packed out tonight."

Aeneas gave Star his hand to sniff who recognized him as an old friend. "You are so beautiful," he said to Star.

According to human criteria, many people consider border collies to be at the top of the dog intelligence scale. They are sensitive to human emotion, especially love and affection, and will respond with their own affection. They are social, playful animals and do not like being alone. Their strong intuition allows them to bond with their human family. Having great stamina and powerful bodies, they require frequent exercise. Except for the shedding of fur, they make good housemates.

The bond between Sheri and Star was intimate and loving. She communicated by hand signs and voice and at times intuitively.

"We were discussing the new operating systems on the market," Henry said. "What's your opinion?"

"And now they're being given away free. What's up, anyway? Who will benefit? We won't," Sheri answered. She appeared disgusted.

"I guess sales are way down and the industry's hope is that a free OS will increase business," Aeneas replied.

"Yeh. How?" Henry finished his wine and waved for another.

"I wonder if the CEOs know," Sheri said.

"My advice is to put your savings into a very secure place, which would not be the financial market. Remember the dot.com bust. It took out the high tech areas of San Francisco and south bay – Silicon Valley.

"Hi, guys." The voice appeared from the crowd around them. Natalie Torres pushed a chair to their table and sat. They all waved to the waitress and the newcomer ordered a glass of chardonnay. Sheri had not placed her order yet, so she asked for chardonnay.

They brought Natalie up to date about their discussion of new OSs and they were off and running. By the time the waitress returned with the ladies' orders, the men were ready for a refill. It was to be a fun night.

After her third glass of wine Natalie with a glee in her eyes said, "Please listen with care. I have a high tale to tell and its truth value may be zero." They drew their heads together to hear every word.

"Well, the word in the marketplace is that all these new OSs being offered free are basically the same. They have the identical kernel in their code. The differences are the apps packaged with them. It's a game among the CEOs of the top computer firms to discover whose brand is the favorite. They believe we're a bunch yokels and they can sell us anything with the proper promotion."

She leaned back in her chair and looked at the others. At first they were astounded and then they all broke out laughing and giggling.

"That's hilarious. But I can understand their thinking," Sheri said.

"I like it. I like it," Henry added.

"Whether the tale has any truth value makes no difference. It's still a great story," Aeneas said.

"And here is additional information just released. The OSs have big security holes that allow the government to listen in on your computer. I don't know the truth value but think about it," Sheri said. Then she playfully put a finger to her mouth.

"Now the government is trying to force Apple to create software that will allow federal agents to access encoded data," Natalie said with disdain.

"Once a trapdoor is made, it can't be closed. Everyone from identity stealers to terrorists like IS will be able to enter," Henry said knowledgeably.

"All security has been destroyed. Thank you, Mr. FBI," Aeneas retorted.

"The group of weirdo hackers who spend all their time designing malware will be extremely happy. The government will be doing the heavy lifting for them," Sheri replied angrily.

"Yeh, the sick geeks who want to bring down the internet – they'll have a field day," Henry added.

"I'm happy that the FBI found an alternate method to access the encrypted data on the iPhone and dropped the suit against Apple," Aeneas noted.

"Will they tell Apple the technique used?" Sheri asked.

"The issue is here to stay and Congress must deal with it," Henry said.

"If the feds ever declare encryption illegal -- " Natalie commented.

"More likely they'll want the key to the encryption," Aeneas replied.

"Holy of holies. Once the feds have the key, the bad guys will soon have a copy of the key," Henry retorted.

"I don't understand them. How can anyone be so mean-spirited and cruel?" Natalie asked.

"They have a deep personality problem," Aeneas responded. He sipped some wine and then realized the wine was nearly gone.

"More like a conflicted soul," Sheri said.

Henry noticed his glass was empty and waved for the server. When she arrived, they all ordered refills. It was to be a great Friday night.

A cold light reflected off the burnished bluish steel machine as it was moving toward him; its six arms were extension rods with claws at the end. The arms were waving in the air seeking something to grab. A dome, its control center, rose above the machine's body. An electronic eye revolved in a 360 degree circle – searching, seeking. Then its laser beam found him and the machine quickly moved toward him – the six claws open to grab him.

Aeneas was terrified. He looked about. Standing in an open space resembling a junkyard, he was uncertain where to hide. The machine's laser beam was checking all junk for human presence with its built-in sensitivity to human physical vitals. He hid behind a battered car. The machine saw him, and the arms pushed aside the scrap metal in front of him. A safe haven was unavailable.

He ran and ran dodging around junk heaps. He could not get out of the yard. The only exit was blocked by his adversary, who kept narrowing in on him. He was penned in. He had to find a place of safety, a place to catch his breath and rest.

He saw a pile of junk that had space underneath it. If he could squeeze into the small space, maybe his attacker would lose track of him. At least he could rest for a moment. He rushed toward the junk pile, but he stopped abruptly when one of arms swung across his path. The monster was there. Backing up, he retreated to the side. The monster was steadily moving toward him.

He ran about the yard until his legs were too tired to move any further. He was backed up to the wall of a concrete shop building. He sank to the ground panting. He put his hands up in front of his face to ward off the brutality of the coming attack.

Suddenly, the gloom of the junkyard was dissipated by a brilliant illumination shining from above. A city of light appeared. He was overjoyed. Just as startling, he found himself in the command chair of the machine. In front of him were the controls to the massive computer system, the electronic brain of the machine. Beside him in another command chair was a woman he had never met. He looked at her and smiled. She returned the smile.

"I'm Sophie Eagles. Remember me?" She reached over and grasped his hand.

A set of memories flooded his mind. He was overcome with surprise and joy. Sophie had been his flame in high school and they had been a hot number.

He especially remembered the senior prom – how lovely she looked. He had bought her a corsage of small pink roses which nicely matched her gown. They danced together with perfection. Other memories of fun times they had together engulfed his mind: the senior picnic, the walks in the cool of a summer evening, ice skating in the winter, and the time in March of their senior year when her folks were away visiting relatives and he stayed the weekend at her place. They bonded and knew they were soul mates.

After graduation Sophie went to Northwestern University and Aeneas dropped out. Everyone was upset, including the families who been planning on a summer wedding. And he was banished from their social group. He felt empty but now had his computer and its world of high tech. At first the high tech world of computers completely filled him, but recently he was feeling empty again. His soul was hiding.

"Oh, my god, Sophie. Is it really you?" He squeezed back.

"Who were you expecting?" She started giggling just like she used to.

He knew. He could tell her giggle. The innocent-like amusement was its trademark. He got up from his chair and moved over to hers and hugged her. "My god, it's true."

"Aeneas , please sit down. You're rocking the boat, so to speak."

"I don't understand. Why are we both in the command center sitting in equal control chairs?"

"Simple. We are entangled and became so when we were dating."

"Entangled? Like subatomic particles?"

"Yes. That's the paradigm. What Einstein called 'spooky action at a distance' -- the behavior of a particle simultaneously influences others that have been involved with it wherever they are."

A strong feeling of love filled him and he wanted to be with her again. He kissed her.

She felt his intense desire and said, "I'm afraid we can't as before. I died two years ago and have been waiting for you to reach an understanding of your basic self. Now we will be together forever – all on the psychic level of course. I'm part of the inner self – your woman image.

He gazed at her with tenderness. An understanding spread through his mind. His soul brightened.

Sunlight was blazing through the bedroom window. Aeneas opened his eyes and stretched. He glanced at the clock – ten am. Wow, what a night I had. And the dream, a terrifying one that ended joyfully. Perhaps I'll tell Peaches. He admired Peaches for her intelligence and intuition.

He got up, went to the kitchen, made coffee, and went into the social room. Sitting, he sipped coffee and observed the ideas moving in and out of consciousness. He had taken up a limited form of meditation with Peaches' encouragement. So he was familiar with depth psychology and the writings of Carl Jung. Peaches had assisted with explanations of main concepts. He decided he would spend today studying psi zone and psychic phenomena. It was a sign. Ha, he thought, now I'm speaking the language.

She woke troubled. The dream that had faded away before her waking was a recurring one. It appeared in slightly different versions. The basic image was a mirror or some reflective surface. In the one she had woken from she was standing in front of the mirror attached to the dresser in her bedroom. She used the mirror for grooming and preparing herself for daily activities. When she looked into the mirror, she shrank back in horror. Her reflection was not there. The mirror reflected the furnishings in the bedroom but – she was absent. The mirror stared back at her: I don't know you, it was telling her. Where am I, she wondered? I've lost contact with my true self.

Other times the reflective surface differed. Once she sat down beside a pool to rest after hiking for an hour. She had her camera with her to capture the glory of nature. She enjoyed photographing images reflected on water. So she snapped a few photos of the pool and was startled to discover that her image was not there – trees, stones, the sky, but no Peaches Peoples.

My god, she thought. Have I vanished? How can that be? Then she regained her balance remembering that Aeneas had spent the day with her and he didn't notice anything amiss. She needed to discuss her mirror dream with someone, and Aeneas was the best one to share her troubles with.

Peaches and Aeneas sat in her living room next to each other on the couch sipping white wine before dinner. He was spending more time at her apartment, and she enjoyed his company. She smiled – I'm becoming more domestic and I think I like the new role. She had never really fancied Aeneas as a soul mate, but a new perception of him was growing. His charm was touching her deeply. She wondered if he reciprocated the feeling. She decided she would starting testing his feelings toward her besides being a business partner.

"Aeneas, I've been having a troubling dream that recurs. I'd like to share it with you."

Aeneas put his wine glass down on the table and with concern in his voice said, "Please Peaches, share with me. You're my best friend and I'd like to help."

Alert, she sensed something different about him. He was more – what? She would have to consider carefully his change.

"The dream involves a reflective surface like a mirror or water and my image is not present." She proceeded to describe the version she had in the early morning.

"My god, that's heavy," he said.

"It bothers me – way down deep in my soul. I feel lost and just don't understand it."

They sat quietly as Aeneas pondered the problem. A voice broke the silence -- a voice from nowhere: "Yes, Peaches, you've lost yourself."

Aeneas bolted upright. "Of course. Your self is missing."

Peaches smiled weakly, not quite certain about the meaning of his statement. She waited for him to explain.

"Virgil pointed out the obvious. Since all parts of a dream stem from one's primary personality, the dream seems to be asking you about your basic self, who you really are, the bedrock of your self-identity."

Peaches giggled like a teenager. "Something opened -- a portal of discovery. Yes, I can feel the source. Rafé and Sandra have talked about ideas of this nature. I'm understanding."

The disembodied voice spoke again, "Think Zen."

"Of course. The ego is nothing – a hollow conceit. It has no substance so it isn't reflected in a mirror."

Aeneas laughed. "We're a pair of nobodies – nowhere people."

"We've no roots. Blowing in the wind like tumbleweed."

"As the balladeer sings, 'What's it like without a home.'"

"I think I get it. My present quest is to find my basic self, whatever that may be. At the moment I'm unknown to myself."

"Use the challenges of our missing manuscript case to fuel your quest."

An intense intuition filled Aeneas' mind. Now was the time for his part in their new intimacy – a sharing of inner thoughts. "I had a weird dream last night too. Would you like to hear it and help me understand it?"

Peaches felt warmth toward her friend. a definite turning point in their relationship. "Yes, I'd be happy to listen and assist you."

He felt very confident now and described the machine dream. His embarrassment was evident when he talked about Sophie Eagles. Peaches recognized his yearning to open his soul to her. Finishing the description of the machine dream, he sat back and looked at her expectantly. He trusted her wisdom.

She smiled and patted him on the knee. "This certainly is entanglement, if not downright serendipity," she said and laughed.

Aeneas felt relieved and laughed too. She understood.

"We both have a similar challenge -- discover our basic self. You need to cultivate your inner woman, and I require a total overhaul – both my inner woman and inner man are deficient."

"The queen and king, I think, are the esoteric terms."

"I believe I read something about them in Carl Jung's writings. Such insight he had and the ability to share with others," Peaches replied.

"Let's work on it together and use our present case to access our true self," Aeneas said.

Suddenly they were hugging and laughing.

Chapter 19

After breakfasting at one of the old hippie restaurants on Haight Street, they meandered through Golden Gate Park. It was a lovely day, warm with a cool ocean breeze flowing inland. Nature was alive. They watched a great blue heron fishing for its meal and observed rabbits and squirrels searching for food. When they reached the bison field on Kennedy Drive, they stopped and sat on a bench, watching the beautiful animals grazing.

"I was amazed when I learned about the bison in Golden Gate Park." He smiled at her and winked.

"A pair was brought into the park in 1890. A few arrived later and of course they reproduced," she answered.

"Over a hundred years – I'm even more astonished."

"Tell me more about the horse-breeding program." Rafé clasped Alan's hand.

"Okay, but let me gather my thoughts." He stared at the bison for a few moments. "The program started back in 1994 to rejuvenate our culture by reestablishing our ancient relationship with the herd. A special project has been set up to involve the youth and reconnect them to our history.

"The first horses reached the Nez Perce before 1700 and have a dominant role in our lives. We were one of the few tribes to breed horses and perhaps the first one. The official theory is the horses had come up from the south and the Spanish. A few alternate notions suggest they had escaped from the French or Russian fur traders."

"But it doesn't matter, does it?"

"No, definitely not. Once horses had become our brothers and sisters, our lifestyle changed drastically. Hunting bison, our primary source of sustenance, changed. It became easier to find herds because we could now travel further distances. We could ride in among the herd and select a specific animal for killing. Our horses were trained to bring the hunter alongside the selected animal, and when the horse heard the arrow leave the bow, it closed in on the mortally wounded bison and separated it from the herd."

"Oh, my, but that's very dangerous."

"Yes. With the wrong move both horse and rider would be killed. The Appaloosa that we bred had quick feet and was very strong and intelligent. The Appaloosa was surefooted enough to climb up and down the narrow trails of our homeland. We mated the Appaloosa with an ancient breed from Turkmenistan in Asia, the Akhal-Teke. We call the offspring the Nez Perce horse, which has excellent strength and endurance. Our horse breeders traveled the world seeking the proper mate for the Appaloosa. Who could guess we would find it in Asia?"

They rose from the bench and began walking toward the ocean. "How did you become involved in magic?"

"I owe the present enthusiasm to the Garlands. I met them at Ocean Delights on Ocean Avenue soon after I arrived in the city. In fact they became surrogate family. Shasta befriended me as an aunt and Ralph taught me about the wonderful realm of magic. He's a semiretired stage magician and was seeking an assistant for a new show. I accepted."

They walked hand-in-hand along the Great Highway northward until they reached the Cliff House, a famous restaurant that had been renovated by the park service. They stopped and went in for a midday snack. Sitting at a table by the windows, they looked out at the ocean. The tide was coming in, and rocks were sinking below the ocean surface. A flock of pelicans flew overhead and then plunked into the ocean, sending up large sprays of water. The seals sunbathing on the rocks being swallowed by rising tide swam to the rocky cliff shores of the nearby Parklands. South along the shoreline surfers with their surfboards were enjoying the high waves rolling onto the beach. A carefree moment – two friends were enjoying nature's bounty. Their souls touched, encouraged by the harmonious surroundings.

They paid the luncheon bill and left, heading east on Point Lobos Avenue until they reached the entrance to Sutro Heights Hill Park. The park had been the garden residence of Adolph Sutro, a former city mayor. They stood at the low garden retaining wall, gazing out over the ocean, and watched three fishing boats plying their trade.

Staring at the ocean as waves moved onto the beach, they watched the rocks vanish beneath the rising tide. Alan said, "The coming and going of the tide is mysterious. The work of our sister the moon rock circling the earth, the rocks disappear into nothingness and then reappear from nothingness."

"It's a mystical idea," Rafé replied. She gazed at the moving waves. "Another idea is that the ocean suggests the unconscious and the rocks are moving into consciousness or out of it."

They stood in silence watching the tidal flow – the earth breathing in and out. Rafé laughed. Alan turned toward her with a questioning look. "I've a magic routine that I learned from Ralph using a magic stone," she said.

"Oh, what is it?" Alan asked.

She opened her shoulder bag and rummaged around in it for a few moments. Taking out a small stone, she showed it to Alan, who took the stone and felt it. "It's smooth and rounded. Must have been in water. Did you find it on the beach?"

She smiled. "Actually, I found it in a creek on my reservation. It has the power of the sacred creek."

"How do you use it?"

"Please keep the stone warm in your hands while I get a packet of tarot cards." Rafé removed a cloth pouch from her shoulder bag and took out some cards. "These are the major arcana. As I spread the cards, please choose one."

Holding the stone in one hand, Alan removed a card from the packet with the other hand.

"Okay, look at the card, remember it, but don't show it to me. Now place it face down on top of the deck and then rubbed it with the sacred stone."

Alan followed directions. "Done," he remarked.

"While I shuffle the deck, please visualize the selected card and project the image into the packet. Use the stone as a power source."

She shuffled the deck several times and then cut it twice. "Now please touch the top of the packet with the stone."

After he did as requested, she turned over the top card. It was the Sun card. "Is this your chosen card?"

"Awesome. That was excellent. Of course, it's my card. It shows a naked child riding a horse bareback. Looks like a garden of some sort in the background. What's the meaning?"

"The Sun card tells about your personality. You're part of nature and prefer a simple life style rather than the contemporary technology. Mother earth is the source of your creativeness. You have the potential to achieve your goals in whatever areas you're interested in."

Alan laughed. "Thank you for the compliments, Rafé. You're a sweetheart."

She stared at him with serious intent. "Alan, I just read the card. Of course, I agree with it, but it's the card speaking. Remember, you chose the card."

For a moment he was taken aback. Then he said, "Perhaps the card chose me."

"More likely, the magic stone linked the card with you. In that sense you both chose each other." She smiled brightly.

"Are you suggesting medicine power?"

"Isn't medicine power magical, mysterious, and sacred?"

He laughed. "Rafé, your insights continue to boggle my intellect." He kissed her on the cheek. She turned and gave him a full kiss.

Looking into her eyes, he caressed her hair. "I have another question."

"Yes?"

"I related to the child riding the horse, remembering when I was young and my father put me on a horse and led us around the corral. I felt on top of the world. Such joy. What is the meaning of the child and horse?"

"We all have a child in us and the horse is our body that the child must learn to control. What's sad is that most of us forsake our child. It's shut in its little room, sullen, forgotten, unloved, and often besieged by fear and frustration. Suddenly it erupts with anger and temper tantrums. Humans are the silliest and most foolish creatures on earth when the child breaks loose. We must care for our child and help it mature along with us."

"Wow. Amazing thoughts. Where did you discover them?"

"Peyote Woman taught me – my spiritual guide. I've learned so much from her."

"There's a Native American Church on the reservation. When I go home, I'm going to learn more about it. I'm feeling it'll be an immense help."

"Oh, Alan, do attend a few meetings and found out what the Peyote Path will do for you."

"When I go home again, I'd love to have you join me."

She smiled filled with radiance. "I'd enjoy visiting your home."

He touched her cheek. "I was thinking of you joining me permanently."

She touched his lips with her fingers. "Shh. Not now. Let's get to know each other well and create a strong bond before we talk about permanent togetherness.

He smiled as he removed his flute from its leather pouch and played a lyrical melody in harmony with the surroundings. When he had finished, Rafé said, "That's not the flute you played the other day. It certainly sounds different."

"This is my medium size flute and is keyed to C sharp."

"Rafé. Hi," a voice called out.

They turned in the direction of the voice. Peaches and Aeneas walked up. "Alan, meet Peaches and Aeneas, friends and employers for my cyberspace research. The data I collect will assist them in solving the strange mystery of a stolen manuscript."

"Was that you playing the flute? It was wonderful," Peaches said.

"Rafé and her friend Sandra Kingfisher have been a great help so far," Aeneas commented, returning to the original line of thought.

"So you two are friends of the Garlands?" Alan inquired.

"We work for Shasta. She writes novels about our adventures as a detective agency," Peaches answered. Rafé had told her about Alan, a Nez Perce from Idaho. She took an instant liking to him. On the spur of the moment she said, "Would you two join us for dinner this Friday night? Aeneas will be eating at my place and we would enjoy the company." Peaches looked at them with pleasure in her eyes.

Rafé and Alan gazed at each other and then Rafé said, "We'd be delighted. What time?"

"Around six pm would be fine, time enough for some wine and conversation," Peaches answered. "Oh, please bring your flute." She and Aeneas left the happy couple and began a tour of the garden, pausing to view the sculptures scattered about and inspecting the plant life. When they came to a stone bench in a sheltered alcove, Peaches said, "Let's sit here and absorb the atmosphere."

They held hands, listening to the birds singing and enjoying the cool breeze flowing in from the ocean. A time to relax and release all their concerns and worries.

"I'd like to share a secret with you." She looked at him intently and squeezed his hand.

"Please. I'm your friend," he replied.

"I've a deep desire for privacy. And I don't want Virgil's eyes and ears always watching me. At first I didn't think anything about his ever-presence, but recently I've become annoyed by it. The older I get, the more I desire personal solitude. I want to control the presence of others, including Virgil. Is there any way to turn him off for awhile?" She had a pleading tone in her voice.

Aeneas was quiet. Finally, he said, "I know what you mean. I'm getting tired of his constant monitoring of my activities while at home or in the office. I can add some subroutines without him knowing it. Thus, being unaware that he's been shut down, he won't freak out. The challenge is dealing with his internal clock. If he realizes he lacks memory for a certain time period, he'll worry and ask me to remedy the problem. I'll work on it."

"Thank you, dear. I feel better already."

Aeneas was alerted to her word 'dear' which she had never called him before. "And you're my dearest friend," he replied and squeezed her hand. Her sweet smile was a kiss of life brightening his soul.

It was Friday evening a few minutes before six pm. Peaches was bustling about the social room, making certain everything was ready for her guests. The door bell chimed and, when she opened the front door, Rafé and Alan were standing there. As they were entering the apartment, Alan gave her a bottle of wine with a ribbon tied around. "Our gift for your hospitably," he said.

Smiling brightly, Peaches accepted the gift, "How thoughtful," she said, "thank you so much."

Aeneas stepped forward, also thanking them, and suggested they should seat themselves.

"We'll save your gift for dinner," Peaches remarked. She took the bottle into the kitchen.

"I'll serve the house wine now." Aeneas winked. "Would you like red or white?"

"Red," they both answered.

When they were settled, sipping wine, Peaches looked intently at Alan, who was even more handsome than she remembered. "Please tell us about the Nez Perce people. I know every little about the native people of the northwest."

"Yes. Your community's life history and your role in it," Aeneas said.

Alan began a short summary of the Nez Perce, but Peaches and Aeneas had many questions seeking more details and further expansion of the subject. He paused and Peaches said, "Please stop here, Alan. I should check on dinner." A few minutes later she returned and sat down again. "It'll be awhile. Please continue."

Alan opened his bandolier bag, which Rafé had given him, and removed a long leather bag from which he took out a flute. "Shall I play a serenade?" he asked. Rafé smiled. The bag had been crafted by her cousin and exhibited the bead work design of Potawatomi origin.

"Please," Peaches replied.

The sweet melody flowed through the room. Aeneas had his eyes closed, caught up in a personal reverie. When Alan had finished, they all applauded. Rafé had gleam in her eyes.

"Wow," Aeneas said, "I'm not used to that type of sound."

"It's beautiful." Peaches commented.

Rafé said, "He has four flutes of different sizes and keys."

"This is my favorite flute and is F sharp," Alan responded.

"Please play another song," Aeneas requested.

When Alan was done, Peaches said that she would check on dinner. She shortly returned and announced dinner was being served. Peaches had fixed an old fashioned Indiana meal: steak, baked potatoes with everything, string beans, and a fresh green salad. During the meal everyone shared personal stories.

After dinner Peaches asked Rafé to perform some of her magic routines portraying Native American stories. Rafé happily obliged by offering the routines she did at Ocean Delights. After the applause, Alan suggested she do the new one she was working on.

Rafé laughingly said, "Ok, but I don't have all the moves worked out yet." She pointed to Alan. "My new one is part of the Nez Perce creation story. If Alan would be the storyteller, I'll stage some sleights I've prepared so far." As Alan told about the monster and coyote, Rafé executed the moves she was confident about doing.

"Now it's your turn," Rafé said and nodded at Peaches and Aeneas.

"Yes, what were some of your most intriguing cases?" Alan asked Peaches and Aeneas.

Peaches glanced at Aeneas. "One that comes to mind was the case of the missing chess set."

"It was an antique set made of ivory. Worth at least $12,000," Aeneas added.

Peaches continued the story, "We had help from our friend Mary Rainbow, owner of the Rainbow Inn on Oceans Avenue. She had been the world chess champion and had retired undefeated. Our clues were chess problems – win in two or three moves."

"The thief was a game player and challenged us with the puzzles," Aeneas remarked.

"Mary solved the problems and the answer lay in the pattern produced by the solutions. We were able to located the thief and where he had hid the chess set." Peaches appeared pleased.

"What other cases?" Alan asked.

Peaches and Aeneas described three other exciting cases.

By ten pm Rafé and Alan were ready to leave. They thanked Peaches and Aeneas for a wonderful evening and promised to host the next dinner party.

As they walked under the star lit sky, Alan took his flute and softly played an evening serenade. Rafé was delighted as she listened to the courtship melody.

Chapter 20

She stood at the window of her study overlooking the backyard garden, observing the diversity of plants. A redwood tree was growing in one corner away from the house. Scattered about were flowering perennials and annuals. Interspersed among the flowers were drought resistant bushes, primarily types of fuchsias that hummingbirds like so much. Her thoughts wandered forth into nature's living room, dissipating anxieties and worries. She realized she was at a crossroad in her creative project writing 'Lazarus' Gospel.'

Turning, she walked to the plants next to the desk and carefully examined each plant for possible insect infestation, damping-off, or other damage. Several orchids were flowering. She considered them for a few minutes, enjoying their beauty, before heading for her thinking chair, an old fashioned rocking chair with padded back and seat.

Shasta Garland was in the process of making important decisions. In the morning's mail a two-day priority envelope was delivered. She even had to sign for it. It was from Spenser Blake, who obviously felt secure enough to use the US Postal Service to communicate with her. The envelope contained comments and dialogue for the manuscript. She wasn't certain whether he wanted her to insert the exact dialogue or her own phrasing with some personal irony. She would phone and ask.

Some of the dialogue was silly and puerile. She would dislike readers to believe she had lost her writing skill. If she infused the dialogue with irony and satire, she wouldn't lose her reputation.

Getting up, she went to the phone and called Blake but got the answering machine. Leaving a message to call as soon possible, she sat down at the computer and opened her mind to the voice of her Muse.

Peaches Peoples prepared for another journey to Marcus Scarpia's library. He maintained a regular schedule for studying ancient texts and working in the small laboratory.

Peaches had called an early morning brain-storming session. As she and

Aeneas were finishing their pastry breakfast and enjoying their third cup of coffee, Virgil was waiting patiently, or so it seemed from appearances. Actually the supercomputer was diligently gathering data on all the main characters in the investigation.

"Well, we have a quandary. Cat Midnight has supernormal talents, and he could destroy our carefully laid plan to spy on Scarpia. Any solutions or possible keys we can utilize to unlock the answers to our dilemma?" Peaches gazed at Aeneas and then peered into Virgil's electronic eyes.

After a few moments, Virgil said, "I do have a suggestion that may cancel Midnight's security talent."

Peaches and Aeneas became alert and smiled at each other. "Well, Virgil, what do you have to offer?" Peaches asked.

"Yes, we're all on edge – waiting."

"I have been studying the behavior of cats, especially the relationship between male and female – their dynamics and courtship rituals. What if the scent of a female in heat were placed in one of the four ceiling corners? Would not Midnight be attracted and perhaps spend some time at that corner, sniffing and looking for the female? With Midnight distracted, Peaches could select one of the other corners to dwell in, safe from Midnight's perimeter defense."

"Brilliant." Peaches was awed by the elegance of the solution.

After the surprise left his countenance, Aeneas raised a practical question, "Where do we obtain the female scent?"

"I will analyze the chemical ingredients in the scent and you can buy and mix them – your own alchemical project, Aeneas."

"Of course, we don't know how long the scent will distract Midnight, but it is worth trying. Excellent."

"A printout of the chemical ingredients is in the printer's tray," Virgil said.

Aeneas picked up the list of chemicals. "The scheme has me wired. I'm on my way." He rushed out of the office.

Aeneas had inserted a tiny atomizer in one of the two microchips attached to the cat necklace that gave Peaches the ability to visit the astral dimension.

Observing the room, she watched Scarpia reading a book and taking notes. Midnight was nowhere to be seen, so she sprayed a little female cat scent into a ceiling corner and moved over to the opposite corner. Stakeouts were usually dull but a necessary part of an investigation. She zoomed in on the text Scarpia was reading. It was written in an archaic script and was illustrated with images. The text appeared to be written in Greek, at least the letters reminded her of the Greek alphabet. Virgil notified her that it was Greek.

Scarpia picked up a magnifying-glass and scrutinized an image on the page he was reading. Then he drew a diagram in his journal and wrote some comments, implying to Peaches that he was seeking an interpretation of the passage.

She was startled by what she saw and zoomed in for a closer, more detailed view of the image. What a weird picture, she thought. In the central foreground were two men dressed in medieval clothes and joined at the leg. They shared the same middle leg. In the background was a leaf-covered tree – birds were sitting on the branches while delicious fruit hung from the boughs.

Examining Scarpia's commentary on the image, she tried to discover any hidden meaning but was unable to. All the words in the text and the commentary were gibberish to her. She transmitted a copy of the page and Scarpia's comments to Virgil, who should be able to search the world's databases and find the import.

Nodding to himself, Marcus walked over to a bookcase at one end of the room and removed a large leather bound volume with gold tooling. It appeared to have rag paper pages. The title was *Liber de Homunculus* authored by Abelard of Seville. When he opened to the title page, she noticed that the book was published in Seville in 1595. He turned to a specific page, and Peaches zoomed in to examine the beautiful illuminations. He took Doug's 'Lazarus Gospel' book and leafed through it until he reached a certain page. He then compared the text in both volumes. The text of *Liber* was in Latin and that of 'Lazarus Gospel' was in Greek. Since she could not read either language, she sent copies to Virgil for translation and analysis.

She heard a meow and watched Midnight enter the study. The cat leaped onto the desk and sat down next to the books and began purring.

"Ah, Midnight, how are you. Some adventures on the agenda for tonight." Scarpia rubbed behind the cat's ears. "Well, go about your business.

I've work to do." He returned to comparing the texts.

Midnight bounded onto the top shelf behind the desk and then stepped onto the ceiling molding forming the border. The cat paused, its head turning from side to side as it sniffed the air. Then Midnight cautiously moved toward the scent-filled corner. Sitting down, he gazed upward at the ceiling corner and began purring, a loving, romantic sound.

She had not noticed earlier that the border molding had images incised in it. They appeared to be occult symbols. She sent photos of them to Virgil and requested Virgil to collect all available data on Abelard's *Liber* as soon as possible. She was already familiar with the contents of Doug's manuscript. In a few minutes she began receiving data about *Liber* from Virgil.

Liber discussed details, methods, and operations for resurrection and the making of a homunculus, which Virgil had discovered were analogies for making the elixir of life. Resurrection is a technique for bringing life into an inanimate (dead) body and a homunculus requires the presence of a life force similar to resurrection. Scarpia had bought the book at an antiquarian rare book store in Seville four years ago.

Midnight continued to purr to the invisible female. It is working, Peaches thought, but for how long? It's a test and I will be ready to withdraw swiftly if Midnight becomes interested in my corner.

She observed Scarpia as he studied the ancient texts. She had decided to transmit copies of all the pages he was reading. From the corner of her eye she perceived a movement – Midnight had gracefully jumped to the desk and reclined on his bed.

Marcus rose and walked to the laboratory. The black cat sat up and watched. The scholar removed a jar labeled salts of magnesia from the shelf and opened it. He scooped an ounce of salts out of the jar and put them into a flask resting in a metal stand.

Then he chanted, "A-la – ala-ka-zam. Sim. Sala. Bim. Arise fiery spirits of the burning chaos. I call you forth. Cleanse the dross from the sulfuric salts." He held up the flask.

Peaches was amazed when a red flaming light shown in the flask. A bright flash – like lightning -- and the flame was gone.

He placed the flask back in the stand. Taking a bottle from the shelf, he poured a small amount of liquid into the flask. Again he chanted, "A-la – ala-ka-zam. Sim. Sala. Bim." He raised the flask and continued, "Come forth watery spirits from the abyssal depths. Oh, Mercury of Life revivify these salts."

Peaches could hardly believe her eyes. A bluish mist filled the flask. The mist brightened and suddenly vanished. After inserting a stopper in the flask's mouth, Scarpia placed it in a wood box and closed the lid. "The Mercurial essence must remain in the dark until the moon passes Saturn again."

Midnight meowed in agreement and then curled up on the desk. Marcus returned to the desk. Before sitting down, he peered around the room, especially at ceiling level. "Midnight," he said, "I am intuiting we're being observed. Yet you found the room to be secure. How strange." He stood and walked over to a basin on a pedestal. "I will check the water mirror for any hidden intruders."

Peaches decided her visiting time was over and returned to her living room. Aeneas was present with a glass of orange juice for her refreshment. He returned from the kitchen with a plate of chocolate chip cookies, which he set on the side table.

As he munched on a cookie and Peaches drank orange juice, they discussed what they knew so far about Marcus' project.

"Well, we now have definite proof Scarpia is our culprit. As yet we don't know the reason Doug's manuscript is important to him. Hmm, the elixir of life or fountain of youth has many labels. And it is a life creating force."

Aeneas reached for another cookie. "Creating the elixir empowers the creator with an immense cosmic force. Does he visualize himself as a god governing the universe? Can pride reach so high?"

"Now we know what to look for. I don't think we should tell Doug yet."

"We can tell him we have a favorite candidate for the thief but no hard evidence."

"We will do more research and maintain regular surveillance. I will ask our research team Sandra and Rafé to perform their cyber magic. And Virgil has his magic. Let us go into action."

Putting the phone down, Doug Balentine puffed vigorously on his pipe. Blowing the smoke out, he smiled. Peaches had phoned and given him un update. They had not located the whereabouts of 'Lazarus Gospel.' They did have evidence that one of the members of the meeting had taken it but no solid incriminating evidence for legal action.

The insurance claims adjuster had visited him and he provided the same scenario as he did for Peaches. In fact he told the adjuster he had hired Peaches from whom she could obtain reports. The adjuster was pleased with a detective firm being employed but said the company would also hire an investigator. After a wait of a month Doug would receive a million dollars for the lost manuscript. Then he could pay off his debts, set some money aside, putting it into a savings account, and get back to his scholar pursuits. Let the rotten financial marketplace go its own way.

He had an intuition that an essential key to the Jesus-Lazarus relationship lay embedded in the story, a key no one had discovered, yet at least not published. If he were the first – exuberance filled his soul. He would be renowned: asked to give lectures at important conferences and offered the best teaching positions.

Actually he did not need to wait until he received the insurance money; he could start now, but he had to be certain his servants did not discover the real text. He walked over to the collection of ancient manuscripts. Climbing a short ladder, he reached into a corner on the top shelf and removed the true copy of 'Lazarus Gospel.' He carried it over to the study table and sat down. Opening it to the beginning of the tale, Doug examined the text carefully and made notes when he believed the idea was linked to the key.

A bell chimed and a green light flashed on next to the door. He had locked the door and required his servants to announce their presence. Doug stood and went over to the door, inquiring through a speaking system. "Yes, what is it?" he asked.

His valet Archie Jeeves answered, "Would you like your nightcap now, sir?"

He looked up at the clock hanging above the mantle. He was amazed. The time had gone by faster than he was aware.

"Yes, I would Jeeves. I will close up my work and be ready for a nightcap in five minutes"

He returned 'Lazarus Gospel' to its hiding spot. He sat down in his reading chair and opened a journal of biblical studies. Shortly Jeeves returned with the nightcap, a fine brandy, and rang the study's bell. Doug pressed a door unlock button in the arm of the chair. The valet entered and served his master.

"Thank you, Jeeves, that'll be all for tonight."

"Have a pleasant night, sir," Jeeves said as he left the room.

After Jeeves left, Doug picked up the copy of *Pride and Prejudice* and opened it to the bookmarked page. He sipped some brandy, savoring its delicate taste. Then he stepped in the world of Jane Austen, leaving his daily concerns behind.

Chapter 21

Dwight walked into the bedroom and over to the bed. Sandra was sleeping quietly on her side. He smiled and was touched by her inner beauty which shone forth. He bent over and kissed her on the check and whispered, "Sandra, sleepyhead, time to rise." She muttered and opened her eyes. Dwight was looking at her. He sat on the edge of the bed and caressed her hair. "Coffee is ready. Shall I bring you a cup?"

Sandra yawned and rolled onto her back. Then she sat up. "No, I'll come to the kitchen."

Dwight got up and left the bedroom, returning to the kitchen where he was preparing one of his special omelets. Sandra groomed herself, put on a robe, and joined Dwight. She sat down at the table where he put a cup of coffee. She sipped the hot beverage. "Yummy. Very tasty. I need it. It's hard waking up." When she had drained the cup, he refilled it.

"Did you sleep well?"

"Oh, so peaceful. I haven't had such a pleasant sleep in ages. Thanks for letting me sack in."

"Breakfast will be ready soon – an omelet, toast, and a bowl of strawberries and blueberries. Do you want some milk on the fruit?"

"Yes, a little bit – not much."

She gazed out the kitchen window at the children and their parents in Dolores Park. Dwight and his roommate Craig Takemitsu rented a flat in a three story apartment building, located in the San Francisco Mission District. The original Spanish Mission was close by. The church, also known as Mission Dolores, was built with the forced labor of the Ohlone people under the supervision of the Spanish padres and military. It was dedicated in 1791 and is the oldest surviving building in San Francisco. The original façade is still in place, but the remainder of the church has been updated and is used for the administration of the mission and a museum. A small cemetery is located on the grounds. A new church in the form of a basilica was completed in 1918. It holds services and is a popular venue for concerts.

The Spanish constructed a number of missions throughout California to protect their territory from other countries and convert the indigenousness population to Christianity. The missions served as a hub for the Spanish settlers who colonized the land.

When she had eaten the fruit, she started on the omelet. "The omelet is delicious. What are all ingredients?"

"It's a secret. I'm planning to put all my recipes into an eBook. You'll be the first to get a copy."

"I'm tired of research. Let's just kick back and watch the day flow by."

"I agree. We'll go to Dolores Park and take in some sun and fresh air," Dwight said.

After washing the dishes and tidying up the kitchen, they left for the park. A slight, cool breeze was blowing in from the ocean and held the temperature down to the low seventies. The Mission District is considered to be one of the warmest parts of the city. They walked across the street and up the grassy slope that's at the south end of the park. They found a place on the slope and sat down. They watched children running about playing various games. Adults were on blankets spread on the ground or seated on one of the few benches. The ubiquitous dogs were running about chasing each other.

"Dwight dear, why did you choose computers and electronic media for a career?"

He laughed. "I didn't choose it, but it chose me. I've' always had a strong interest in mechanics and a talent for math. Lowell High School, which I attended, had funds for a high tech lab. All students were required to learn the operation of a computer."

"Dwight, I know that. Remember I went to Lowell also. Fiat Scientia." She giggled.

His face turned reddish and a warm glow appeared. "I'm sorry, honey. I wasn't thinking and got caught up in answering your question. You know, it's a wonder we didn't met while studying there. The school's motto 'Let there be knowledge' really touched me. It was an intellectual paradise."

"For me too. But please continue."

"Well, I fell in love with electronic technology and spent after school hours at the lab. Both my physics and math teachers supervised the lab different days of the week. They recognized my talent and encouraged me in that direction. In fact they helped me get a scholarship at S.F State by writing letters of recommendation that highly praised my ability. I hope to complete my PhD thesis next year. I told you what it was?"

"Only in general terms. So spill the details."

"It focuses on methods to surf cyberspace and their influence on society. But since I've met you, I decided to sneak in the topic of surfing psi-space, but I have to word it carefully because my advisers will only accept the existence of the electromagnetic dimension of reality. They would laugh me out of school if I wrote clearly and directly about psi-space and its link to cyberspace. You're an excellent wordsmith. Perhaps you could assist me."

"I'd be delighted. I'll give the problem some deep and serious thought." She hugged him and they kissed each other.

"Let's stroll along Mission Street and see what's happening. There's always something of interest."

They left Dolores Park and walked east along Eighteenth Street until they reached Mission Street where they turned south.

"I'm starting to feel like a midday snack. Let's check the restaurants," Dwight said.

Walking south along Mission, they paused at El Toreador, a well-known Mexican restaurant. After reading the menu posted on the front window, they entered and found themselves a table in a quiet corner of the café. When they had finished their lunch of enchiladas verde, they left and continued walking south on Mission.

They were holding hands and, when Dwight paused, he pulled Sandra toward him. "I've some news about our research project. Would you like to hear it now or later?" he said.

"Now is fine," Sandra answered.

"I've learned more about Carlyle Quincebury's stroke. A rumor was going around campus before the incident that Quincebury had certain enemies he was trying to harm or at least prevent their actions that might be detrimental to him. At first I didn't think much of the rumor, but after researching his daily activities for a year before the stoke, I came up with evidence he had it in for Ralph Garland because of Ralph's work at the Institute of CIN. For some reason Ralph's psi talents bothered him and he wanted to damage them."

"Well, well. now that's intriguing. So Rafé's vision was correct. They'll be glad to know the truth."

They continued south on Mission until they reached Twenty-fourth Street and turned right onto it and walked west. Twenty-fourth was in the heart of the Latino community. They saw signs posted in shop windows protesting the development of the area into a high priced condo and apartment neighborhood. The employees of profitable high tech firms could well afford the costs, and the people who had lived there for generations were being pushed out. Wealthy developers had friends in city government who assisted in the gentrification of the Mission.

At Valencia Street they turned north and strolled back to Eighteenth, stopping at shops to browse. It was early evening when they reached Dwight's apartment.

Chapter 22

After a pleasant dinner Spenser Blake retired to his library and sat in a comfy reading chair. He thought about the day's events. He had visited Shasta in late afternoon and learned about her progress. She was further along than he had expected and the progress pleased him. After coffee and a satisfying social conversation, which give him more information about the Garlands, he took the copies she had made of the material and left. Smiling, he was in particular amused by the cats. Yes, the Garland exuded positive energy.

He stood and walked to the desk where a briefcase was set. Beside it, Theo his Abyssinian napped. He patted her. "Guarding the manuscript – thank you." She purred. Removing a large envelope from the briefcase, he placed it on the desk. Sitting down, he emptied the envelope and started reading the material. Spenser smiled. His plan was working so far. Shasta had written a fair amount of the story and listed episodes to be composed. He read through the written sections and made comments and suggestions. Several times her ideas had inspired his own thinking. He liked the character Marcus Scarpia, who was just bizarre enough to possess a warped intellect.

She had not written anything about the Lazarus-Jesus affair, the central theme of the tale. She wanted to wait until she was inspired. Ah, these creative souls, he thought, to be so open, waiting for the imagination to flow. As a scholar he was unable to give up the control of his intellect: peel away layers of debris and meaninglessness until the truth was revealed. Keeping his intellect honed was a necessary mandate and there was no time for leisurely daydreaming.

Creative artists like Shasta maintained the sacredness in the world, certainly not the players in the marketplace. The imagination was a portal to the invisible realm and artists kept it open. He could do a little bit by building a firewall to protect the portal.

When he was a teenager, painting touched his soul. His works were good, that is, correct composition and conventional subject matter. He enjoyed painting landscapes with their many colors and forms. Learning that the creative imagination was a vehicle for gaining knowledge, he spent many hours in his studio. He looked up at the wall facing him and admired a landscape he had painted when he was eighteen. It was the only one he could save from his father's rage.

His father was angry and told him he should take up a manly profession, like banking or law, and be a success. Being on the top floor was his father's metaphor for success, and Spenser should be working hard now to gain entry.

Spenser turned his back on his father's demands and retreated further into himself. He was safe taking religion as a profession as long as he followed his father's beliefs. So now was the opportunity to achieve what he had always desired to do: publish his own beliefs, especially about controversial biblical topics. An inner warmth arose as he reflected on the prospect.

Silence reigned, except for the quiet turning of pages, in Marcus Scarpia's library. Midnight was curled up on the desk, snoozing but with his ears alert while Marcus sat hunched over, studying two books whose pages were open. They were Abelard of Seville's *Liber de Homunculus* and Doug Balentine's 'Lazarus Gospel.'

Peaches, sitting in her eagle's nest, was fascinated by the illumination of the page in *Liber*, so she zoomed in for a closer examination. The illumination portrayed a woman who was dressed in a white gown, wearing a crown, and stood within a chemical flask. The interior of the flask was blue in color. Scrolls with Latin words swirled around the flask. Below the flask was a Latin text which continued onto the facing page.

Virgil quickly beamed Peaches a translation of the words as it received the transmission. The scroll above the flask, which was in the center of the illumination, contained the words 'Elixir of Life.' Virgil added that the phrase also meant 'Elixir of Immortality.' Some of the phrases in the swirling scrolls were 'dissolve and coagulate,' 'as above so below,' 'the matter is everywhere but we are blind,' 'seek the green lion,' and 'the sun devours the moon.'

Although the words were now in English, she did not understand their meaning within the alchemical context. Obviously, they were extremely symbolic and required a special glossary. The text beginning below the illumination and continuing onto the facing page had the same obdurate quality and eluded her present comprehension. When she returned to her living room, she would begin an in-depth study of alchemy.

Marcus wrote some comments in the journal and then turned the page of *Liber*. The next image was a knight with the head of the sun riding a lion who was fighting a naked woman with the head of the moon on the back of a griffin. He picked up the magnifying glass and carefully examined the image. He draw a copy of the image in the journal and jotted down several notes.

Quite mysterious, Peaches thought. It is a battle between sun and moon whatever chemicals or processes they refer to. Why is the moon naked and not the sun? Oh, I see. the moon is new and not receiving any light from the sun. The sun is on a lion, the power of earth while the moon is riding a griffin, a combination of earth and sky powers.

Marcus moved on to the next bookmarked page in *Liber*, which he studied with the magnifying glass. The illumination was a knight in armor who is standing on a fountain with double bowls. One foot is on one bowl and the other foot on the second bowl. White liquid from the bowl on the right flows into gold colored liquid on the left and then out onto the ground. The knight is holding a shield in his left hand and a sword in his right hand. The shield has a Latin phrase indicating double water written on it. Each fountain bowl has a child standing in it urinating. Is urine actually called for here? Interesting. Obviously the image deals with the blending of the two powers or waters. She presumed that they are the sun and moon – white for moon and gold for sun.

She did pick up a few ideas from the main text, which discussed the four stages in the chemical process of making the elixir of life. The text seemed to convey specific details for the different stages. She was amazed at the use of color and its apparent links to these stages.

Okay, Peaches thought, I have a lot to ponder and many questions to resolve. Marcus' research is not as simple and straightforward as I first imagined. What is his true agenda? When I discover his purpose, I can deal with the issue of Doug's missing manuscript.

She was about ready to leave when Marcus spoke to Midnight who lifted his head, his ears alert. "See, Midnight, the 'Gospel' does contain the keys to the elixir. The story of Lazarus' resurrection is the center of our little drama. Biblical scholars still have not realized that the key to Jesus' power lies hidden in the storyline."

Marcus stood and began pacing about the library, speaking aloud, "You know, Midnight, when all the links are discerned and the pattern they create is understood, the true meaning is clear." Pausing, he flipped to a page in *Liber de Homunculus*. "Right here, we're told how to produce our Homunculus, our little man, our golem of ancient tradition. Creating the little man involves harnessing the life force and infusing it into dead matter. A form of resurrection just as much as the power Jesus applied to Lazarus."

Midnight sat up and watched Marcus walk over to the laboratory at the far end of the room. The wizard picked up a piece of mandrake root and showed it to Midnight, who was now staring intently at Marcus. "Here is the prime matter, our philosopher's stone in its raw state. The Mandragora root, another little man and a member of the nightshade family, shares a correspondence with our homunculus, the red philosopher's stone, the magnum opus of our art." A wry grin crossed Midnight's face.

Taking the piece of mandrake root, Marcus sliced it into slivers and placed them into a marble mortar. Picking up a marble pestle, he ground the small pieces into a powder which was poured into a pelican flask, the vessel of a circulatory distillation apparatus.

He took a flask from the wood box. Holding it to the light, he scrutinized the reddish liquid. "Yes," he muttered, "Saturn has played his part." He poured some of the reddish liquid into the flask with the mandrake powder. Then he started the heating process – the amount of heat produced by a setting hen.

"The salt is prepared. The mercury will separate the sulfur from its body. Patience is our virtue now. The required time for the process is about a moon quarter or one week. Tonight is first quarter, so we'll check in on full moon." He left the study, but Midnight remained scrutinizing the ceiling corners.

Peaches retreated to her home, looking forward to the orange juice Aeneas had ready.

Once she finished the orange juice and felt refreshed, Peaches with the aid of Virgil told Aeneas the events she had witnessed in Scarpia's library. Images of the illuminations were viewed on the 42 inch TV monitor and brought enthusiastic responses from Aeneas. Then they watched Marcus make the chemical concoction.

Virgil interjected basic data about the Mandragora or mandrake, a perennial which grows around the Mediterranean region. Its roots are often shaped like a small human body. It has been used in magic rituals since ancient times and is still used today by many Wicca groups. It is a powerful hallucinogenic and narcotic and when taken in large quantities can induce delirium and unconsciousness. It has been a part of traditional herbal pharmacopeia and used to treat diseases.

"Wow," Aeneas exclaimed. "And Marcus is making a concoction with it? Does he plan to drink it, do you think?"

"What's the purpose of the liquid made from the salts of magnesia and some other liquid?" Peaches wondered aloud.

"My surmise is that the compound liquid is to extract the essence of the mandrake," Virgil responded.

"Well, we may learn more when the concoction is completed."

"Yes, patience is a virtue."

Chapter 23

Sitting on a bench in South Park – a recently gentrified neighborhood of San Francisco, Lenny Sawyer watched cyberniks and other young people return to their jobs after the lunch break. He was glum, filled with self-pity and vengeance. He was no longer part of the group of employed cyberniks. He was unemployed. His anger flayed against those who had participated in his fall. But he was not totally destitute.

Anger illuminated the day disaster had struck. He was fired. Don, Carlyle's live-in servant, had come to his room summing him to the library. When he entered, he found CFO Abbott X. Tyler and the firm's lawyers headed by Todd Lowe, who was executor of Carlyle's will. Lowe now held Carlyle's power after his death. Carlyle Quincebury had suffered a heart attack and died during the night.

Bless his vicious soul, Lenny thought. A feeling of scorn warmed Lenny. But the warmth vanished quickly when the terms of the will pertaining to him were read. Carlyle's vengeance was directed toward him too, not just at the Garlands. Lenny lost his good paying job and was given a bad eye in the computer security industry. No work where Carlyle's many companies, headed by Madrone Advanced Systems, LLC, were influential.

He was not totally destroyed. Carlyle did give him severance pay, including a year's lease on an apartment in South Park. And here he was, watching the world go by.

Lenny was not the kind of person who gave up easily. After a month of self-pity he had bought a week's ad in the job wanted section of the *Chronicle* and was waiting for a response. So he could justify his idleness.

He watched a tall man, who was wearing a light gray raincoat as protection against the damp fog flowing in from the ocean, cross the intersection and walk toward him. Reaching Lenny seated on the bench, the man said, "I'm Douglas Balentine and seeking a computer expert by the name of Lenny Sawyer." The stranger pulled a job advertisement from his pocket and showed it to Lenny.

"You're wearing the maroon beret as the ID. May I speak with you about a job." The news did not brighten Lenny's attitude much, but still a job...

"Yes, that's me, Mr. Balentine."

Sitting on the bench beside Lenny, Balentine said, "Please, everyone calls me Doug. I'm in need of a computer expert and can offer a fine business package. Are you interested?"

"Tell me about the job and its pay. You know I have a bad reputation. Carlyle Quincebury, even in death, wants a piece of me. If you are a go, I'll listen to your proposal."

Seated at the control center of his computer system, Lenny Sawyer surveyed the workstation. He had accepted Doug Balentine's offer and was very satisfied with his life at the moment. Besides a weekly salary, he was provided with a two room suite and meals at Doug's mansion. The servants, Jeeves and Gladys, were quite amiable and left him alone but were always ready to respond to his requests. He wasn't earning as much as he was before, but with no rent or daily food costs to pay he invested most of his funds in a powerful computer system, building a high tech workstation – not as good as Carlyle had, but it was a start. Living in, he performed any jobs that his boss needed at the moment and had the remainder of the week to follow his own interests. He wasn't on duty twenty-four/seven as he had been for Carlyle, and he didn't need to hide his personal agenda and work. He was free to do whatever he wanted when the boss didn't need him for a project.

The main project he was working on involved cataloging Doug's immense book and manuscript collection. Doug had hired a professional librarian, Stacey Wilder. Lenny worked with her, operating the computer system. The books were organized using the Library of Congress standards. The data was placed on flash drives for storage and easy retrieval. Ultimately the books would be scanned into a digital format. His boss wanted a digital format of the whole collection stored safely and securely in a cloud. The project would require several years to accomplish, and everyone understood the long period of time that was necessary. Doug was in no particular hurry and saw the process as slow and precise. Lenny was happy with the arrangement.

His first personal project was to refine the program X-KEY, a lite version of NSA's X-KEYSCORE, by adding several subroutines. His program could monitor the movements of surfers in real time and collect data of the sites they visited and contacts they made. He also developed a lite form of Carlyle's DOG, the massive data collector. His program, DOG-2, had calibrated parameters which filtered out unwanted data. He now spent more time surfing cyberspace and protecting his turf.

He decided to avenge himself by devising plots to hamper business operations of Madrone Advanced Systems, LLC. He added the firm to the large group of databases from which he gathered information. Many of Madrone's secrets would be worth thousands of dollars to other corporations. The primary challenge was finding purchasers who would buy the data. He knew that many firms would refuse such transactions, fearing being caught with illegally gained insider information. Some might report his offer to sell to the authorities. So he had to choose carefully those he contacted. He set up a secure database which contained groups of corporations based on their potential willingness to conspire with him. He would also offer a service to collect specific data that a firm might want.

Working with Stacey, he learned the library system of cataloging and coding. He was amazed at its efficiency. Inspired by the library system, he constructed a special structure for his corporate needs.

The danger and intrigue juiced his fancy and added another element of joy to the job. His fantasy was flying high.

"Someone is after us. Quick, into the sacred node over here," Sandra called out to Dwight. Her voice sang through the astral field and alerted him. He glanced behind him and saw another surfer in hot pursuit. He followed Sandra into the sacred node, which she cloaked after he was inside.

Safe now, they watched the threat glide by without noticing their presence. Sandra's ability to cloak sacred nodes had protected them many times from harm.

"It's Tau-2," Dwight said.

"Lenny Sawyer, Carlyle's employee," Sandra confirmed.

"He believes he owns all the world's databases and is very protective. I told you, Sandra, he could cause us harm," Dwight said.

They waited a few minutes until they felt certain Tau-2 was not returning. Then they left the sacred node and headed to the Occult Guild's database, which included names of members and those interested in the occult and a presentation of occult subjects. They were searching for as much material on Marcus Scarpia and his project as they could find.

They arrived at a firewall with the words 'gold cui cult' imprinted on it. "Whoa!" Dwight exclaimed and pointed at the three words.

"That's an anagram, isn't it?" Sandra said. "What are the original words?"

"I got it!" Dwight was ecstatic. "Occult Guild." Being an expert at code, Dwight easily rearranged the letters until he had words he knew.

"That's wonderful. The Occult Guild site." Sandra said. "Is 'cui' a word?" she asked.

"It has several usages. I've seen it used as an acronym for controlled unclassified information – what the government does when it wants to hide embarrassing data. But its earlier and more common use is for copper-iodine compound –cui.

Dwight took his electronic decoder and passed it over the firewall's surface. Numbers appeared on the digital screen. When the operation was finished, he pressed the enter button on the decoder. The firewall vanished and they entered a narrow corridor which ended at another firewall protected portal. Sandra examined the firewall and discovered hidden within it an ID scanner for the left hand. Her ability to cloak gave her the opposite talent to peer through a cloaked area.

"Dwight, the ID scanner requires the left hand of a male. Place your left hand here." She pointed to an area on the firewall's surface.

Dwight obliged and the second firewall vanished. The pair entered a long, dark corridor and glided down it to a third door which appeared impassible. The surface image was that of a book with a lock. All they needed was the key.

"Not everyone will have a key. So one must be hidden around the door," Sandra commented. Using her talent to peer through a cloaked area, Sandra scanned the door frame and discovered a small hole concealed by a stone. The key was there. She retrieved it and, unlocking the firewall, opened the book. Knowledge streamed out and filled the immediate area. Words and images glided and swirled about, interlinking with each other. They seemed palpable like they could be held. The two mates were stunned.

As Sandra turned the book's pages, Dwight electronically copied them and stored them in a flash memory, which would be given to Peaches.

"What an amazing amount of data," Dwight remarked.

"Peaches will be happy," Sandra noted.

After copying the last page, Dwight said, "The memory is nearly full. Luck is on our side."

Closing the book, Sandra set the lock. Then they left the occult repository deep in the earth and, keeping an eye open for Lenny, headed home.

Gliding through cyberspace, Lenny spotted a surfer with the tag PI. He had noticed PI several times and searched for the person's identity and bio. Learning that the tag PI was owned by Peaches Peoples, a close friend of the Garlands, he decided to follow her. If she went to one of his databases, he would deal harshly with her; otherwise, he was curious about PI's agenda.

The Garlands would also receive their punishment for causing the fall in his fortunes. If it weren't for Ralph Garland, Carlyle would not have had his debilitating stroke and Lenny would still be administrative executive of Madrone. Perhaps he could harm the Garlands through one of their friends.

He stayed far enough away so she would not be worried about him. Suddenly, PI vanished. Checking the coordinates on X-KEY, he realized she had left the electromagnetic field at a junction with psi-space. Entering the junction she had passed through, he survey the surrounding area. She was not visible. Of course, cloaking was easily accomplished here. A powerful mind could work wonders in the psi field, including spinning an invisibility shield around itself.

Next time he sighted her, he would capture her with his cyber-net. Then he realized he did not have a plan for using the captive to punish the Garlands. Until he had one, he would refrain from imprisoning PI.

He continued his travels and headed toward a region he had recently discovered. Islands were grouped in a spiral pattern. He initiated a X-KEY subroutine which sent a probe to each island. The probe would gather basic data about the island.

As he waited for the data collection, his tele-monitor blinked. He was wanted at home base. Probably Stacey had a new project for him to do. He would view the data later after the gathering was completed.

When he returned to home base, he found a very upset Stacey. The program had frozen several times and strange things had happened, producing error messages. He told her that he would have the system fixed and up-and-running soon.

He rang for Archie and requested a cold bottle of steam beer. His boss had agreed to stock his favorite brand of steam beer. Lenny was in heaven. What a great deal he had.

He sat down at the command center and put on his wireless headphones. He inserted a special CD into the player and started it. The CD was an anthology of 1980s songs culled from the great American Songbook and performed by various well-known bands. He took swig of beer and settled in to solve the program issue.

When he was ready, he keyed in his ID and password as system administrator. Then he opened the library cataloging program and moved down to the source code folder. Using the UNIX toolkit, he inspected the code for flaws or bugs. It was a time-consuming and tedious process but had to be done. After a careful search, he found the problem area. Replacing the faulty code with correct code, he saved the work and closed the source code folder. Then he ran the software. It worked smoothly – no glitches occurred.

He texted Stacey that the problem had been solved and she could get back to her cataloging. He looked at the beer bottle and realized it was empty, so he rang Archie and ordered another. Now he could review the data the probes had gathered about the cluster of islands he had discovered. The data for each island included its name, geographical features and types of flora and fauna, and any strange phenomena.

Out of the whole group Anna Island had caught his attention. The probe had spotted a source of the elixir of life. Recent cyber chatter was centering on esoteric processes and the elixir of life was one frequently mentioned. He had learned that it referred to renewal and longevity -- the fabled fountain of youth or immortality. He would investigate the situation. He would use its power and perhaps even sell some of it. He would make a fortune.

He set the GPS coordinates and entered cyberspace. As he moved toward

Anna Island, he pictured himself as the man he should be: wealthy and powerful. He would set up an equity corporation and buy controlling interest in Madrone Advanced Systems and other security and surveillance firms. He would sit atop of an immense empire of data collecting and storage operations. He who controlled the information ruled the world and he would control all the data, which would be at his fingertips.

Hovering over Anna Island, he sent a probe to pinpoint the exact location of the elixir source. When the GPS coordinates were furnished, he begin to descend but paused suddenly. A strange phenomenon was happening. A surfer was gliding by. It had no tag and more unusual it did not act like a particle, which is the way surfers moved, but as a wave. He had never seen or heard about such a thing. He was dumbfound. He made a quick decision to follow the wave surfer to its IP address and then ascertain its identity.

When he reached the wave's home base, he entered the data into X-KEY and looked at his viewer. The IP was the same as PI's. Obviously, it was part of Peaches People's team. He was worried. The wave left no traces as surfers normally do. Even the best cannot eliminate all their tracks. But the wave had no tracks to leave. It passed through space and then, like a wave on the surface of water, was gone. Space was the same as before the wave's passage. An aha struck him. He would devise a program to track and tag wave movement. He headed back to his home base to start developing the program.

Chapter 24

A beautiful morning – the sun was shining and a cooling breeze flowed inland from the San Francisco Bay. Birds were filling the garden with melodious songs. Spenser walked slowly around his garden until he reached the lotus pond. He sat down on a chair beside the pond and breathed in the fragrant aromas of the brightly colored flowers surrounding the pond. He watched hummingbirds moving swiftly from flower to flower, gathering nectar.

Ah, the lotus, a primordial symbol of life. He stared at the flowers rising on their long stems from the muddy waters of human existence. Their beauty and purity were unstained by human desires and attachments. He was growing several different plants which covered the pond's surface with a multi-colored patina. The opening of a flower's petals portrayed the expansion of his soul as it reached heavenly toward the divine. Here lay the force of creation and cosmic renewal. And he was seeking his own renewal and spiritual resurrection. But he could not shed desires as easily as the flower could water. The water of human existence clung to him and he was mired in personal agendas. Utmost in his mind and fueled by years of frustration and anger was the need to prove himself better than most of his conservative colleagues. Yes, he saw the egotism behind the project to publish his ideas in a novel. He laughed. He a searcher after truth was building a façade of fiction, yet when he admonished himself, he had to admit that truth was conveyed even if it was in a form different from what he normally used. Does the form of presentation make a difference? For a long time he had thought so, writing scholarly articles and essays for a select group of biblical investigators.

Remembering when he was a teenager who realized art was a way to share the truth about human existence, he smiled. The art courses he took in high school provided him with excellent skills. He did well in the classes and devoted himself to his art. He had hoped such devotion would please his father, but it had the opposite effect. His father angrily told him that his goals were wrong and he must stop wasting his energy on frivolous activities. His mother, though, approved and supported his artistic aspirations.

He was fascinated by form and color and attempted some abstract paintings, but these did not win his mother's support. She could not understand them. As long as he painted conventional themes, he gained her approval.

One day when he entered his studio, he found Father there viewing his work. He had just finished an abstract painting. Father had flown into a rage when he saw it. Grabbing a pointed-tipped palette knife, Father ripped the canvas to shreds. Calling Spenser out as a wimp and wastrel, Father stormed out of the studio, slamming the door behind him. After that Spenser stuck to the tried-and-true conservative style. He had realized that the safe way to live was by creating a conventional, conservative persona. And he did. He was a skillful artist. But now he was ready to blossom forth. He was filled with enthusiasm and energy.

So he was now renewing himself by resurrecting his basic beliefs about life. He had hidden them in a concealed and safe corner of his mind, protected from his father's wrath. How sweet be revenge, yet it would taint the flower of his soul. He knew the correct answer: give up the project -- call it off. He would meditate on the issue. Of course such an action was a form of denial and a refusal to let go. Then a profound hope filled his soul. Perhaps meditation would give him the strength to rise from the mud of life and his selfishness.

He glanced at the Rock of Ages, nodding his head in agreement. He aimed for spiritual attainment and would shape his soul toward that goal. Humming the gospel hymn, he stood and walked back to the house. So involved in his dilemma he did not notice Theo kitty walking beside him. Entering the kitchen, he walked through it and out into the hallway. Theo had her own cat door she could enter any time she wished.

Pausing at Maud Hubbard's suite, he knocked on the door. His housekeeper had two rooms, which she occupied: a bedroom and a sitting room, plus a private bathroom. He had a maid who did the cleaning and laundry, but she lived elsewhere. Maud not only controlled the household budget but also reported directly to the trustee. Spenser was the last to know of any budgetary issues.

Maud opened the door. "I'll be out for dinner tonight. My usual breakfast in the morning," he said. Smiling, he turned and walked down the hall to his private sanctum, a place of silence and positive energy. He deliberated a moment and then entered. Hearing a meow, he looked down at his feet and saw Theo, who quickly hurried into the room before the door was shut.

The chamber had two windows opening onto the garden. The lotus pond was clearly visible. He placed the mat where he could view the pond and sat in a half-lotus position. Theo sat beside him. "Theo, I have a dilemma I must resolve. You can assist by opening to your higher consciousness." The Abyssinian smiled and sat up straight in a regal posture.

When he was much younger, he could achieve a full lotus, but age brought the stiffening of joints, and he was no longer able to execute it. The half lotus still provided good support for the upright vertical position of the body, allowing spiritual energy to travel downwards from the heavens above and enter the lotus portal on top of the head, flowing along the spinal column to the base, kundalini, and move back upwards to its heavenly source. He thought of the process as spiritual breathing -- in and out, a continuous cycle of nourishment.

Moving deep within beyond the window of perception, he allowed all his thoughts to flow by without concern. They were nothing but hollow clusters of letters linked to associated emotions. The thoughts were meaningless unless he gave them meaning.

Emptying his mind, he sat in the half lotus position until he had an answer. The project would be a perfect challenge to spread the good word without personal attachment. He would be walking a thin line between ego satisfaction and the purity of sharing the truth. Spenser felt an inner brightness, realizing that the truth was a divine attribute and a cleansing of the soul. Standing up, he left the spiritual sanctum and retired to his bedroom to dress for his dinner outing. Theo followed quietly.

After finishing with the cleanup chores, she returned to the living room and sat at her private table. Removing the profile from the envelope, she began reading. Several times she paused and glanced over at the kitties who were curled up on the couch, but their ears were raised and alert. "This is weird" and "This is bizarre," she said to them a few times.

When she had concluded and placed the document on the table, a shock wave flowed through her body. Then she started giggling, which became boisterous laughter. The kitties were now staring at her. Getting up, she went over to the couch and sat down between them and commenced rubbing behind their ears. Both purred with approval. "Well, my loves, have I not been taken or what?" Misdirection is what Ralph might call the deception, she thought. If Sandra's report was accurate, Spenser Blake was different from what he presented to the public. His inner man was inconsistent with the outer persona. So, she wondered, what is your purpose in all this madness, Mr. Blake?

She looked at her wristwatch. It was 3;30 pm and happy hour would be soon. Ralph would definitely be intrigued by Mr. Blake's magical personality. She was anxious to learn her husband's insights.

☨

Shasta was reading her journal entries for today when Ralph entered from the kitchen and handed her a martini. He placed his glass on the side table and sat down on the couch. Karma crawled onto his lap, and he rubbed behind her ears. Shasta heard the quiet purring and, glancing at Karma, smiled approvingly.

"Well, Sandra Kingfisher delivered the detailed profile on Spenser Blake this morning. Actually, she arrived while I was thinking about Spenser and the visit we had yesterday. He liked the novel in its present state and provided some suggestions and comments. The whole project can be viewed as an act from an absurd drama." She was now repressing a strong urge to giggle.

Ralph noticed her behavior. "What on earth are you going on about?"

She couldn't help herself. She laughed. "Spenser Blake is a fake, a fraud." And she proceeded to relate the truth about Blake.

After Shasta had finished the story, Ralph also laughed. "Spenser Blake a fake? I'm flabbergasted, though I'm not surprised. There seemed to be a wrongness around him."

"At least he's not what he pretends to be." Shasta sipped the extra dry martini and stared intently at her husband.

"A hidden agenda aided by skillful misdirection -- traits of a good magician. If we only knew the secret desire motivating him, we could gain a better comprehension of the Lazarus Mystery."

"Obviously, the project is an important part of his goal, whatever that might be."

"Let's have Sandra continue her research on him, especially his interest in the Lazarus story."

"Also she can give us a detailed bibliography of his published writings."

"Some emotion deep within his soul motivates him. We need to understand what it is."

Chapter 25

Sitting in her astral travel chair, Peaches said to Aeneas, "I'm sensing a strong anticipation. I think tonight we'll learn an important part of Scarpia's agenda."

Aeneas gently squeezed her hand. "I can feel your energy. Yes, tonight his secret is revealed."

She smiled at him. "I'm off."

When Peaches entered her nest in the ceiling of Marcus' study, he was smiling. He walked over to the desk, patted the black cat, and lifted up Abelard of Seville's *Liber de Homunculus*. Turning to a bookmarked page, he compared the comments he had written in his journal to the book's text. The page had two illuminations. Peaches zoomed in for a closer look. The first was a green lion holding a human head signifying the sun in its mouth. Blood was dripping from the lion's mouth. A scroll with Latin phrases was above the image.

The next was a man dressed in red garments wearing a crown. He looked like the king who was waiting for the queen. He was standing in a flask which was primarily blue with a red bottom. The image was at the top of the page. Scrolls with Latin phrases curled around it. Below was a Latin text.

Marcus flipped to another page and sighed deeply. The illumination portrayed a man and woman, both naked, embracing each other having intercourse. They were in a pool of water. They wore the crowns of queen and king. The queen was on top of the king. One or both had wings, but it was hard to tell. Marcus checked a journal entry and chuckled.

He put the *Liber* down and picked up the 'Gospel.' "Now, Midnight, while we are waiting for the first stage of our extraction to finish, we will have some fun. I'll tell you the amusing story of Lazarus and Jesus and read passages from Doug's book." Midnight emitted what to Peaches sounded like a deep belly laugh and wagged his tail.

With the 'Gospel' opened in one hand, Marcus paced about the room, laughing. In tune with his master Midnight meowed softly.

Peaches sat quietly in the ceiling corner with its bird's eye view, intent upon observing the unfolding drama. She felt Marcus was about to reveal a profound secret.

"Midnight, I will give a contemporary translation and commentary on Lazarus' absurd story. Remember, Jesus had restored Lazarus to life after four days in the tomb. Later Jesus returned to Bethany. Entering the house, he hugged and kissed his closest friend, his beloved disciple. During the evening conversation Jesus asked Lazarus how he had been."

Marcus peered at Midnight who smiled knowingly. "Now listen to this inane drama between these two close friends. It is insufferable."

He flipped a couple pages and began reading, "Here's Lazarus speaking to Jesus. 'I will tell you the truth, Jesus. You have said it will free me. I have been miserable, more unhappy than I have ever been,' Lazarus moaned."

"He hasn't smiled since you departed after restoring him to life," Martha, Lazarus' sister, complained in a sorrowful voice.

Of course, Jesus was puzzled. "Why is that, my dearest friend?"

Midnight watched Marcus prance around the study gesturing.

Lazarus' bitterness infected the room. "I have realized how meaningless life is. From birth to death our existence is a constant struggle without much reward: pain, suffering, sickness, the death of loved ones. So you speak of resurrection after death, one in heaven. Why didn't you let me go there? Why bring me back? Why sentence me to more torture and anguish?"

Midnight nodded in approval, wagging his tail.

Jesus was shocked. "God has given you the gift of life and I've restored it to you, my beloved friend."

Lazarus raised his voice, "You call me 'Beloved Friend.' How can that be? If you loved me so much, you would never have brought me back to life. God's great gift – a big lie. If you had truly loved me, you would have allowed me to go to heaven. My daily activities are tedious, dreary routines that I've been doing all my adult life."

Martha, of course, tried to apologize and restore harmony. "Oh, Lazarus, don't be so critical. Jesus, he has been complaining endlessly. I just don't understand him anymore. He certainly has changed."

"Jesus, my beloved friend, I have experienced death and restoration. Been there and done it. You have preached that you and the Father are the resurrection and you will die and be restored. Well, let me tell what it was like for me. It was not pleasant. During the four days between the death of my body and its restoration, I had terrifying visions. I was in a room and saw a rack of limp bodies hanging along the wall. My body marked Lazarus was among them. I looked at it and saw myself as a side of mutton. I was nauseous. Bile rose in my throat and I nearly choked on it."

Lazarus cringed and his face had turned pale. "Even now remembering the sight of my limp body is frightening and repulsive. Then three men entered the room. One carried a wood chest which he opened. The men took out of the chest what appeared to be me, but as a deflated person. I watched petrified as they inserted the person into the body marked Lazarus. One man said to the others, 'We have replaced his life force and spirit. We will carry the restored body to the large flat stone at the entrance of the tomb and then depart. Jesus will be here soon and resurrect his beloved disciple Lazarus.'"

"What about that, Midnight? Isn't that a fantastic but foolish vision? Well, Lazarus has more to say on the subject." Midnight released a low meow and stretched his front legs forward before sitting back up and smiling at Marcus.

Speaking directly to Midnight, the wizard said, "Lazarus articulates his thoughts clearly."

"Jesus, waiting for your arrival seemed like an eternity. I kept thinking – is that death, limp bodies hanging from a rack and people's awareness sitting there with the bodies? Later I wondered if I would get someone else's body at the end of time with full resurrection? The vision was unnerving and I didn't enjoy it."

"But Lazarus, you were not suffering, and strange visions can occur after the body dies and before the soul goes to the Father."

Pointing to Martha, Lazarus said, "Look at the useless suffering you and Mary bear – really all women. The pain of your monthly menses, the second class social status you endure, the burden of childbearing and raising the children. No, it is totally unfair. Besides, I am a servant to the Great Sanhedrin, which controls my life and freedom."

In a soothing voice Jesus said, "Oh, Lazarus, my beloved friend, how can you say such things. Believe in me and you will have everlasting life."

Anger shook Lazarus. He yelled, "You are an arrogant and selfish fool."

A fiery fervor shone in Jesus' eyes. "I am the resurrection and the life: he who believes in me will live, even though he dies."

Lazarus trembled with fury. "Once I believed in you as the Son of God and that all things were possible in the glory of God. But now my eyes are opened and I recognize you as a vain, puffed up, egotist. You waited two extra days before coming to Bethany and restoring my life."

Jesus answered, "I did it for the glory of the Lord, that He works in wondrous ways and in Him is life eternal."

Lazarus jumped up filled with rage. "The desert heat has impaired your mind. You have become as crazy as John the Baptist." Shaking his fist at Jesus, Lazarus vehemently shouted, "You are no more the Son of God than I am." He stalked out of the house.

Midnight wagged his white-tipped tail and grinned.

Jesus was perplexed. "What has happened to my most beloved disciple? To him I have revealed my greatest secrets. Now his mind is soiled with evil." And Jesus sat and wept. "Oh, Lord, forgive him for he knows not what he does."

Martha bowed to Jesus, wringing her hands. "Oh, Jesus dearest, my brother has changed since his resurrection. I know him not."

Jesus was sorely grieved. "I shall leave. I do not wish to give my friend more anguish than he has now."

Mary, Lazarus' other sister, now spoke to her beloved friend, "Please do not depart, dear Jesus. We have planned a social gathering, a party to honor you before Passover. We have been planning it for weeks and have invited your family, disciples, and friends. Even your favorite, Mary of Magdalene, has agreed to attend."

As Jesus began to rise, Mary put her hands on his shoulders and gently pushed him down. She knelt at his feet, removed his dusty sandals, and anointed his dirt-encrusted feet with expensive perfume. Afterwards she dried his feet with her long hair. "My beloved Lord, please forgive my brother and stay with us until Passover. We would be honored."

Jesus acknowledged their love, "Mary and Martha, beloved sisters, I will stay and ask my Father's forgiveness for Lazarus."

Marcus stopped pacing, walked over to the desk, and laid Doug's 'Gospel' on it. He rubbed Midnight behind his ears. "Well, my black wizard, have you ever heard such drivel? An asinine, absurd story concocted for the feebleminded. Where is the spiritual meaning? Obviously it is meant for the common taste. Now back to the important things: making the elixir of life." Midnight chortled, stretched his back and lay down on the desk, realizing the drama was over.

A bong sounded from the laboratory. Marcus walked over to the table where the mandrake powder was being distilled. He turned off the heating unit and picked up the flask and studied its contents carefully. Nodding his approval, he said, "Ah, Midnight, our preparation is ready for the next stage of fermentation."

He strode over to the desk, patted the large black cat on his head and spoke confidentially to him, "Midnight, if nature can perform marvels, I can use nature's laws and forces to perform my own alchemy. For example, the Higgs Field exists throughout the universe and it can impart mass to subatomic particles. The Field has its special particle, the Higgs Boson, which interacts with other particles and sometimes is called the 'God particle.' Yes, indeed, if nature can give mass to particles, I should be able to impart a life force into inanimate bodies. And that my dear friend is what we are going to do. We will follow the guiding path of Hermes' craft: As Above, So Below."

Peaches was totally amazed by the spectacle Marcus had staged. She now felt she had a better understanding of his agenda. She retreated to her living room, looking forward to the glass of orange juice Aeneas had waiting for her. They could now devise a plan to retrieve Doug's 'Lazarus Gospel.'

Chapter 26

Peaches sat on the couch drinking orange juice thinking about the talk-fest with two witty and brilliant young ladies, Rafé Courbet and Sandra Kingfisher. Their enthusiasm and high energetic sparkle nourished her aging body. Their social event was fun, entertaining, and enlightening. She learned much about cyber and psi-spaces. Facts about the spiritual path enhanced the conversation. She knew she would never possess Rafé and Sandra's talents, and she appreciated them and could increase her own skills. They would teach her to surf all psi-space so she was not limited to the throat chakra only and happily agreed.

Peaches had asked Sandra to do more research and gather all the data she could find about a photon gun and invisibility cloaking. Now was the moment. She savored its joy and was riding a wave of intense exuberance. Her decision to spend time with fun activities and friends, not all the time on investigations, was paying off. She arose from the chair and headed toward the kitchen.

She filled a cup with coffee and headed back to the social room. Sitting down in a chair, she picked up a document from the side table and began reading it.

A broad smile covering his face, Aeneas unlocked the front door of Peaches' apartment and entered. She glanced up from the document she was reading. He said, "I've a gift for you." He held out his hand and she noticed a small object. She took it and turned it over examining the device. "And what do I do with it?"

"It's a cloaking device and will make you invisible."

"You're joking."

"He isn't. He's quite serious." Virgil's voice boomed from the silence.

Peaches scrutinized the device and stared at Aeneas quizzically. "Now that I'm set up, please give the details."

"I've a strange tale to report," Virgil told Peaches. "I was surfing cyberspace searching for new data when I happened to witness a fascinating adventure. Three surfers were tracking each other. Two seemed to form a team and the third was the odd guy out. The tags of the two teammates were elf and stealth while the third was Tau-2, who was following, or at least trying to, the other two. All three played an amazing stunt. First they were in cyberspace and suddenly vanished, only a little later reappearing again. I've developed probes which will attach to any surfer. I sent out a few probes when the three were visible. When any vanished, the probe went along. I have analyzed the data the probe gathered when it went into the invisible realm and I am very disturbed."

Aeneas abruptly entered the conversation. "I believe Virgil has discovered the psi field and denies its existence."

"I did not." Virgil was very indignant. "Psi fields cannot exist because they are not part of the electromagnetic field, which is the only one in the cosmos."

"That's okay, Virgil. We will not insert the existence of a psi field into your database." Aeneas wanted to placate the super computer.

"Please, Virgil, let's get back to your adventure," Peaches said.

"Yes. The probe absorbed weird anomalies in the invisible space. I do not understand anything about the space's attributes. I will investigate further. As I continued data-gathering, I learned of an innovation Madrone Advanced Systems, LLC, a security and data collecting business empire, has developed with utmost secrecy. I downloaded the data with blueprints and all. It is called a photon gun which will cause objects to become invisible. It was an interesting project to build one. Now you have it, dear leader. Aeneas will demonstrate its operation."

"Well. Show me," she said to Aeneas.

He demonstrated the way the device operated, the function of each key and the small screen. She was enchanted and a little bewildered. After she had heard the instructions, she switched it on and two voices spoke at once: "You are invisible, dear leader," and "You can defeat Scarpia now." She turned it off and sat back in the chair, smiling.

Aeneas laughed. "What's your impression of the cloaking device?"

"I'm totally amazed," she answered. "And Virgil, thank you for making the photon gun. Your initiative is excellent. When we finish the case and receive our pay, you can have any improvements you desire."

With a slight tone of pride in his voice Virgil said, "Thank you for your praise. I'll let Aeneas know my wants."

"Yes, indeed. Well, let us make our plans and retrieve Doug's manuscript. And we will also considered the best plan for returning it."

After the last visit to Scarpia's library, Peaches would not be surprised at anything that happened tonight. She looked at Aeneas and nodded. She was there, witnessing Marcus at work. She had learned a few techniques for quickly reaching the remote viewing location and arrived two seconds later.

What? she asked herself. Something is off. She sensed a wrongness. Marcus is upset. Another unexpected incident?

After laying down on the desk the book he was reading, Marcus Scarpia stood and walked slowly over to the laboratory. A grimace was etched on his face. The smell was all wrong. He sniffed. A putrid odor was emerging from the flask with the ash of distillate. He picked up the flask and waved it beneath his nose, sniffing. Yes, a definite putrid smell with a slight taint of bitterness. The directions stated the odor would be sweet. He scrutinized the ash closely. It was a black encrusted clump of residue. It should be flaky and light brown. Did he misunderstand the directions or was the code in error?

He put the flask down on the workbench and walked quickly back to his desk. Picking up Abelard of Seville's *Liber de Homunculus*, he opened it to a specific page. Carefully reading the text, he compared it to Doug's 'Lazarus Gospel.' He frowned. Alerted, Midnight sat up and examined his master. The black cat howled softly with a growl mixed in. Marcus looked at Midnight and nodded. "So, you agree, eh. We've been swindled and deceived. That rascal Doug had a bogus copy of the Lazarus manuscript. What a fraud. Let's visit Doug's home and see if he has the real manuscript. We'll visit his place tonight. I can't wait. The fraud has damaged my schedule."

Marcus rubbed behind Midnight's ears. The black cat purred contentedly. Marcus turned, took a jacket from the coat rack, and left the study. Midnight stretched, then leaped to floor, and followed his master.

Somewhat astounded, Peaches returned to her living room. After enjoying a glass of orange juice, she related to Aeneas what she had witnessed in Marcus' study. Aeneas was rather surprised but also amused. "So the swindler gets swindled. Perhaps there is justice in the world."

Peaches decided to visit Doug's home also and observe the activities of Marcus and Doug, if he was present. Instead of remote viewing, she decided to go to Doug's home in her physical body. She was anxious to try the photon gun. Putting the cloaking device, the photon gun, in her purse, she left. Aeneas had wanted to go with her until she pointed out the cloak of invisibility only worked for one person.

Parking the car a half block from her destination, Peaches strolled along the sidewalk casually. When she reached the path to Doug's house, she turned onto it and moved quickly to the front door. She had noticed a light on in his study and was not going to take any chances he might be home. She rang the doorbell several times. No one answered and yet the study light remained on. Ah, she thought, Doug's out and Marcus is in the study searching for the 'Lazarus Gospel.' I have no need to worry, she told herself. I have the cloaking device which will protect me.

She tried opening the door and discovered it was locked. As she removed a set of lock picks from her shoulder bag, she remembered the history of the kit. Leroy Betzner, one of her fellow students in criminology at the Fort Wayne campus of Indiana University, had given it to her as a birthday present. Not only had she used the set frequently since then but cherished it for her friendship with Leroy. She easily unlocked the front door. Entering quickly, she closed the door after her. She stood in the hall and listened. The only sounds came from the study. Taking the photon gun from her purse, she switched it on.

The study door was partially open and light spread outward into the hall. There was enough space to squeeze between the door and frame. Standing inside the room, she surveyed it. Marcus was searching the roll top desk drawers. Rummaging through one drawer after another, Marcus had a disappointed mien. He's in such a hurry that he's leaving the drawer contents in disarray, she realized. Midnight was seated on the desk, a roguish grin played upon his face.

Marcus found a bill of sale from a French seller of ancient manuscripts. So Doug had purchased the 'Lazarus Gospel' and had a fake copy made, which he left out as bait. For some reason, perhaps for an insurance claim, he wanted it stolen. Marcus did not care about the reason; he wanted the original manuscript.

In frustration he looked about. Then he began a diligent search of the books, which was his last and only hope. If it was locked in the safe, he was out of luck. Searching each shelf took time, but it had to be done.

Wagging his tail, Midnight meowed and hopped down from the desk. He walked over to the bookshelves and leaped to the top shelf. The cat sat down and stared at the end of the row of books.

Marcus walked over and looked up at Midnight, who had a very pleased smile on his face. Marcus took the bookshelf ladder and climbed to the top shelf. There was 'Lazarus Gospel' hidden from view. The wizard took it down and carried it over to the table and sat down. He leafed through it and was satisfied it was the original and not another fake. Scratching behind the cat's ears, he said, "Well, done, Midnight. I will give you a special meal when we get home."

As Marcus was tidying the study so Doug would be unaware of the intruders, Peaches on silent tiptoes left and headed home.

Aeneas was waiting for her with a glass of orange juice and was intrigued by the new complications she related. So now Marcus did have the manuscript. What should they do? Take it from Marcus and return it to Doug or only notify Doug so he could inform the police? But he did not want to do that as he had told the team when he hired them. The team decided to give the matter serious thought.

Chapter 27

Perched in her invisible niche, Peaches with excited anticipation watched Marcus Scarpia. With the authentic 'Gospel' now in his possession Marcus will reveal more of his hidden agenda, she realized. He rose from the desk, strode to the book shelves, and retrieved Abelard of Seville's *Liber de Homunculu*. He carried it to the desk and laid it beside 'Lazarus Gospel.' Opening it, he compared the pages to the 'Gospel.' He wrote some notes on a notepad and tore the page from the pad. He went to the laboratory, putting the notes on the worktable.

Glancing back at the desk where Midnight was sitting upright, he said, "Now Midnight, we shall perform our experiment again, following the correct recipe." The black cat smiled knowingly.

Opening a jar, he removed a chunk of mandrake root. He cut a small piece from it and replaced the root back into the jar, which he closed. He sliced the piece of mandrake into slivers, which he placed into a marble mortar. Picking up a marble pestle, he ground the small pieces into a powder, which was poured into a pelican flask,

"Now, Midnight, again we start with the prime matter, our philosopher's stone in its raw state." The cat's face lit up with an ironic grin.

He removed a flask from a wood box. Studying the reddish liquid in the flask, he nodded approval. "The power of Saturn is still present." He mumbled.

Some of the reddish liquid was poured into the flask with the mandrake powder. He took a jar labeled salts of boron from the shelf. He opened it and measured an ounce of boron, which he put into the pelican flask. Then he took another bottle from the shelf, removed the cap, and put an eye dropper into it. He squeezed the rubber top of the pipette and fluid filled the chamber. Taking the dropper out of the bottle, he held it over the pelican flask and emptied its contents. "Some essence of fuchsia will assist Mercury," he mumbled. He followed the same procedure with another bottle, adding the fluid to the pelican flask. "The essence of mint purifies the sulfuric action," he muttered.

Then he started the heating process with a very low heat. "We have prepared the salt. The recipe in the fake 'Gospel' was incomplete. All the proper ingredients have now been added. The mercury will separate the sulfur from its body. We must wait until the next lunar quarter for completion. But we'll look in on the process frequently just in case we've been tricked again.

He was buoyant, filled with high hopes of success. He picked up the 'Gospel.' "Now, Midnight, while we are waiting for the first stage of our extraction to finish, we will have some fun.

We'll discover the true story of Jesus and Lazarus. I'll read passages from Doug's book and make comments." Midnight meowed deeply in a mocking fashion and wagged his white-tipped tail.

Holding the 'Gospel' open, Marcus roamed about the room, chortling. In tune with his master Midnight meowed softly, a feline laugh.

Peaches sat in suspense in her hidden space, focused with complete attention on the new reading of the 'Lazarus Gospel.' How different would the true version be from the fake one? What secret would now be revealed?

"Midnight, here's my up-to-date translation and the latest word on the affair. It's still ridiculous as before but in a different manner. A quick review of the background. The prologue to the story. Jesus had restored Lazarus to life after four days in the tomb. Later Jesus returned to Bethany. Entering Lazarus' house, he hugged and kissed his closest friend, his beloved disciple. During the evening conversation Jesus asked Lazarus how he had been. Of course, Jesus expected to hear positive news."

Marcus smirked at Midnight who smiled knowingly. "Now listen to this idiotic spectacle between these two dear friends. It is unbelievable."

He turned a few pages and began reading, "Here's Lazarus speaking to Jesus. 'I will speak plainly, Jesus. You have said the truth will free me. I have been miserable, more melancholic than I have ever been,' Lazarus groaned."

"He hasn't smiled since you departed after restoring him to life," Martha, Lazarus' sister, grumbled.

Jesus was definitely perplexed. "What is the matter, my beloved friend?"

Midnight observed Marcus strut around the room gesturing.

Lazarus' bitterness infected the house. "Life is meaningless. There is no purpose to it. Our existence is a constant struggle without any reward: only pain, suffering, sickness, the death of loved ones. You talk about resurrection after death, one in heaven. I have a serious question. Why didn't you let me go to heaven? You brought me back to this living hell. Why did you condemn me to more suffering and anguish?"

Midnight meowed in approval, thumping his tail on the desk.

Jesus was shocked. "God gave you the gift of life and it has been restored to you, my dearest friend."

Lazarus raised his voice in anger, "You call me 'Dearest Friend.' How can that be so? If you loved me so much, why did you bring me back to life? God's great gift – humbug. If you really loved me, you would have sent me to heaven. I would be free from life's pains, living in bliss. But no, I've returned to my daily drudgery, doing all the tedious, dreary routines that I've been doing my whole life."

Martha, tears streaming down her face, sought to apologize and restore harmony. "Oh, Lazarus, don't be so disapproving. Jesus, he has been grumbling endlessly. I just don't understand him anymore. He has changed so much."

"Jesus, my beloved friend, I have experienced death and restoration. Been there and done it. You have preached that you and the Father are the resurrection and you will die and be restored. Well, let me tell you what it was like for me. It was hellish. During the four days between the death of my body and its restoration, I had terrifying visions. I was in a room and saw a rack of limp bodies hanging along the wall. A body marked Lazarus was among them. I looked at it and saw myself as a side of mutton. I was nauseous. Bile rose in my throat and I nearly choked on it."

Lazarus cringed. His face turned pale. "Remembering the sight of my limp body is terrifying and repulsive. Then three angels entered the room. One carried a wood chest which he opened. The angels took out of the chest what appeared to be me, but as a deflated soul. I watched petrified as they inserted the soul into the body marked Lazarus. One angel said to the others, 'We have replaced his life force and spirit. We will carry the restored body to the large flat stone at the entrance of the tomb and then depart. Jesus will be here soon and resurrect his beloved disciple Lazarus.'"

"What about that, Midnight? Isn't that a fantastic but ludicrous vision? Ho, ho, ho. Lazarus isn't finished yet." Midnight meowed, echoing his master, and stretched his front legs forward before sitting back up and smil_ng at Marcus.

Facing Midnight, the scholar said, "Lazarus states his thoughts clearly."

"Jesus, my wait for your arrival was like an eternity. I kept thinking – is that death, limp bodies hanging from a rack and people's souls sitting there with the bodies? Later I was worried I would get someone else's body at the end of time with full resurrection. The vision was unnerving and I loathed it mightily."

"But Lazarus, you were not suffering, and strange visions can occur after the body dies and before the soul goes to the Father."

Pointing to Martha, Lazarus said, "Look at the useless suffering you and Mary bear – really all women. The pain of your monthly menses, the second class social status you endure, the burden of childbearing and raising the children. No, it is totally unfair. Besides, I am a servant to the Great Sanhedrin, which controls my life and freedom."

In a soothing voice Jesus said, "Oh, Lazarus, my beloved friend, I have given you secrets the other discipline have not received. Believe in me and you will have everlasting life."

"Master, you brought me back to life. Then tell me the secret for resurrection. Wash away my anger," he pleaded.

"You have heard me call myself the Son of Man and others have said I'm the Son of God."

"Yes, I have."

"I am both, the Son of Man and the Son of God."

"How can that be?" Lazarus was perplexed.

"I was born of woman and God is my father. We are all the Children of Man and the Children of God."

"But what does that mean? I don't understand."

"I am a human like you and the Father has planted within me the divine seed, which I have nourished."

"The divine seed?"

"We are fields for the sowing of the Father's goodness. You have heard me say that the Father is within us. To know God enter the inner mansion."

"I still don't understand."

"Our parents give us our body and God gives us our soul. The spirit is God's touch of life, the great mystery."

"Can I feel God's touch?"

"You have not been spending much time in the inner mansion with the Lord, Lazarus. You are spending more time in the marketplace arguing with the Pharisees."

"I have been defending our cause. They attack you unfairly. I am correcting their false beliefs."

"Do not bother with them. They cannot hurt us. Instead listen to the Father. Your body is no longer the same as before your resurrection."

"What do you mean?"

"The divine seed is growing. Nurture it."

"I did sit in my inner mansion, Jesus, but I heard nothing. No one spoke, giving me advice."

"I will tell you Lazarus that your physical body now has sacred power, which you can tap and use for healing and blessing. As the Father's seed grows into a sacred plant, your hands will become the Father's tool. Feed the hungry, heal the sick, cast out demons, bless the righteous, and pray for the souls of all God's children. Your soul must open to the spirit. In their love for each other they will become one. And God will bless you."

"In the silence and darkness of night I think about what you have taught – the secrets you have revealed to me, but I only grasp a little bit of your meaning. Can't you speak plainly to me without metaphor, lay out the basic thoughts as the farmer lays out the rows in his field?"

"Lazarus, more is concealed than revealed. Your understanding will grow and the truth shall become clearer. After the seeds are planted, they wait for the rain to sprout. And the sunlight and rain and warmth nurture the little sprouts and they will grow stronger. You are God's plant and need the Father's light and spirit and love. Embrace them and you will gain access to the divine mysteries. Your consciousness will the climb the staircase to Heaven."

"Give me a sign."

"You are the sign."

"Me?"

"You have changed since your restoration. You are a different Lazarus."

"Oh yes, he has changed Jesus," Martha said with a worried look on her face.

"I haven't. Not at all. I'm doing the same daily drudgery. I'm arguing with the same Pharisees. Only I'm just feeling more despair."

"Go into your heart and listen to the still, small voice – your spiritual guide. You will discover how you have changed. The secrets I have given you will become clear. Much will be revealed."

"I don't know. I just don't know. I'm so depressed. I want to die and sleep forever." Lazarus sunk into deeper despair.

"God has given you life. Cherish it."

"Oh, Jesus, help him see. We don't know what to do," Martha pleaded.

Scarpia paused. Midnight wagged his white-tipped tail and grinned. The scholar looked back at the page and continued.

Jesus was perplexed. "What has happened to you, my most beloved disciple? To you I have revealed my greatest secrets. Now your mind is soiled with evil." And Jesus sat and wept. "Oh, Lord, forgive him for he knows not what he does."

Martha bowed to Jesus, wringing her hands. "Oh, Jesus dearest, my brother has so changed since his resurrection. I know him not."

Jesus was sorely grieved. "I shall leave. I do not wish to give you, my beloved friend, more anguish than you have now."

Mary, Lazarus' other sister, now spoke to her beloved friend, "Please do not depart, dear Jesus. We have planned a social gathering, a party to honor you before Passover. We have been planning it for weeks and have invited your family, disciples, and friends. Even your favorite, Mary of Magdalene, has agreed to attend."

As Jesus began to rise, Mary put her hands on his shoulders and gently pushed him down. She knelt at his feet, removed his dusty sandals, and anointed his dirt-encrusted feet with expensive perfume. Afterwards she dried his feet with her long hair. "My beloved Lord, please forgive my brother and stay with us until Passover. We would be honored."

Jesus acknowledged their love. "Mary and Martha, beloved sisters, I will stay and ask my Father's forgiveness for Lazarus." He looked at Lazarus sitting alone and sullen.

Lazarus shook his head as if awaking. "Oh, yes, Jesus, forgive me. Please stay for the Passover," he begged. A darkness shone in his eyes and he cried, His sisters sat beside him and comforted him as Jesus prayed.

Scarpia put the book down on the desk and bent over laughing. "Such drivel. Midnight, can this be the real Gospel? The sentiments are superficial. The logic is absurd. Did Doug pull another switch on us. Perhaps the true

Gospel is locked in the safe or – and I wouldn't be surprised – Doug never owned a true 'Lazarus Gospel.'

The black cat stood up and revolved in a circle, howling. Then he sat down and cleaned his front paws.

The wizard opened the *Liber* at a bookmarked page, studying it thoughtfully. Putting it down, he picked up the 'Lazarus Gospel' and carefully checked a few pages. Carrying the 'Gospel' with him, he walked to the laboratory. He studied the pelican flask, noting that it was glowing with an orange light.

"Yes, Midnight, the first stage has the correct signature. It is here where most mishaps occur. I'm more certain than ever that we finally have the true manuscript." He grinned at the black cat, who meowed deeply.

Peaches decided to leave and report her findings to Aeneas.

ço ❋ ೧

Aeneas stared at her expectantly as she sat in her travel chair and drank orange juice. His silence caught her attention.

"What?" Peaches asked.

"'What?' is my question too," Aeneas replied. "What happened at today's session?"

"It was amazing. Virgil, play the episode on the TV monitor."

"Wait." Aeneas jumped up and hurried into the kitchen and then rushed back with a plate of chocolate chip cookies and a mug of coffee. "Okay. Let it roll, Virgil."

After they had witnessed Marcus' antics and presentation of the Lazarus story as it was conveyed in the authentic manuscript, they discussed the import of the event.

"It certainly ended differently from the earlier version," Aeneas commented.

"I thought this story was more uplifting and positive," Peaches remarked.

"Yeh. The previous rendition was very nihilistic – a drastic difference in tone," Aeneas said.

"Both versions were very dramatic and emotional, too much so. I doubt very much they are factually correct depictions of what really occurred. Both versions suggested authorship by different writers with their own agenda,

But what would constitute a reliable source?" Virgil asked.

"So Marcus got stung again," Aeneas said.

"He seemed to believe the recipe in the authentic edition was correct. At least in the first stage the concoction had the proper color signature," Peaches answered.

"He indicated that the whole process would take a lunar cycle for completion," Aeneas said.

"I'm curious about Marcus' personality. What's his world view? His thinking is so bizarre," Peaches said.

"And his logic. It doesn't come close to what I think of as logic," Aeneas commented.

"I thought both versions of the story had their own logic," Peaches said.

"The idea of creating a homunculus! What's logical about that?" Aeneas inquired.

"Aeneas, maybe there's some truth about the idea. Remember how shocked you were when Gloria told us about astral travel and the chakra system. I was too for that matter," Peaches replied.

Aeneas held up his hand in surrender. "You win. I was also startled when the Garlands related their remote viewing and OBE episodes."

"Experience is the test and verification of the idea. I learned that from Rafé and Sandra too," Peaches replied.

"It may be symbolic," Virgil announced. "The idea sometimes refers to the philosopher's stone or the inner man or woman."

"A psychological encounter with one's self." Aeneas was pensive.

"An important point to consider: it was Lazarus who was portrayed differently." Peaches said.

"He was the catalyst who influenced the message." Aeneas had an insight. A light shone in his eyes.

"Remember that the first version of the story contained the incorrect recipe," Virgil stated.

"So he makes the elixir of life. Then what? Is he actually going to create a little man?" Aeneas wondered.

"Or will he drink the water of immortality and have eternal youth?" Peaches responded.

"We don't know his next step. I have nothing in my database for making a prediction," Virgil said.

"We'll wait and watch. But I'm leaning toward taking action and removing the 'Gospel' from his possession. I'm anxious to resolve the case," Peaches said.

"Let's sleep on the issue and decide tomorrow," Aeneas answered.

"Aeneas, I need to relax and have fun. Let's go to one of your favorite bistros tonight."

"Agreed. I'm ready for fun too. How about Smarty?" Aeneas asked.

"Let's go now. What are we waiting for?" Peaches laughed.

"Good night, Virgil," they both said.

Chapter 28

Enjoying her morning outing in astral space, Peaches had a strange feeling, intuiting someone was following and spying on her. She recognized the ID tag. It was Lenny Sawyer. A few days earlier he had tried to capture her, so she spun toward his approach, ready to defend herself with a cyber shield. But she would have to halt and remain stationary; otherwise, the shield would vanish. She waited for Lenny to make his attack.

Virgil had constructed the shield based on principles of the photon gun. The shield used particles from the electromagnetic field to enclose an area of space and protect it from penetration by anything outside it. Lenny was using a cyber net to capture surfers. It was similar to the shield and enclosed and immobilized the surfer. But Virgil's shield could change the polarization of the net and dissolve it.

Now he sped by engrossed in a different agenda. He did not even notice me, she realized. What was he up to? She turned and pursued him, staying far enough behind so he would not notice her. A portal loomed ahead. Lenny zoomed through without slowing. Peaches paused a moment and felt its sacredness. She then continued her journey tracking Lenny.

He landed on a small island covered with trees and flowering plants and disappeared into the wilderness. She followed and alighted on the island. Sitting down on a fallen log, she considered her situation. I have entered a magical realm after going through a sacred portal. I will explore the land and experience any other realities available.

After crossing the island, she decided it was a lovely place to live for awhile, like a weekend camp. Finding a charming clearing, she built a lean-to for shelter and gathered bedding material. Now all she required was a food source and she could live here in her paradise. She sat, listening to the bird songs, embraced by the sacredness of the place, as memories of summers in Indiana came to mind when she worked on neighboring farms and camped out a lot.

In a joyful mood she stood and went to a rocky area of the beach and gathered stones to construct a hearth. After stacking firewood beside the open hearth, she left her nest and explored more of the island. She paused frequently to observe the colorful birds that sang such sweet songs. Since she was constantly looking up at the treetops for birds, she stopped when she had an amazing vision.

Hanging from the upper branches of a very leafy tree were clusters of what appeared to be feathers of a brightly colored bird. Was she viewing a bird's boudoir? She watched them closely. They fluttered in the breeze, moving to the rhythm of the wind. Suddenly, a cluster broke off a branch and dropped to the ground near her feet. She picked up the bundle and marveled at its beauty. Magically, the binding loosened and the feathers dropped – all but one which stayed in her hand. The feather, the size of an eagle feather, had an image of a ruby-throated hummingbird. She wondered about the reason for the feather to remain in her hand. She waved the feather in a circular motion and up and down.

She was delighted with the feel and sensitivity of the feather. Had it chosen her? Was it her personal feather and no one else's?

Chuckling, she stuck the feather into her belt and continued her exploration. She came to a small pool with water bubbling up like a fountain. Sitting on a rock next to the pool, she meditated on her situation. The mystery island was certainly a pleasant place, almost like her vision of paradise, at least for now. But were there darker realms she could not discern, realms where foul and horrible monsters lurked?

"Hello, Peaches Peoples." The voice was gentle, filled with charm.

Peaches peered around searching for the person who greeted her by name on the enchanted island. Then she noticed a bluish light hovering over the pool. She rubbed her eyes. Was she dreaming?

When she opened her eyes, she perceived the bluish light had transformed into an Anna's hummingbird. "What's happening?" she cried aloud.

"Do not be frightened, Peaches." The hummingbird flew close to her face in a friendly manner. "I am a sylph, a spirit of the air, one of the four basic elements. My name is Anna. The feather you have is my shield and herald."

Peaches was puzzled and bewildered. "I'm missing something. I don't understand." She looked at Anna expectantly.

"I am your guardian spirit, your genius in the ancient sense of the word. You can also think of me as your Muse."

"How powerful is your magic?"

"It is rather weak. I am not a wizard. I cannot create miracles."

"How can you assist me?"

"I will always be at your side, whether visible or not. I will protect you to the extent of my ability. I will be your inspiration, mentor, and source of wisdom. More importantly, I will help you regain your perfect Self."

A dawning light spread through her mind. An awareness touched her soul. Yet she was puzzled. "But why me and at this moment?"

"Everyone has a guiding spirit, but most never recognize it. The ego must acknowledge it and accept its assistance; otherwise, it will weaken and die from lack of love. It requires a strong, intimate bond with its soul mate."

"And this enchanted island I am on?"

"It is named Anna Island since it is my home. It is one of the mythic Isles of Nephele, located in the upper heavens."

Peaches had an inspiration, an intuitive thought. "Is an allegorical meaning involved here? Like these isles represent upper consciousness?"

"Very good, Peaches. We are speaking an allegorical, symbolic language. It has been called the language of the birds. It is the appropriate language of discourse for attaining the perfect Self."

"And of course in the shape of a bird you speak it." Peaches laughed.

"Peaches, we're both speaking it now. And you comprehend it."

"So what fate led me here? What am I supposed to learn?"

"Not only is the isle my home, but it is also yours. A place to restore yourself and prepare for the next stage in your transformative journey. Consider the realm below you as the unconscious. A tiny region of it is lighted with awareness but most is in darkness, like the universe which contains mostly dark matter, impenetrable to human understanding. Yes, the darkness hides monsters, which are of your making. Here in the upper regions of heaven you will have the opportunity to increase the brightness and range of awareness in your soul and decrease the darkness."

She realized that the path she was on would reveal secrets that would empower the spiritual intuition.

"Come. I want to show you something special." Through a meadow of bright flowers Anna led her to a glen. "This is the fountain of living waters."

Water flowed over a small cliff into a pool set in a green glen. The pool was bottomless, and the water sank deep into the earth. Seated beside the pool was a huge human-shaped creature, a golem. It was impassive like a rock.

As Peaches was marveling at the sight, into the glen rushed Lenny, his eyes dazzling with greed and saying that it was all his. He looked about. A huge stone-like creature sat beside the pool. Silence reigned around the motionless golem.

"Who are you? What are you doing here on my property? Get off. Go away into the savage forests where violence rages." Lenny was angry. He dashed at the dumb form who rose up and gave Lenny a mighty blow, knocking him into the primeval forest. Lenny was quickly pounced upon by hungry, feral animals. His shrieks abruptly ended.

Peaches looked at Hummingbird who nodded in agreement. Anna spoke, "No one owns life which has roots in the divine source. Only those who are worthy may dip their cups in the pool of immortality. Meditate well and bind your soul and spirit. When you are ready, I'll come for you."

Unexpectedly, she said to Anna, "I am feeling sleepy."

"Yes, you have had a busy day and now require a refreshing slumber." Anna fluttered her wings and Peaches fell into a deep, peaceful sleep.

She was peering through a gate at white liquid. She stepped forward and moved along a gold colored path, which ascended toward a hilltop. Around her was a meadow of grasses and flowers. She paused frequently and looked out over the landscape. A slight breeze flowed through the grasses, moving them to nature's rhythm. Birds were singing their songs. Insects went about their business securing food.

When had she reached the top of the hill, she found a chair designed like a throne and a table. A book was on the table. She felt a sacredness here. Looking up, she was illuminated by a bright glow and saw the moon shining down on her. She was the only presence she could detect.

Picking up the book, she carried it over to the chair and sat. Hmmm, she thought, this is like a throne. I can sense its power. She settled in and felt power fill her. It made her feel she could accomplish anything. Opening the book, she discovered to her surprise it was her biography with film clips and everything. Now intrigued she read the book from beginning to end. On the last page Peaches Peoples found her true self. The real self was a holographic image staring back at her. She gasped. Assisted by the chair's power, she kissed the image and stepped into the hologram becoming one with it.

Now she remembered the rabbit vision she had as a teenager. So she had followed the path to the moon and discovered her true self. It felt good. She felt complete.

Suddenly the throne rose, levitating and gliding westward to the horizon. Fascinated she watched the landscape go by underneath. Surprised when it stopped, she looked down and saw an island. Then she realized it was Anna Island. She had an aha. She would ask Aeneas to spend next weekend with her there. On Monday she would broach the subject.

Her heart filled with joy at the prospect of a weekend with Aeneas on the island. When she returned, she would make a list of things they would need, especially a chair like hers so she could lead him there. And there she was – back in her social room resting on her favorite chair. Rising from the chair, she walked over to the desk, sat, and started working on a list of items they would need. Virgil would be absent, she smiled to herself.

Sitting in her astral chair as she called it, Peaches looked over at Aeneas who was busy working on his tablet. The chair, from which she could enter the chakra energy levels and travel psi-space, had become her favorite location in her apartment and most sacred too. She definitely had changed since she had become able to surf cyberspace. She watched Aeneas her best friend. There was something adorable about him. It was the twinkle in his eyes, an expression of his soul when he looked at her. Were they in love? When she was younger, she had a few romances, and now with the youthful energy of Rafé and Sandra around her she felt more like she was in her middle twenties than early thirties. And it felt good.

Aeneas was cute enough, but it was the inner glow that touched her soul. An image of Anna Hummingbird appeared and she knew. She would take Aeneas to her island. He was adventurous enough to accept the offer. But he would require his own astral chair. and she had already made a list of items to get, which included an astral chair.

"Aeneas, would you go surfing with me? I know a pleasant island paradise where we could spend time together and refresh ourselves."

He glanced up and smiled. "Virgil sleep," Aeneas called out.

"What was that with Virgil?" she asked.

"He's now asleep or turned off for two hours when he'll automatically come back on. He won't know he was turned off. What I said were the two words that perform the magic."

"So you solved the clock issue?"

"Yes. Do you want to hear what I did?"

Peaches chuckled. She would not understand. "No thanks. It's enough to have the magic words at my command."

He was delighted for the offer to surf with her to an island paradise. "When?" he asked.

"Tomorrow I will purchase an astral chair like mine. This weekend I will lead you to beautiful Anna Island."

It was a beautiful morning when Aeneas arrived at Peaches' apartment. After they had coffee and pastry for breakfast, Peaches pointed to objects laying on the astral chairs. "These goodies are supplies for our weekend adventure. Hop into your chair, grab my hand, and we will take off."

The next thing Aeneas knew they were standing in a clearing in a forest setting. Glancing around, he noticed Peaches seemed to be having a conversation with a red-throated hummingbird. Peaches turned to Aeneas. "Come over here," she said. "This is Anna Hummingbird and we are on her island, which we can use if we take care of it."

Anna acknowledged Aeneas, who, embarrassed, gave a partial bow.

"Anna, please show us the fountain of youth and tell us the tale of Lenny Sawyer," Peaches requested.

Anna flew ahead and they followed along a trail lined on both sides with lovely blossoms. They reached a green glen where water flowed over a small cliff into a pool, which was bottomless, and the water sank deep into the earth.

"There is the fountain of living waters," Peaches told Aeneas.

"At the moment it is only fresh unpolluted spring water," Anna said.

Peaches glanced around the pool, searching for the huge golem.

She told Aeneas, "When I was here at the pool before Lenny Sawyer arrived, a huge stone-like human figure, a golem, was sitting over there. Lenny was so greedy he charged the golem trying to remove it from the glen. The golem grabbed Lenny and threw him into the forest where monstrous creatures tore him apart for their meal."

Aeneas was amazed and filled with love. "You weren't hurt?"

"No, Anna held her shield of protective power around me."

Aeneas took Peaches in his arms and gave her a tender hug. "I don't know what I would do without you." He hugged her again. She responded with a more sexual squeeze and kissed him on the mouth.

He took her hand and they sat down beside the waters of life. The surface of the pool was calm and clear. They could see their reflections, two smiling faces, happy and carefree.

"I have always admired you and now I realize how strong my love is. We have been close friends, but I have hidden my love. I can't anymore." He hugged her.

She drew his head to her breast and cuddled him, smothering him with kisses. "Oh, my dear, Aeneas, we were soul mates and did not know until now." She heard the song of Anna and faced the hummingbird. "Thank you, Anna, for opening our unconscious to our true selves. Our hidden love has flowed through the portal of conscious, opening our eyes to each other." Anna nodded her head in agreement and then flew away.

They sat contentedly beside the fountain of elixir for awhile, silent and spiritually bonded. Then they rose and walked back to their camp, open to nature's force.

"If you would get the fire going, I'll prepare dinner," Peaches said.

Aeneas walked over to the hearth and rearranged some of the stones for better heating. Then he placed two flat stones at the edge of the fire pit. They would serve as warming plates. He put a reflector oven on one of the stones. Next he put some sticks into the pit and lit them. Adding larger sticks as the fire grew, he created a hot bed of coals. The over fire grill stood next to the hearth.

Peaches unpacked the dinner food: beef patties, buns, condiments, and potato salad. She sliced two tomatoes before uncorking a bottle of red wine. She looked over at Aeneas. "Is the fire ready yet?"

"Yes," he answered. Placing the grill over the hot coals, he said, "Bring on the burgers and buns."

She put four patties into a skillet, which Aeneas took and placed on the grill. The four buns were placed on the reflector oven. After pouring two glasses of wine, she gave one to Aeneas.

He raised his glass. "A toast to our camping weekend." They touched glasses and sipped wine as the burgers cooked.

When the patties were ready, she took the skillet from the grill and put it on a warming plate. "Come and get your burger," she called out.

Aeneas took a plate and walked over to the hearth. He picked up a warm bun and spread mustard and mayo on the two sides. Then with a spatula he scooped up a burger, putting it on the bun. Adding several tomato slices, he closed the bun and bit into it. "Yummy. It sure is good." Taking another bite, he smiled at her as she was fixing her burger. He added some potato salad to the plate and sat down beside Peaches. Silence pervade the camp as they enjoyed dinner.

Once they had finished, Aeneas remarked, "Nothing beats an outdoor picnic. I always have a big appetite."

Peaches giggled. She felt like she was in her teens on a camp-out with her beau. "Now's the cleanup part," she said. "You can heat water for the dishes."

Once the dishes were washed and the grill and oven removed from the hearth, they sat and exchanged personal life stories and secrets, which they had never shared before. Sleeping under the stars, they awoke refreshed. After breakfast they explored the island and especially its sandy beaches where they found shells to their liking.

In the late afternoon they returned to Peaches' apartment, promising to spend more leisure time on Anna Island. In fact each weekend was designated Anna Island outing.

Virgil inquired about their whereabouts for the past two days. He was given the bare facts. He did not need to know how they had discovered their love; besides he was not programmed for emotions.

Chapter 29

She was sitting in her car a block from Marcus Scarpia's house, waiting for Virgil to notify her that Marcus had left. The team had agreed on a plan: take the original manuscript from Marcus and then play it by ear. Marcus would wondered how it had vanished.

While she was waiting, her mind entertained memories. Camping out with Aeneas on Anna Island had touched her deeply. She was delighted that he took so well to outdoor living. She had worried that since he was a city boy he would not like leaving the comforts of 'civilization' at home. But he actually enjoyed himself. He had remarked that he was happy to be away from his normal high tech world. She smiled. Being with him in her kind of world had enhanced their bond. She discovered another part of his personality, one she never knew existed. She was looking forward to the coming weekend. It would be their fourth outing to Anna Island.

A chime sounded on her cell phone. The text stated that Marcus had left. She looked down the street and saw his figure walking away. After waiting ten minutes in case he returned for something, she got out of the car and strolled toward the house, up the sidewalk with bushes on either side, and stopped on the porch. She rang the doorbell and when no one answered, she took the key especially made for her by Aeneas' locksmith friend Lance Thomas. She unlocked the front door and entered as if she lived there. Switching on the protective cloak in case someone was in the house, in particular, the large black cat Midnight, she walked to the study door, which was locked.

Removing another key from her purse – Lance had made keys for all the household's locks – she opened the door and quickly stepped through and shut it. There was no sense having Midnight check out the study while she was present.

It did not take her very long to locate the manuscript since she had been visiting via the astral plane quite frequently. Placing the book on the desk, she decided to inspect the study because of her curiosity.

She surveyed the large collection of books, noting the variety of subject matter. Selecting books from the occult-magic section, she opened them and glanced through the pages. Because of the occult material Sandra had collected for her, she recognized some of the authors: Hermes Trismegistus, Nicolas Flamel, H. C. Agrippa, John Dee, Robert Fludd, Eliphas Levi, Arthur E. Waite. As she was re-shelving a book by Fulcanelli, she paused. A still, small voice spoke to her. Leaving the book shelves, she walked over to the work table Marcus used for reading purposes. Picking up pieces of paper, she saw images had been drawn on them. She studied the images but could not understand them. Now she wished she was wearing the cat charm necklace so the images could be sent to Virgil.

Her concentration was broken when she heard scratching on the study door. Midnight wanted entranced, she thought. She knew cats disliked closed doors.

Quickly, she went to the lab section, found an empty flask and filled it with the elixir of life concoction. Pushing a stopper into the mouth, she put it into her shoulder bag along with Doug's original manuscript. Removing a note she and her team had composed, she left it on the desk underneath a miniature skull, no doubt a reminder of his little man. The message on the note stated:

> Marcus Scarpia. Your hospitality is substandard. I have taken
> the recipe book and gone to seek better lodgings. Also I have
> taken a flask of the elixir of life and will complete its prepara-
> tion. The Little Man.

She debated about the best way to handle Midnight. She could open the door, allowing the cat to enter, and then quickly shut it, locking him in. Would he set up a howl or take a nap on the desk, waiting for his master's return?

The scratching stopped and she listened intently. After five minutes she felt safe leaving the room. Quietly, she opened the door, peering around the hallway, stepped out and locked the door.

She heard a meow and paused. Standing in the doorway to the kitchen was Midnight. He turned and entered the room. After a few steps he stopped, turned, and looked toward her. She stood silently. Midnight changed directions and bounded toward Peaches. When the cat reached her, he rubbed against her legs and meowed more loudly. All right, she thought, he is aware of my presence and probably wants more munches. She entered the kitchen, found a box of dry food, and poured some into his bowl. While he was eating, she left the kitchen and hurried to the front door. Silently, she opened it, and looked outside. Quickly, she left, closing and locking the door behind her. She walked confidently to her car still protected by the cloak of invisibility. When she reached the car, she bent low to put the key into the lock and switched off the photon gun. She got into the car and drove home. Mission accomplished.

Peaches removed the Cuban cigar from her mouth and asked, "We have the 'Lazarus Gospel.' How shall we proceed?"

Virgil immediately answered, "Take it to Balentine. Receive your pay. The case is closed."

Aeneas had been deliberating and finally said, "Ask Scarpia to come to the office. We'll confront him. Discover his purpose. Then we return the manuscript." He gave Peaches a knowing look and rubbed his hands.

"Why do you want to confront him?" Virgil asked.

"I'm curious about his motivation. Why did he steal the book?" Aeneas answered.

"I have no interest in the mind of an irrational human," Virgil replied.

"Okay, you guys. I'll settle the debate. We invite Scarpia to the office. See if we can learn his motivation and purpose. I'm definitely interested in understanding human behavior, which for the most part is irrational. After a social visit with Scarpia, we return the manuscript to Doug. Agree?"

Aeneas and Virgil gave their approval.

"Okay. How do we explain we knew he had the book?" Virgil asked.

"I don't believe we should tell him about my astral travel or the photon gun," Peaches answered.

"Why, not. He's a wizard and into magic," Aeneas remarked.

"Do we want to go public with our secret toolkit? No." Virgil was adamant.

"We won't tell him anything. We'll just wheedle his motivation from him with our brilliant cross examination techniques." Peaches smiled, noticing the delight on Aeneas' face.

Peaches looked at her watch. It was 11 am. Scarpia should be arriving soon. She had mailed him a registered letter stating that they represented someone who called himself the Little Man and they had a book he might be interested in. Scarpia phoned and made the appointment. Peaches smiled to herself when he had asked for more details about the book, but she had stated that he could ask during their meeting.

She was sipping coffee and chewing on a Cuban cigar, daydreaming about the coming weekend outing with Aeneas on Anna Island. Had she become obsessed with the weekend jaunts? Or was it something deeper: a growing love for Aeneas? Her reverie was broken when Aeneas announced over the intercom that Marcus Scarpia had arrived. Aeneas opened the door and ushered Scarpia into Peaches' office. She stood and offered a handshake. "Please sit down in the easy chair," she said.

"Thank you." He looked about the office, noting that the furniture had seen better times. Scratches were visible on the desktop. The cushioned seat of the easy chair was lumpy. The other chair had scratches on its surface and lacked any cushioning. He was surprised that he didn't see a computer. A smirked crossed his face. They obviously are at the bottom of the food chain. Nothing to worry about here, he thought. He then sat back in the chair with his hands clasped. And waited.

She stared at him. A knowing smile played on her mouth. They sat in silence for a few moments. He became uneasy and anxious. Then he blurted, "You said you had a book that the Little Man had given you. What is the book?"

"The Little Man called it 'Lazarus Gospel' and said it was a rare and ancient manuscript containing a description of the Jesus-Lazarus affair. He had taken it from you and wanted us to return it to its rightful owner Doug Balentine. But first we were to contact you and found out why you had stolen the book."

"What! I didn't steal the book," Scarpia exclaimed.

"Now, Scarpia, it was in your possession illegally." She gave him a knowing look. "What would the police believe if we told them?"

"Tell the police?"

"Of course. Balentine will report its return to his insurance company whom I'm sure would tell the police. Wouldn't you agree that's the most likely scenario?"

"You have the book, but what evidence do you have that I ever had the book?"

"Why, the Little Man would verify the fact since he took it from you."

"The Little Man?" Scarpia chortled and shook his head in disbelief. "There's no such person as the Little Man."

"Then who gave us the book?"

"Yes, indeed. I want to know that." Scarpia was puzzled.

Aeneas jumped into the discussion. "Scarpia, are you suggesting we took the book from you?"

"Well, how did you get it?"

"Why is the book so important to you?"

"I'm interested in the topic and doing some research on it."

"You're saying that the Little Man doesn't exist and that we may have taken the book from you?"

"If you have the book, I want to verify if it's the same book we're talking about."

"You mean Balentine's 'Lazarus Gospel,' which he said offered a new interpretation of their friendship?"

"Yes, yes, of course. Can I see it?"

"Why did you take it in the first place? Balentine didn't give it to you, did he?"

Scarpia took a handkerchief from his pocket and wiped the sweat from his face. Worry lines were visible on his forehead. "Why, I just borrowed it." He stared at Peaches, trying to appear nonchalant, but his attitude showed uncertainty.

"Balentine told us that it had disappeared after last month's meeting. He didn't loan it to anyone."

"Well, no, I didn't get a chance to talk to him." He wiped his face again. The uncertainty became pervasive, coloring his countenance. "I was looking at it when the meeting adjourned and took it with me. I looked for him, but he had departed and Jeeves was ushering us all out the front door. I was planning to phone and tell him not to worry and I would return it the next meeting. I guess I forgot." He looked at them with an unhappy expression.

"Well, we'll return it to him. Shall we tell him that you're sorry you didn't get to inform him that you borrowed it."

"Oh, yes, please. I'm very sorry. I didn't mean to cause so much fuss. Tell him I apologize." He smiled weakly and sighed.

"And that's what we'll do. We have a written statement offering your apologies to Balentine. If you would sign it, we'll give it to him along with the book." She handed him the statement.

"Could I see the book?" he pleaded after signing the apology.

"Of course. Aeneas, please get the book."

After a few minutes Aeneas returned with the book and opened it for Scarpia to view.

"Yes, that's the 'Lazarus Gospel.' It was very intriguing to read about their friendship."

"Why was the book was so helpful to your research?"

"I'm interested in the esoteric aspects of ancient culture. There's an essay in the book on alchemy and the making of the philosopher's stone. An essay on pharmacology dealing with the elixir of life. The Jesus-Lazarus story itself contains clues about their attitude toward death and the tree of life. Things of that sort." He smiled and nodded, believing he had extracted himself from a dangerous predicament.

Aeneas took the book back and left the office. Peaches stood, offering her hand. "Thank you, Scarpia, for helping to resolve a difficult situation."

Peaches smiled as Aeneas came back into the room after Scarpia had left the office. "That went well," he said.

"Yes, it was very easy. Now we can notify both Doug and his insurance company."

"I'm looking forward to the reward," Virgil said. "I can use more memory -- as much as we can afford."

Aeneas and Peaches laughed. "Of course, Virgil, I'll install more memory for you," Aeneas answered.

The Peoples Investigation team stood on the porch of Doug Balentine's mansion. Peaches rang the bell while Aeneas waited behind her holding a ten by twelve inch box containing the 'Lazarus Gospel.' When the door opened, Archie Jeeves stared at them, then smiled, and invited them in.

"The master is waiting for you," he said. Turning, he led them to the library.

Doug looked up when they entered. He stepped toward them with his hands out. "You have it. How wonderful," he cried joyously. Taking the box from Aeneas, he placed it on the table and opened it, removing the book. He leafed through the manuscript, nodding. "Yes, yes, yes," he said, "I don't know how I can thank you. You have performed way beyond expectations."

Peaches commented wryly, "As long our bill is paid, we are happy too. Besides, your insurance company has offered a $10,000 reward for recovery of the book or evidence leading to its recovery. We've already applied for the reward."

"Oh, my, yes. I've just talked to the claims department and the company is happy with the results. The check will be in the mail tomorrow. But please be seated and tell me about the recovery. All the gory details." Doug chuckled. He pointed to three chairs set in a conversational circle.

After the team had sat down in comfy arm chairs, Doug asked, "Would you like a drink to celebrated? I know I would. Archie, I'll have brandy. Get Peaches and her partner whatever they want."

Peaches looked at Aeneas and smiled. "I'd like a brandy too," she said. Aeneas asked for the same.

Archie walked over to the small bar built into the wood paneled wall and poured three brandies from a decanter. Once he had served the drinks, he retired from the library.

"Here's to your success." Doug raised his glass in a toast and sipped. The team followed him. Doug sat back in his chair. "I'm all ears to hear the story."

The team with Virgil's input had devised a plausible story to explain the recovery of the manuscript. "Well, there's not too much to tell. We closely watched three members of your monthly group who seemed most likely to be the culprit. Marcus Scarpia topped the list as the best candidate. We discovered the manuscript hidden in his library."

Doug interrupted. "How did you accomplish that?"

Peaches smiled. "Let's say, it's a need to know situation. Our method would not be admissible in a court of law."

"Oh, yes, of course." Doug chuckled knowingly. Sensing an irregularity on their part added to his amusement.

"Once we had the gospel in our possession, we confronted Marcus. We threatened him with police action if he didn't justify his purpose for taking the gospel. He's clever and realized the game was up and he needed to explain his way out of a potentially criminal situation. He stated that at the last meeting he was examining the manuscript, which you had left on the table for their inspection, when the meeting was adjourned, and everyone left the library. He thought he would just borrow the gospel for closer perusal. He was going to ask you if he could, but you had already disappeared. He believed you wouldn't mind if he took it home and returned it the next meeting. He was going to phone so you wouldn't worry, but he was so excited reading the gospel that phoning you slipped from his mind."

"I see. He was only borrowing it, certainly not a crime, but it did cause me worry and anxiety, and of course payment for your recovery. I'll talk with my lawyers about receiving just compensation for the harm and pain he caused."

Peaches reached into her shoulder bag and removed a folded piece of paper. Holding it up, she said, "Here is a signed apology. Scarpia was very sorry to have put you to such trouble." She handed the paper to Doug, who took it and read it.

"Thank you, Peaches. I may need this confession if my lawyers suggest a lawsuit to recover damages." Doug stuck the paper in his pocket.

As the team sipped their brandy, Doug went to his desk, sat down, and wrote a check for their services. He looked up, a seriousness passing over his countenance, and asked them, "Did he give any reasons for his intense interest in the gospel?"

"Nothing that we could understand. It was all too esoteric. Something about a little man, elixir of life, philosopher's stone, the tree of life, and some other incomprehensible symbols."

"Ah, yes, very esoteric, indeed." Doug stood up and walked over to Peaches. He handed her the check. "I can't thank you enough for recovering this precious manuscript," he said.

They stood up to leave and when they turned toward the study door, they saw Archie standing there. He escorted them to the front door and let them out.

On their way back to the car they looked at each other shrewdly. "Well, well, well," Peaches said, "there's something wrong with the whole scene we were in."

"I agree," Aeneas said, "Doug is hiding something."

"Indeed. He was overly thankful and took our explanation without much hesitation."

"Did he already know who the thief was?"

"Perhaps, he didn't want the gospel found – for insurance purposes."

"Of course, that makes sense. The $10,000 reward is a tiny fraction of the one million dollar claim the company would have to pay."

"If he has received any money for the loss, he'll have to return it."

"Well, we've completed our mission and made a tidy sum for our efforts. Besides, it was a fun adventure."

After they had left, Doug took the 'Lazarus Gospel' and placed it in the safe, which he shut and locked. The recovery was very unexpected, he thought. I'll need to devise another plan to 'lose' the manuscript. So Marcus was inspecting the work for esoteric symbols. The ones Ms. Peoples mentioned remind me of alchemy and renaissance magic. I wonder if he is seeking the same subject I am?

He filed his pipe and sat down in his reading chair, puffing on the pipe and blowing the smoke into the air. He watched the white clouds drift and vanish into nothingness. He let his mind wander.

When his computer expert, Lenny Sawyer had not returned after three days absence, Doug considered hiring an employment agency to search for a replacement. But now with the manuscript found, the insurance payment would be given back. He still had the original financial problems. He would postpone the cataloging project until the funds were available. So much bad luck had fallen upon him.

He was too unhappy to read *Pride and Prejudice* tonight.

Chapter 30

Peaches finished eating the Danish sweet roll, wiped her hands on a paper napkin, and sipped coffee. "I wonder what's been happening in the world the last few days? We've been so busy with the 'Lazarus Gospel' I've been out of touch."

Without looking up from the book he was reading, Aeneas mumbled something unintelligible and continued eating his pastry. Peaches picked up the morning *Chronicle*. She glanced at the headline and articles above the fold. Nothing caught her interest. She turned to below the fold. A story brought a beam of light from her eyes. She read the story aloud so Aeneas could hear it.

"Listen to this," she said.

Biblical Scholar Arrested

A well-known biblical scholar and magician Marcus Scarpia was running around naked in front of his house last night. Neighbors called the police, who found him in a delirious mental state muttering words like 'Homunculus,' 'golem,' 'mandrake,' and 'elixir.' The medical team was called and they escorted him to the psychiatric unit at General Hospital. No one understands what triggered Scarpia's delirium. Perhaps the black cat, sitting on the porch, wagging his white-tipped tail and observing the activities, had better insight. The cat had a happy grin on his face.

Aeneas cracked up laughing and Peaches joined him. "There is justice in the world," Virgil offered.

Ralph poured another round of freshly brewed coffee and settled back to finish his bowl of fresh fruit.

Shasta pointed to the paper. "Did you notice the article in the morning's paper about the weird behavior of Marcus Scarpia? I think I have heard about him."

"Oh, my, of course, I have, when proof-reading the novel for Spenser Blake, and I read the article about his strange actions."

"I imagine Spenser will be delighted to hear about Scarpia's escapades."

They laughed and giggled. Ralph stood up, walked over to Shasta, hugged and kissed her. "You have opened the portal to the Muse."

"The flow between cyber and psi spaces is unimpeded."

Afterword and Acknowledgements

Important ideas derived from contemporary scientific disciplines are embedded in the story and influence thematic material. Those interested in the latest ideas and proposals in quantum physics, cosmology, and psychology, including psychic phenomena, will find numerous fine books and articles, cogent and accessible, on these disciplines. The internet, our global Commons, provides extensive research facilities.

Many excellent books have been written about Native American culture. Both the Potawatomi and Nez Perce nations have websites, which present their history and cultural values.

These two books are helpful for understanding the Native American Church: *Rueben Snake, Your Humble Serpent: Indian Visionary and Activist* by Rueben Snake and *Peyote Religious Art* by Daniel C. Swan. Rueben Snake was a Native American activist and roadman who fought to maintain the integrity of the Native American Church against the onslaughts of the federal and state governments in their attempt to destroy the Church.

Research data on stealth technology can be found online. Articles in the journal *Science* discuss cloaking research at the US Department of Energy's Lawrence Berkeley National Laboratory and the University of California, Berkeley and at the University of Texas, Austin. Some articles on invisibility can be read online at *Science*'s website.

For those interested in the federal government's massive surveillance and data-collecting systems, details are available online. Wikipedia, especially, has very useful information. Glenn Greenwald's *No Place to Hide* is another valuable source for understanding government spy operations. An important book that sheds light on the dark side of the federal government is David Talbot's *The Devil's Chessboard*. The book centers on former CIA Director Allen Dulles and his many intrigues, both legal and illegal.

The portrayal of cyberspace and psi-space surfing is creatively derived from ideas and data on psychic research. The magical routines performed in the story are either well-known effects of the magical craft or imaginatively shaped from basic principles. The magical craft is an art and has been since the beginning of human culture. Like all the arts, it is based on a foundation of knowledge acquired and refined over the centuries.

For a thoughtful presentation of the Beloved Disciple issue, go to http://www.gospel-mysteries.net/beloved-disciple.html

Contemporary technology has given rise to serious social-political issues. The recent FBI attempts to force Apple Corporation to design software to access individual iPhones are a dangerous use of government power. Besides the issue of privacy is the one of involuntary servitude, which is prohibited by the constitution. Can the government under the name of national security or for any other reason compel individuals or companies to perform specific acts against their will? Because the technology for enslavement is available does not mean it should be used for that purpose. Creating software with backdoors and other insecure portals will enhance the ability of hackers to enter an electronic device. Criminals will have an easier time gaining access. It is an invitation for criminal activity.

Even though the specific threat to an IT company has been removed, the issue is now part of our daily life and will continue to be a potential threat to the public welfare. Knowledgeable and wise people must examine the ramifications of the new technology and set policy for its use. A forward looking perspective is required: what will be the implications unto the seventh generation of our brave new world.

Without the encouragement and advice from my friends this book could not exist. I am profoundly grateful for their part in the making of the story. Mary, my companion and partner, has been the greatest source of inspiration, and I deeply appreciate her support by designing the cover.

Note on Author

John Caris has been a college teacher for thirty-six years, thirty-three of them at City College of San Francisco, where he has taught Humanities and English. His previously published books are *Dancing Magicians, A Tale of Psychic Activities*; *Hermes Beckons, A Tale of Alchemy and Magic*; *Foundation for a New Consciousness*; and *Reality Inspector*, a novel set in San Francisco involving a world championship chess match and computer hacking at the Federal Reserve Bank.

John and his wife Mary have been residing in San Francisco for over forty-five years.

Visit their web site Ye Olde Consciousness Shoppe at westgate-house.com.